The Killing of Strangers

The Killing of Strangers

A NOVEL

Jerry Holt

Lucky Press

The Killing of Strangers

This book is a work of fiction and a product of the author's imagination. Any resemblance to persons, living or dead, is entirely coincidental and the relationship between fictional and/or historical characters and the events described within this book are done so in a fictitious manner.

2nd printing 2008

Lucky Press, LLC
PO Box 754
Athens, OH 45701
To order call, toll-free: 866-308-6235 ext. 6
Available at Amazon.com and by special order at fine booksellers, or email the publisher at books@luckypress.com

www.luckypress.com

ISBN-10: 0-9776300-4-8
ISBN-13: 978-0-9776300-4-2
Library of Congress Number: 2006005383

Book design by Janice M. Phelps

PRINTED IN THE UNITED STATES OF AMERICA

LIBRARY OF CONGRESS CATALOGING-IN-PUBLICATION DATA

Holt, Jerry, 1942-
  The killing of strangers : a novel / Jerry Holt.
    p. cm.
  ISBN-13: 978-0-9776300-4-2 (trade pbk. : alk. paper)
  ISBN-10: 0-9776300-4-8 (trade pbk. : alk. paper)
  1. Kent State Shootings, Kent, Ohio, 1970--Fiction. 2. Bodyguards--Fiction. 3. Ohio--Fiction.
I. Title.
PS3608.O4943594K55 2006
813'.6--dc22
                          2006005383

To Victoria

Acknowledgments

Any work of fiction which attempts to incorporate actual history is going to be heavily dependent upon research. I am indebted to many sources, chief among them William Gordon's *Four Dead in Ohio;* James Michener's *Kent State,* and *Kent State and May Fourth, a Social Perspective* by Thomas Hensley and Jerry M. Lewis; also Brian Richards. The Kent State May 4 Center has also proved to be more than valuable. Individuals who contributed insight to this manuscript in various forms include Russ Eichner, Daniel Saez, Leah Campbell, Fran Tiburzio, Melissa Holley, Sharon Short, Barbara Heckart, Kathy Trocheck and especially Alyson Cay. Finally, I want to thank the Antioch Writers' Workshop, a truly inspiring community of peers.

ONE

The morning of the day Lucifer Jones came back from the dead, it snowed like hell. It was late March already, but we can still get a good one in Southern Ohio at that time of year. But even if it hadn't been for Lucifer and the snow, I'd have had other reasons to remember that day. For one thing, I got fired, and for another, I met Corrie Blake.

Start with getting fired, since that began my day. It was a little after eight and I was into my second cup of Folgers, sitting on my sofa and warily watching the lead sky through the sliding glass door on my little balcony. I have the second floor of the old Two Rivers Shoe Company, which was cut up into apartments after shoes and steel and every other industry but the coke plant folded its tent around here in the late Fifties. And that's pretty much what my balcony looks out on: the rotting corpse of downtown Two Rivers. Fortunately, I can also see the Kentucky hills just across the Ohio River in the distance, which are always worth looking at. So is the Scioto — pronounced Sigh-Oh-ta — which joins the Ohio at the southwest edge of town, but the Ohio is far more impressive. Once upon a time it would have been possible to see it from where I was sitting, but in 1937 the town finally flooded one too many times, and thus a levee was built that stands seventy-two feet high.

I could also see the tops of a couple of buildings on the Two Rivers College campus, which so far as I knew then was still my place of employment. I'd been working Security there for nearly two years, mostly the night shift. The school has just over three thousand students, most of them commuters, so I'd spent most of those nights double-checking locks or jimmying car windows for students who had locked up their keys. Security was boring work, but it suited my life and I would have been content to keep on doing it. But then the phone rang.

"Samuel Haggard?" The woman's voice was unfamiliar.

"Speaking," I said.

"Hold for Ms. Denning, please." I heard myself being flicked into the AT&T limbo known as Call Waiting.

Ms. Denning — Rosalyn Denning — I did know. She was twenty-nine years old, and she held a doctorate from the University of South Carolina. She was assistant to the president at Two Rivers College, and she was downright beautiful to look at. But on the one social evening we'd ever shared, I'd found myself forgetting about her looks because the woman was so much fun to listen to. Her voice reminded me of strong tea with honey, and her stories — reminiscences of growing up black in the south, of being a first-generation college graduate, and of living a life so worth the telling — caught me up completely. I'd been surprised as hell that she'd ever agreed to go out with me, and very pleased we'd had such a good time: good steaks down at the Ribber and an electric, sweaty couple of hours listening to Jim Miller's Blues Band at Thompson's down by the shoelace factory. When she called the next day to tell me that she'd had so much fun we'd better not do it again, I'd told her I wouldn't have thought she'd pull rank on me. But no, she'd said: it wasn't that. And don't get any dumbass ideas, because it wasn't the black-white thing, that Old Crap as she put it, either.

"That's good," I'd said like a dipshit fool, "because I wouldn't care even if you were a — What's Spock?"

"A Vulcan."

"Yeah."

"Well, I'm not. I'm a sharecropper's daughter who worked my black ass off to get where I am. I made a promise to my daddy to do this, and I'm keeping it. Later on I'll do something else. Hope you're around, Sam. In the meantime — see ya."

That had been last summer, but I still thought about Rosalyn Denning sometimes. I'd even hoped she'd call me. But this one didn't sound like the call I had in mind.

"Sam," her voice: that voice, the same one. "Hi."

"Hi," I said.

"We need to talk. I—" She stopped. "Oh, hell. Come over."

"Okay. Thirty minutes?"

"Make it fifteen. I have a board meeting." She hung up.

I slugged down the rest of my coffee, pulled on my heavy coat, locked up, and went down the stairs. Once outside, the wind hit me like an angry lover's slap. The wind rarely blows hard here: the enclosure of the valley won't let it. But this morning had brought something mean and bone-cold whipping down from the hills: something brutal.

I walked the two blocks down to Second and headed across the parking lot for the Performing Arts Center toward Administration. I stuck my hands deep in my pockets and wished I'd worn some gloves. In fact, I was feeling generally defenseless by the time I made it to the main building. From a few feet away I could see Phil Pixley just inside the glass doors, pushing one open for me.

"Pix," I said, huffing in, "it's cold."

"It's the end of the world. End of life on this planet, as we know it. River's going to freeze, you wait. Just like it froze in '89." He sniffed. "When's tickets?" he demanded.

Pix was a good enough guy, but not exactly a linear thinker. Weathered and gnomish with a face like a chamois, he was senior maintenance and the Administration Building had been his janitorial kingdom for nearly thirty years. Some people thought he was crazy, but I could usually follow him. Here he was not inquiring about tickets to the end of the world, but about when tickets might go on sale for the Cincinnati Reds baseball season. Since this was the year of the strike, I certainly didn't have the answer. But I wasn't going to tell Pix that: he'd told me long ago that as far as he was concerned baseball was the one thing in the world that made any sense.

"Maybe this ought to be the year you get into basketball," I told him.

"Fuck basketball," he replied, and slumped down the hall.

The president's suite was spacious for a campus of this size. A college girl sporting braided brown hair and granny glasses out of 1968 sat behind the regular secretary's desk, peering hard at a computer screen.

"Hi," I said. "Where's Pat?"

She looked up, distracted. "Oh," she said. "She's out today. I think her car wouldn't start."

"Sam Haggard. I'm to see Ms. Denning."

Behind the glasses, her eyes revealed dark knowledge. By that point I knew it: I was on the block. I gave an inner sigh and sat back. The girl picked up the phone and buzzed into Rosalyn's office. She announced my presence, and then hung up. "Go on back," she said, and returned to her computer screen.

I'd never been in Rosalyn's office before. It was just off the president's, a comfortable room with a bay window and a round conference table. Rosalyn was at that table, elbow deep in manila folders. She greeted me without getting up and gestured to the chair across from her. I sat.

She threw down her pen and put both arms on the table before her, lacing her fingers. "You're fired," she said without preamble.

"The hell you say."

"I don't say it. The president does. And since he and the board are still honeymooning, that means the board is going to say it, too. Only they'll call it a layoff."

This time I sighed for all the world to hear. "Effective when?" I asked her.

"Now," she said. "We have a severance check for you."

"Whatever happened to two-weeks notice?"

"The check takes care of that."

I looked over her shoulder, out at the sky. It had begun spitting something that wasn't quite snow but wasn't quite sleet. Call it snert.

"Do I get a reason?" I asked her.

"Complaint. It's Professor DeShong."

I'd already known, too, that it would be DeShong. Rosalyn leaned back with her arms on the sides of her chair, waiting for my reaction. She was still beautiful. Even more, maybe.

"One complaint and I'm out?" I asked her.

"The school has a lot riding on him. The book about — Who? — "

"Kierkegaard," I said.

"Yeah. I knew it was some Swede or another. It's supposed to be important. He's a good teacher; students like him, and he's good in the community."

"And you can always get another security guard."

"Something like that."

"The son of a bitch set off the alarm for that entire building over there. The company had to come over at two in the morning and disconnect it. That's the third time he's done it, and he knows good and well the building gets locked at eleven and the alarm goes on."

"He says his biorhythms are better in the middle of the night."

I stood up. "So are Dracula's. Screw his biorhythms."

"You're killing the messenger, Sam. I didn't do it."

I took a breath and sat back down. "I know. Look, Val doesn't have anything to do with this. I was doing the job. I wasn't supposed to let him in there."

She got up and came around the table, all five-nine or so of her. She looked wonderful: crisp and cool and every bit the executive in a tailored blue suit and sheer stockings and sensible heels that were still high enough to show off her legs. It was hard to keep my mind on getting fired. She sat in the other visitor's chair and leaned toward me a little. "Sam, that wasn't the problem," she said. "It's what you said on the fire escape."

I exhaled all over again. "He shouldn't have tried to go up the fire escape."

"No question. But 'Get your fat ass out of that window' is just not professional. Sam, and— "

I stopped her. "That's what this is about?"

She leaned back and drummed her fingers on the side of the chair.

"It's what he objects to. He says it's harassment, and he says it's not the first time. He says that ever since he moved in with Val— "

"I haven't come around there once. I'm the guy she threw out, remember?"

"I know that. And I know you were very close to your . . . to Val's boy."

"That's a good question, isn't it? What do I call Linc now? Is he my ex-stepson? What the hell is he?"

She stood up. "This isn't going anywhere," she said.

"Will it do me any good to talk to Griff?" I asked her. The school had one of those presidents who insisted that everybody call him by his first name. His full name was Griffin Bell, and he was on his first baccalaureate school assignment, fresh from junior college in Oregon. Griff was maybe forty-five, but he looked older, showing the perpetual weariness of somebody who started every day by getting clubbed with a sockful of shit. He was the sort of man you could vaguely like, but never feel close to.

"It won't," Rosalyn said. "And besides, he's in Columbus."

I got up, too. "Okay," I said. "That it?"

"You need to turn in your uniforms and your radio. And your keys. The gun's yours, of course, but they might pull your permit unless you need it in your next job. I don't know the rules." She took a breath. "I'm sorry, Sam," she said. "You know I'm fond of you."

"Yeah," I said.

Her eyes flashed, quick and hot. "This hurts, Sam."

"Damn sure does."

"I'm talking about me. Go see Lonnie. He's waiting for you."

I got out of there and crossed the parking lot to what used to be my office, the sleet stinging my face. I was mad. When I had quit the Two Rivers police two years ago, unable to answer another domestic violence squeal or to look at one more woeful result of economic desperation, I'd been damn glad to land a job that was more like hibernation than working. I'd been running from my failed marriage and my wife's adultery and my lost son, and I wanted the monotony of security work; I wanted to traverse the human community around me like a tourist, instead of a lifelong resident. My salary had never seen the bright side of thirty thousand, but I'd long ago stripped my life to essentials anyway. But now that paycheck was gone. *Why the hell didn't the security people ever bother to unionize,* I wondered. Everybody else on that campus belonged to one union or another, including the teachers … most of all the teachers, who were in the habit of threatening a strike every three years when their contracts had to be renegotiated. But not security. We're too busy keeping the peace.

I had a fair head of steam worked up by the time I opened the door, which read "Head of Security." Lonnie Skaggs was behind his desk too, working on a fishing lure.

"I'm fucked," I said, and slammed the door behind me.

"Good morning to you, too, Sam."

"Did you know this was coming?"

"So what if I did? Do I look like I cut any ice around here?"

Lonnie was sixty or so and still wore the bristling crewcut he probably acquired in the military. He was gray and paunchy now, but he'd been a good soldier and later a good cop. I slumped on the sofa against the wall.

"What am I supposed to do?"

"Go fishing. Works for me."

"In this shit?"

"Go ice fishing."

"I hate fishing."

"You hate everything except baseball and blues and that pothead buddy of yours, Ferguson. But you'd like fishing. It's civilized. It's baseball of the kind of sports where you get to kill things."

I rested my head on the back of the couch and shut my eyes. It felt good. After a moment I looked at him again. "Leave Mac Ferguson alone," I said. "He always speaks highly of you. And why don't you go fishing, if you like it so much?"

"The only person Ferguson speaks highly of is his dealer. And as for fishing, I may never do it again. I just like making these damn things." He waved the lure at me. "I like daytime TV, too. Never would have believed it. In these small ways I am preparing myself for retirement. Gonna stay home and eat my meals in bed if I want to and watch *All My Fucking Children.*"

"Lucky you," I said. But I guessed he could if he wanted to. Lonnie had never married and was as alone in the world as I was.

"Watch *Oprah*, too," he said.

"Look, Lonnie. I'm glad you don't need a job, but you're not the one with the problem here. Why don't you moonlight me?"

"We'd get caught. You oughta consider going back to the city cops."

"Yeah, right. I didn't part on the best of terms with those guys, you know. And I don't want that job any more, anyway."

"Then go on up to Columbus or over to Cincinnati."

"Forty-six is a little old to be looking for a job, Lonnie."

"I know your troubles, man, but you're whining."

"Damn right I'm whining."

He inspected his lure again and tossed it on the desk. Beyond his small window, I could see that the sleet had turned to a hard snow.

Then, very quietly, he said, "I might have something for you." Somewhere outside, I heard an ambulance siren: an angry hornet, a warning cry.

"I don't want a loan from you, Lonnie."

"Not a loan, you dickhead. It's a job, but it's — Well, it's short term — if there's still a job at all."

"Doing what?"

"I got a call from some broad last week." He shoved a pair of horn-rims on his nose and dug in his desk. "Here it is," he said, coming up with a Post-It. "Her name's Blake. Corrie Blake. I've got a number."

"What's her story?"

"It's her mother. She says her mother thinks her dead father is suddenly back from the grave, alive and kicking."

"Sounds like she needs a shrink."

"No doubt. It's Crystal Jones. You remember her, right? And that nutcase husband? Satan or Jesus or whatever he called himself? Well, he's the one who's come up for air."

"Crystal Jones," I said. "Oh, shit." I remembered her, all right. The both of them, in fact. Some twenty-five years ago, Lucifer Jones and his wife Crystal were infamous Ohioans: superhippies who were hellbent on tearing the whole counterculture a new asshole. Their actions, from open drug use to flag burning to that memorable day when Crystal auctioned off her haltertop in front of the Ohio University student union, were great press, which the two of them parlayed into local and then national notoriety. Toward the end of their run, they even wound up on *The Dick Cavett Show.*

But then one day Lucifer, self-proclaimed hippie prince of darkness, had up and disappeared. And not on just any day, either. It had been that fateful noon on the Kent State campus, May 4, 1970. The National Guard had started shooting and some kids had died, and a long time later, when somebody thought to look, there was no Lucifer any more.

Nobody could seem to get a line on him — and he was famous enough that he got hunted by experts. Crystal mourned him through her drug haze for a while — publicly, of course — and even got somebody to ghostwrite her autobiography. She had lived in a commune for a while, and then, in the waning days of the era, she'd come home to Two Rivers and to her parents, who were and had always been rich enough to live up on the hill. There had been a couple of bad marriages — and yes; there had been a daughter. Crystal didn't leave her house on the hill much any more, but when she did people still gave her looks. I'd seen her, maybe within the last year, wandering the paperbacks in my friend Mac Ferguson's used book store down the block. She'd looked to me like she belonged on a shelf somewhere in Mac's musty stacks: as if she, too, had been given a quick read and discarded — another pop-culture icon whose fifteen minutes of fame were long since up. I could believe she was seeing ghosts: she seemed herself to be little more than a spectral reminder of the poster girl for *High Times* she had once been.

"Anyway," Lonnie said, "I guess the daughter lives in Columbus now and can't stick around to chase the monsters out from under mom's bed any more. So she's looking for somebody to do the honors till her mother gets over this."

"Why call you? Why not the city guys?"

"Hell, you know the answer to that. They laughed in her face. Seems Mom drinks a bit. Hubby isn't her first hallucination."

"Sounds like a load of crap to me."

Lonnie sighed. "Look, Sam, do you want it or not? If you do, I've got the number." When I didn't immediately reply he added: "Listen. It'll tide you over, maybe."

I realized I was thinking about my coffee table back at the apartment. On it I'd left yesterday's mail, most of it bills. One of them would be new to me: the first payment on a three-year-old Corsica I never should have bought, but that had looked like the cure for what ailed me during my last bout with the Christmas lonelies. I looked out at the sky again. It had really begun to snow now; big, heavy flakes. Why the hell couldn't I have held my temper? Why lose a job over a shit heel like DeShong? Was this all I had left in me? If it was, maybe I ought to hole up in the john with that .38 Police Special that was now the last thing I had to show for two years on this job and . . . *Ah, hell.*

"Give me the number," I told Lonnie and reached across the desk.

He handed the slip of paper over. "Watch out for this bunch," he said. "They're nuts."

"They're the Love Generation," I told him.

"That's what I mean," he called after me, but I didn't answer. I started across the hall to clean out my locker, and then spotted its contents sitting on the front counter. It had been emptied for me. What a day: it wasn't even ten yet, and I'd already disappeared faster than even Lucifer Jones would have dreamed possible.

TWO

I dropped my pitiful belongings at the apartment, then walked across the street to Mac's. He lives where he works, in rooms behind The Wise Old Owl bookstore in the Brewery Arcade. He didn't name it: the original owner did, some fifty years before. That's also the guy who carved the sign which made sure that this was one store that would keep its original name. Hanging above the door was a giant carved owl, wings spread wide against the backdrop of a wooden full moon. There have probably been five owners over the intervening years, and not one ever had the heart to get rid of that owl.

Not that Mac styles himself as being big on heart. He's piled on a lot of layers over the years. I first met him in '69, when we were both in Vietnam. We were in the same company. Mac is the reason I wound up in Two Rivers. He was cynical enough when I first met him, but after he lost both legs to a land mine, he became perpetually testy. He did his time in a rehab program that didn't work, then came home to Two Rivers and bought himself a used book store. Sometime in there he took up with a grand lady named Rita who was big — about twice Mac's size — and whose disposition was as bright as Mac's was dark, and who was willing to put up with the load of discontent Mac dished up every day. They were still together. We were all still together.

The Wise Old Owl is at the back of the arcade, sandwiched in between the Cupid's Retreat Sex Shop and Mr. Larry's Body Piercing.

Cupid's Retreat had been around forever, but the body-piercing place was brand new. As I passed Mr. Larry's door, a young woman suddenly came lurching out. She was chalk white and looked like she was about to heave. I started to ask her if she was all right, but before I could she pitched forward, directly into my arms.

I was lowering her to the floor when Mr. Larry himself arrived, clutching something in his hand. "Here," he said. "Just hold her up."

I did, and he broke a popper under her nose. She revived. Mr. Larry stood her up and braced her by the shoulders. "You're all right," he said. "Go home."

The girl wandered off toward the entrance to the arcade. "You sure she's okay?" I asked Mr. Larry.

He was a big guy with a black ponytail and a look of perpetual irony. He wore a black silk shirt, unbuttoned to the waist, over black Levis and snakeskin cowboy boots. He was probably thirty-five, but he looked more like fifty.

"She's great," he said. "There's no pain in that procedure. It's just the thought of it."

"Of what?"

"Getting your navel pierced. It looks like it'd hurt. It don't, but these girls get themselves crazy." Mr. Larry looked around him and then back at me. "You wanna see hurt? " he said softly. "Take a look at this." He put one hand inside his shirt and pulled forth a gold earring which appeared to be attached to his left nipple. He tugged on the earring, pulling the nipple skin taut.

"Jesus, Mr. Larry," I said.

"Now I ain't gonna tell ya," he said, "that that didn't hurt." He closed his shirt but didn't button it. "Got it done in Columbus," he confided. "And nobody held my fuckin' hand." He stalked off back into his shop, trailing righteous indignation.

Mac was at his usual place behind the counter, surrounded by musty shelves of paperbacks and book-club hardcover editions. The sign over his head announced: "TRADE TWO-FER ONE." The whole store conveyed organized chaos.

"Hiya," I said.

"Fuckya," he replied, holding up two taped fingers. He'd jammed himself pretty good while we were playing Horse from Hell during the false spring the week before. That's Mac's version of the basketball game Horse that we play down at the high school. We only get to use philosophers' names. Last week he beat me two games of Schopenhauer. He's wheelchair bound, but all it's meant to our relationship is that I'm the one who comes to see him most of the time: my stairs require that he be carried up, and he hates it.

"Wasn't my fault," I told him. "Maybe you could get your neighbor to repair it. He seems to be doing surgery over there."

Mac pulled a face. "I know some parts of Mr. Larry I'd like to pierce," he said. "That asshole cowboy faggot blares Michael Bolton music about twenty-four fuckin' hours a day. Do I look like I need Michael Bolton here? Didn't I pay my dues already?"

"One can never retire one's debt to political correctness," I said.

He gave me a sour look and hoisted a coffee cup instead. Mac has always looked a little like a thinner David Crosby to me. I never tell him that because he never could stand those guys except when Neil Young was with them. "Is it snowing?" he demanded. "We're livin' in a fuckin' cave here, ya know."

"It's snowing. And nobody says you have to stay in here. Take Rita out for dinner. Do the town."

"Who says I don't like it in here?"

"You're fucked."

"You're more fucked." He drained off the rest of his coffee.

"I need that Michener book about Kent State. Or anything about the killings."

Mac eyed me. "For what?"

"You wouldn't believe it," I said. "By the way, I'm what you might call laid off."

"For how long?"

"Until they say."

"DeShong nailed you, did he?"

"Yeah."

"Well," said Mac, "he can shit and fall back in it. Piece of garbage. He came in here one time looking for a fuckin' valentine card. Dig that. Does this place look like it sells valentines? What's that Buy-Trade-Used on the glass doing there, anyway? Does that mean fuckin' greeting cards, for Christ's sake?"

I held up my hands. "He's not my valentine. Give me some coffee."

He poured me a cup from the Bunn on the bookcase nearest him. "Anyway," he said. "Screw the sorry asshole."

"That's only half the story. I have another job."

"America," Mac said. "What a country. How'd this come about? affirmative action?"

"Lonnie. And Rosalyn Denning indirectly, I guess. Anyway, I'm giving her the benefit of the doubt."

"The hot piece of ass in the president's office?"

"She works there."

"You oughta be knockin' off some of that."

"We have more of a spiritual relationship," I said.

Mac snorted. "So what kind of bone did they throw you?" he said.

I told him about Crystal and Delbert. At the first mention of Delbert's name he burst out laughing. "Lucifer Jones!" he said. "Shit, I never did believe he was dead."

"Neither does Crystal. You two should hold a sèance."

Mac rolled himself out from behind the counter and motioned for me to follow. We went down the long row that goes to the back of the shop and turned left at the bulging New Age section. A shelf had spilled out, leaving a swirl of Wayne Dyer all over the floor. I picked a couple up.

"Leave 'em," said Mac. "I enjoy puttin' tread marks on that fucker's face."

"Does anybody really buy this stuff?" I asked him.

"It's a major inventory. They read 'em while they're waiting next door for Mr. Larry to tattoo a butterfly on their butts."

"He does that too?"

"We got a regular Renaissance Mutilator over there."

Mac had stopped at a section that was mostly hardbacks, one I knew well: Ohio History. "I could have found this myself," I said.

"Do you see anybody else in here to wait on?" he demanded, and plucked the Michener book off a lower shelf. He handed it to me.

"It's not the best one, you know," he said. "This one's better." He handed me a much thinner volume entitled *The Kent State Coverup*.

"I'll take both," I said. "All of a sudden I have a lot more time to read."

"Bullshit," Mac said. "What did you do all night while you were protecting Floodwall Tech? Meditate?"

"I read," I admitted.

"Don't be ashamed of it," he said. "You got lots of worse sins, Samuel." He wheeled off. I followed him.

I knew where we were going. Mac has what he calls an office at the back of the store which is really a big closet. In an earlier incarnation it really had been an office, but now it's piled high with the detritus of Mac's life. His Bronze Star is back there somewhere, but it would take a team of archaeologists to find it. I followed him in and shut the door behind us. Mac pulled out a spliff which was roughly the size of a ballpark brat, extracted a kitchen match from his pocket, and prepared to fire it up.

"Eye opener," he said. "Want some?" I shook my head.

"Ah well," he said. "Here's to old Stevie Ray." He lit up and dragged deep. The sweet aroma of the smoke took me back to other times, some of them pretty good ones.

"You never smoke any more," he said presently, squinting his eyes against the wreath that now encircled his head.

"Not since I found out the dog was me," I said.

"What dog?"

"The dog in the middle of the living room floor. I read an article once, I think in *Rolling Stone,* that was recalling those dear dead days when we were nineteen and one joint seemed to make it around a room of twenty people. Somebody's dog would always be in the middle of the floor, and the more stoned you got the sillier the dog got."

"Yeah," Mac said. "That was my dog. Stupid fucker got so stoned at one of those parties that he went out to shit and walked right in front of a semi."

"Well, the point is that when you're forty-something and get stoned, nowadays, likely as not, the dog is you. You're the silly one."

"You, maybe," Mac said. "Not me." He took another long toke. "You don't know what you're missing. This is the Brown County strain."

He was talking about superdope, some mindblowing shit that an Ohio State lab assistant supposedly bred years ago. Not that it seemed to faze him any. Mac claims they shot him so full of legal drugs in the VA that he can tolerate anything now. That doesn't mean he never gets crazy, though. Rita could tell you about that, although she wouldn't.

"I need focus," I said. "According to Lonnie, Crystal stays loaded enough for both of us."

"Not many old freaks got outa the Sixties without some kind of dependency. And all the straights got Valium or Zanex or some shit." Mac inhaled deep and held the smoke, talking from the back of his throat. It's a trick only old dopers do well. "I had that cousin, took four hits of acid in one day. Sonuvabitch is under lock and key. Decided he was a comet and tried to jump off the roof of his apartment building. Now he just sends postcards all over hell telling people when he's gonna be overhead."

"Did you know Delbert and Crystal?"

He exhaled, finally. "I knew Crystal. Went to high school with her. She was the fuckin' prom queen. But I never saw anybody take to the hippie life as fast as she did. She went up there to Kent and got her first hit of sunshine and it was all over. Of course, it was probably Delbert gave it to her."

"He wasn't even a student there, evidently."

Mac snuffed the rest of the joint with his fingers and tucked it away in the drawer of his cluttered desk. "Delbert," he said, "frequented the university of life." He wheeled out of the little room and headed back for the front. I toted my books up to the front counter.

"So give me May 4 in one easy lesson," I said.

"Where the fuck were you? Oh yeah, out in the rice paddies, humpin' a water buffalo." He poured himself some more coffee and gestured with the pot at me. I shook my head no. "Well," he said, stirring in sugar, "What you had up there was a nice, quiet little campus. Ohio State was on fucking fire and Athens was damn near in the same situation, but Kent was just as tame as could be. But when Nixon went into Cambodia, all hell broke loose. The SDS came out of the woodwork up there and next thing you knew, they were trying to set fire to the ROTC building."

"Which they did," I said.

"Did they? The fire started, all right. To this day nobody who's talking knows who lit it. But that happened after the Guard had already been called in, on Saturday night. They'd been raising hell down in front of the bars on Water Street for a day and a half before that." Mac grabbed the Michener out of my hands and thumbed around in it for a moment. "Here," he said, and held it out.

There were several pages of pictures, most of them in half-page. Kids in bellbottoms and fatigue jackets, holding Iron City P.O.C. bottles and looking pissed, danced around in front of a flaming trash can in one picture. In another, an older-looking guy sat atop an intersection traffic light, dangling a Vietcong flag.

Mac took the book back. "And here," he said, pointing at another section a little further over. "Here's the ROTC building the next night, on fire."

"I see," I said. The pictures were not unfamiliar to me. Some place in the thoughts I'd put away, Kent State was there, labeled Do Not Open, like lots of other memories from that time. I'd been in country, all right, not due to be rotated for another six months. But every kid soldier in my platoon already knew about My Lai, and there wasn't anything likely to surprise us any more.

"So this detachment's just been over in Akron, working a trucker's strike. And they're tired and they're pissed and now they got to chase what are basically kids their own age around the campus, trying to get close enough to ram a bayonet up their asses. It was like a video game before video games, so many Pacmen and women jumping in and out of the bushes. And by Monday morning they've had it. Nobody knows why the university, in its wisdom, decided to hold classes on that day, but it did. And the kids razz the Guard while they're passing between classes, and the Guard gets even more pissed. They throw tear gas, and the students throw it back at them. Here." He had flipped more pages and now pointed to a picture of a gaunt man, one who also looked a little older than most of the students, hurling back a tear gas canister. The canister left a stream like a jet trail across the sky.

"I know his name," I said, dredging it up. "It's Canfora."

"That's right, Alan Canfora. See, you remember the whole damn thing."

"The word cannister made me think of it."

Mac gave me a hmph, the utterance he reserves for extreme skepticism. "So," he said, "the Guard marches itself down the football practice field, nearly gets cornered, talks things over a few minutes, and then marches here, up Blanket Hill." He tapped another page and another picture, this one of the Guard advancing up the hill. "Now check this," Mac said. "See how some of them seem to be looking back at something? Remember this part?"

I did. Some of these guys would later swear that at this point the students were advancing on them.

"So they get up here to the infamous pagoda, you see," Mac went on, turning to yet another picture, "and somebody maybe yells 'Fire!' It could have been this creep here, right in front. That's Sergeant Ron 'Cyanide' Snyder, a horse's ass so big he actually planted a fucking gun on one of the dead kids. Or it could have been this old fart here in the business suit. Or it could have been God. Maybe Elvis. Nobody knows, or at least nobody ever said."

I looked again at one of the most famous pictures in all the history of the Vietnam years, the one which shows the Guard, several of them semi-crouched, firing back down the hill.

"Wasn't one student, as it turned out, any closer to them than the length of half a football field. They killed four dead, just like Neil Young told us. Nine others got wounded."

"Yeah," I said. "I remember that part too."

"Well," said Mac, "Most people pretty well turned the whole fucking story off after that. White upscale kids gettin' shot and two of them girls? It caused a few ripples. But it wasn't what got our asses out of Nam."

"What did, Mac?" I asked him, just so he could have the satisfaction of giving me the same answer he had for twenty years.

"Pure inertia," he said. "That's all." He produced one of those little stogies of his and flipped his lighter. "We drifted outa that war as smooth as we drifted into it. And the Guard members got exonerated and the students got indicted. And the parents of the dead kids got fifteen thousand bucks a head, and even that took ten years." He ashed. "Like I said: America — it's a great country."

"You're a bitter old fart," I said.

"Got that right. And — Hey!" Mac suddenly wheeled his chair around and dug behind his counter. "Look out," he said, producing a BB gun. He aimed down the aisle just behind me and squeezed off a round. "Got mice," he said.

"Jesus," I said, straightening from my duck. I looked behind me. "Did you get it?"

"Hell, no. Fucker ran behind the Harlequins." He fired another shot and the BB pinged against an old file cabinet at the back of the shop.

"Will you quit that shit?" I said.

"Just workin' my way up to carbon-based life forms. Besides," he said, rummaging again and this time coming up with a gun case. "When they come for me, I'll be wavin' this." He popped open the case and withdrew way too much gun. "Forty-one magnum six shooter," he said.

"Where the hell did you get that thing?"

"Took it in trade," he said indifferently, opening the chamber and spinning the barrel.

"They're not coming for you," I said.

"They're comin' for everybody."

"Where's Rita? You need your medication."

"I got your medication danglin'. Get outa here and let me hunt."

"How much for the books?"

"So! Money! That's different." He pulled his glasses down from the top of his head and inspected the inside cover of both books. "Twenty bucks," he concluded.

"My ass. I'll give you ten."

"Done."

I handed him the ten I already had in my hand. It was always ten.

"It's just I don't have time to fuck with you," he said as he took it. "There's customers bustin' down the door."

"Give Rita my love."

"I'll give her my own."

WHEN I GOT BACK TO THE APARTMENT Linc was there, inspecting my records. Fourteen now and nearly as tall as I was. He was wearing his brown hair pretty long that year and I could see a little freshet of acne around his nose. But God, he was a handsome kid.

"Still too much blues," he said.

"You'll get it when you're older," I told him. "Want a Coke?"

"Sure," he said. I got him a can out of the refrigerator and pulled the tab. "The real stuff," he said as he took it.

"The diet variety gives me a headache. What happened to school?"

"They let us out. There's a hell of a storm coming."

"I heard that." We sat down in the living room. "How's your mom?" I asked him.

"She's crazy," he said. He sipped his Coke.

"If they get this strike over, we'll go to some Reds games," I told him.

"Sure," he said. We sat for a minute. Over his shoulder, I could see out the window that it had begun to snow even harder.

"Do you think they will?" he asked me.

"Will what?"

"Get the strike over."

"They have to. Too much money riding on it."

We sat again.

"Things bad at home?" I asked him.

He sat his Coke can on the coffee table, sat back and pulled on an ear. I had seen him do that for twelve years now, ever since he was very small. "Yeah. They're bad," he said finally.

"Want to stay here tonight? We can get a couple of steaks and a movie."

"Sure," he said.

"Let's do it."

We talked awhile and then went out into the falling snow to walk five blocks to the little meat market in the historic district. We picked out two rib eyes and bought a loaf of Vienna bread. Then we walked over to Front Row Video. The snow was good and thick by this point, but it felt nice to be walking in it with Linc. We looked at the new stuff for a while, but wound up going over to the international shelf and getting *Wages of Fear*. Linc saw it for the first time last year and really liked it, once he quit fighting the subtitles. On the way back to the apartment he said something that got me laughing, and I felt the ice crystals break against my face and thought about the time when he was seven and it snowed so hard the town couldn't move. I couldn't go to work and Linc and Val and I played marathon Monopoly all one Saturday and Val kept hanging on to those railroads. It was a good year, a good time.

THREE

I knew I'd have to call Val sooner or later, so when we got back to the apartment I dialed the number I still knew best. She answered on the first ring.

"Hiya," I said. "He's over here."

She exhaled. I knew her so well I could see the little grimace she was making. "Well, how the hell's he going to get home in this?" she demanded. "It's a blizzard outside, in case you hadn't noticed."

"Just let him stay here tonight. It's supposed to break by morning."

"Running away isn't going to fix what's wrong around here."

"I know."

"I have a different life now, Sam. I want Linc in that life with me. *And not me.* I said nothing.

She took a different track. "I'm sorry about your job," she said.

"Word does get around."

"I mean it. I don't agree with everything Brad does, you know."

"It's okay, Val," I said. "I got another one. That's another reason I'll have him home in the morning."

She sighed. "Brad won't like this."

"Screw him," I said. My civility well had run dry.

"He's trying to be a father to Linc."

"We'll see you in the morning." I hung up.

Somehow it had gotten to be four o'clock. I looked out the window at my little town and found little of it to be visible. It was snowing very hard. I looked over at Linc, who was stoking the fireplace.

"Just use a Duralog," I told him.

"I want the real thing," he said. He was looking for newspaper.

"Well, light a Duralog first and throw a real one on top." I tossed him a box of matches from the bowl on the bookcase. "I have to go out for about an hour and a half," I said. "I'm meeting this woman . . . "

"Meeting a woman?" he said.

"This woman I'm doing some work for."

"Hell, Dad," he said. "I thought you might have something going."

It still hurt to hear him call me that — hurt and felt good at the same time. "Not with this lady," I told him. "She's young enough to be my daughter."

"Maybe she likes old guys."

"Thanks," I said. "I doubt it."

"Then maybe I should come along."

"She's early twenties."

"Sounds about right," he said.

"You're an overachiever," I told him.

He had the fire going now. The flames leapt against the bricks, casting finger shadows.

"Who is she?"

"She's the daughter of some people who were hot stuff in hippie days. The mom lived; the dad died. Or maybe he died. It's not clear. To the mom, anyway."

Linc sat on the couch, propped his feet on the coffee table, and picked up his can. "Sounds interesting," he said.

I told him the story. When I'd finished, he said: "I know all about Kent State. My history teacher's an old freak himself. He was there."

"I'm starting to think everybody was," I said.

"My teacher said that the guy who ought to have stood trial for it was the governor."

"Rhodes."

"Yeah. He said that Nixon told Rhodes to make an example at Kent because he didn't have the balls to do the same thing at Ohio State."

"That's one theory," I said.

"He says the whole thing was set up."

I sat down across from him. "It doesn't make sense any way you look at it. I don't think you'll find good guys and bad guys in this one. Just people at the ends of their ropes."

"He told us you could still see the bullet holes up there."

"Hey," I said. "I've got two books. Take a look at them while I'm gone. They're on the kitchen table."

"I'm thinkin' I might go see Mac," he said. "I got homework, too."

"Great. But I'd bet my Howlin' Wolf records that there's no school tomorrow."

"I don't want your Howlin' Wolf records," Linc said.

"You will," I told him.

PRETTY SOON LINC DID GO DOWN to the bookstore. I said I'd be gone when he got back and he said he had his key. Once alone, I picked up the phone and called Harvey Smoltz down at the police station. He was there.

"You should go home," I said. "It's too cold for crime."

"No shit," he said. "I ever tell you this kind of weather makes Marge horny?"

"I think I'd recall that."

"Well, it does. We got a kid to show for every fucking blizzard ever hit this place. That bad one in '83's where the twins came from."

"Sounds like you get a little randy yourself when the snow flies."

"Randy? Who the fuck's Randy? Is she that stripper we saw in Covington?"

"I wouldn't mention her to Marge."

He sighed. "Ah, well. They say you know you're married a long time when you grab your wife's rear and it feels like your own, but Marge still looks damn good to me. Thirty years this month. Ain't just a day, you know."

"I hear you guys don't want to work for Crystal Jones."

"Crystal," he said. "She's a pain in the ass. Probably a pain in her own ass, the egregious bitch."

I once asked Harvey why he liked to do that, yoke some four-dollar word with slang that way. He said he tried to learn a new word every day and vocabulary building was easier if he could swear at the same time.

"She can't be too much trouble. Doesn't she pretty much sit up there on the hill and do nothing?"

"Nothing? Nah. She drinks. And after she drinks enough she calls the cops. It's got so when we pull up she confuses us with the pizza guy. Been going on for years."

"She's been seeing Delbert for years?"

"Not him. But any number of other spooks. One night it was Jim Morrison, I swear to God. Two or three times a year we get it. And she's always hateful as hell, just fuckin' abusive."

"Are you sure she's drunk?"

"It don't take a one-armed genius to figure that out, Hag. What's all this to you, anyway. She didn't . . . Aw, God. She did."

"Her daughter did. Corrie Blake."

"I hope to hell you know what you're getting into. Crystal likes to OD a lot, too."

"Great."

"Oh, yeah. She'll be a laugh a fuckin' minute. Want my advice, you'll stick with the college job."

"The college and I had a little falling out."

Harvey waited a beat. "You okay, Hag?"

"Yeah, I'm good. I'm fine."

I could picture him shift his weight in that desk chair that always seemed too small for him. He'd be chewing on a pencil eraser by now, an old habit from back when he gave up cigarettes.

"Well," he said. "Take care of yourself."

"Just a second," I said. "What else can you tell me about Crystal?"

"Not a hell of a lot you wouldn't know. She's lived here for years, basically on her daddy's tab. She got somebody to ghostwrite that book a few years ago. She's bat-shit nuts. That's pretty much it."

"What about Delbert?"

"Just as big a fruitcake as you'd think. The asshole got on national TV, though. Better'n I ever did."

"You're a late bloomer, Harv. I can always tell one. Play your cards right and Sally Jesse's in your stars. Where'd Delbert come from, anyway? I know Crystal's from here, but . . . "

"Shit if I know. Crystal brought him home from college. That's all anybody knew about him. After he did a Jimmy Hoffa, there was stuff in the papers. Seems like he was a California kid. Look it up. You know where the library is."

"I will."

"They were just kids, really. Just Bonnie and Clyde on acid."

"Things happened to people fast in those days."

"No shit. I got drafted and married in the same day."

"Anything else ever come over your wire in all these years that would make you think the guy is alive?"

Harvey sighed. "Don't get your head there, Sam. Don't do it. How long did you contract to babysit this bitch?"

"I haven't yet . . . "

"Well, take my advice: Do it, get the money, and get the hell out of there. Get your security job back. Don't fuck with Crystal or her daddy or any of them. They never touched anything that didn't go to shit."

"Thanks for the advice," I said. "Do you know the daughter?"

"I knew her a little. She'd the same age as my oldest, I guess twenty-four. Corrie's a smart girl, smart enough to get away from that family as quick as she could, anyway."

"Her last name's Blake."

"Yeah, she was married to a lawyer up in Columbus for a year or so. Didn't take."

"She and her mother close?"

"I never got that idea. Mom's pretty much on her own. Her father gives her money, but I don't think he has shit to do with her. I'm tellin' ya: Crystal's a major fuckin' hassle."

"I'm supposed to meet the daughter in about an hour."

"Corrie's had a life, I'll tell you that. Crystal tried to home-school her for a while, and then when Crystal fell apart the dad got into it. I think they sent Corrie away to school, pretty much took her out of her mother's hands. Anyway, you can bet she was bounced around. Useta be a nice lookin' girl, but not the kind that wound up buckin' for Miss Teenage Whatever. Corrie was always too far outside the system for that. Like I said, my daughter knew her some. But even that was a long time ago. Corrie hasn't lived in Two Rivers in three, four years at least."

"Thanks, Harv," I said. "Let's grab some lunch next week. I'm buying."

"The Ribber?"

"Sure, The Ribber."

"You're on, Bud. And I'm outa here. You're about to keep me past quittin' time."

"I thought the Two Rivers police never slept."

"This one does. Adios, Sam."

I could see through the window that the snow was just as heavy as it had been. I looked at my Kent State books on the coffee table in front of me. The story was one of the many unsolved mysteries of the century. Who had given the order to fire on those kids, if there had even been an order?

And, as Mac had suggested, the burning of the ROTC building was an even bigger mystery than that. Was there some kind of collusion; some setup by some shadowy arm of a government anxious to make an example in a small, easily controlled situation? I didn't like conspiracy theories, but I could feel the seductive pull of this one, nonetheless.

But I shrugged it off. We were talking about a job of work here, not something of significance. Meal ticket time, and nothing more. I dug out my Post-It, dragged the phone over to the couch, and dialed the number Lonnie had given me.

FOUR

Corrie Blake, the daughter in question, did not seem relieved that I had called. She did, however, agree that I should present myself at her mother's house at five that afternoon. She was so brusque about it that I was surprised when she called back around four to revise that plan.

"Look," she said. "I don't think it will work out for you to come to the house today. Where's someplace I can meet you?"

The snow had continued to fall all day, and from my kitchen window I could see that the city offices' parking lot down by the river was less than a third full. In fact, there was little traffic downtown at all. The only place I knew that was certain to be open was the Huckins House out on 23 North. Back in the Fifties the Huckins had been the city's official roadhouse, but by the late Sixties its once-plush furnishings had become as faded and shabby as its clientele. Somehow, though, it has persisted — mostly because it seemed to never close, or maybe because its aged owner, a rotund geezer named Hardesty Boyle, was just too stubborn to quit. At least the place was in Corrie Blake's general direction.

"I can meet you at the Huckins. If you come down Rosemount, it's just a little way north on 23."

"Do they serve food there?" she wanted to know.

"They used to. I haven't been there for a while." Like, maybe since Jimmy Carter was in office, I thought.

"Well, make sure it didn't close up because of the weather. It's snowing like a bastard out there, you know. If you don't call me back, I'll meet you there at five."

"Okay," I said, and hung up. None of this was doing wonders for my mood, especially not the fact that I hadn't even met Corrie Blake in person yet and she was already treating me like hired help. But I'd spent the early afternoon going over my finances, and I'd been able to calculate that I could maybe go a month without new income. Not much to show for forty-six years on the planet, I'd admitted, then shot the rest of the day trying to argue myself into some renewed self-esteem. Corrie Blake was playing hell with my peptalk.

Even so, I needed a job and she had one. So I dug out my snow boots and then briefly studied my clothes rack, such as it was. Should I wear a tie? With nearly a foot of snow outside already, I bagged that idea. I pulled a clean sweater over my Levi's and grabbed my parka, then went down my inside stairs to the front door.

The snow was falling so fast that I couldn't even see my car in the parking space across the alley. The TV weather bulletins had been calling for "near-blizzard conditions" all day, but if this wasn't a blizzard I never wanted to see one. I tromped over to the Corsica and pried the door open from beneath its mound of snow. My brand-new used car started right up, but I thought the heater was never going to kick in. When it did, I wipered fresh snow off the windshield and pulled very slowly out of the alley and into the street.

I didn't really need to be careful. There was nobody out there. After three blocks I finally saw a city truck dumping rock salt on the frozen street, but my fellow civilians had evidently packed it in long ago. I thought of the rosy glow of living rooms in houses up the hill, Duralogs already cooking full blast in the fireplace; Dad or Mom safe at home after calling it an early work day. Kids out of school probably by noon so the rural buses could still get around. I peered through the snik-snak of my wipers and thought of my own childhood in the southwest, long before I'd parked my existence here. It had snowed only rarely there, but when it did my child's mind had always been filled with a wonderful sense of anticipation, one quickened by the sure knowledge that on the next day or the next one the sun would shine again and this white swirl of hopeful excitement would pass, an insubstantial and momentary pageant.

About the time I got to the railroad bridge I realized that I'd never even bothered to call the Huckins. What the hell was I going to do if I got out here to find the place had called it quits for the day? It was a silly thing to do, made even sillier by the fact that I hadn't forgotten — I just hadn't done it. Ah, well. If worst came to worse, we could talk in the car.

When I finally inched into the parking lot of the Huckins, the sign was still lit up, a dingy beacon in the dusk. Hard to tell why they were bothering, though: there were maybe two other cars in the lot. I pulled into a space near the entrance and got out. The snow had not slacked, but there was no wind and, without the usual sounds of traffic on the highway, a stark and lonely stillness seemed to have settled in. I tromped toward the door, anxious to get inside.

It was pretty lonely inside the Huckins, too. The "Please Seat Yourself" sign was posted at the entrance to the restaurant, which was full of empty tables. Off to my right in the bar, a couple of ball-cap types were drinking beers and shots; probably truckers who had hiked from the Motel 6 up the highway. Behind the bar, leaning against the cash register, was the guy I could swear had been there the last time I'd come. He was maybe my age, skinny with a soccer-ball paunch. His hair was graying and thin, a circumstance for which he compensated with a neatly trimmed moustache. Three men and nobody else in sight. I took a seat at the far end of the bar, where I could watch the front door. From there I could see that somebody, I supposed the bartender, had taken the trouble to build a fire in the hearth just inside the restaurant area. It crackled invitingly, its flames basking the room in cozy illumination. In that light the gouged mahogany of the booths seemed transformed, restored to its heyday of elegance. I almost expected the silence to be broken by the ghostly laughter of people celebrating the end of World War II, or Ike's election to a second term.

The bartender sidled up. He wore one of those permanent-looking name tags, emblazoned with the single word "Bob." He leaned close, as if about to let me in on some conspiracy.

"Some lousy night," he said softly.

"That's a fact," I said. "What did you do? Send everybody home?"

"Cook's still working," he said. "You want a menu?"

"No, but I'm meeting somebody and I think she will," I told him. "I'll just have coffee."

Bob put a cup down in front of me and moved off to fetch the pot. When he returned to pour it, he said: "I'm having a helluva night here."

"Looks pretty quiet to me," I said.

"That's the problem. I went and contracted that OCD, you know."

"OCD?"

"Obsessive-Compulsive Disorder. I been to the shrink about it. Means there's stuff I think I gotta do, or something awful will happen. Like right now, standing here doing nothing, I keep getting the idea that I gotta count every place in this room where the furniture touches the floor. I mean, there's a shitload of chairs in here, man. It's better when I'm busy. Then I get some relief from it."

I looked at him. "Do you think you should be telling me this?" I said.

"I got to, man. One of my compulsions is to tell people I'm obsessive-compulsive." He leaned in and lowered his voice even more. "Who'm I gonna tell? Those jerks down there? They already asked me what kinda beer we have. I have to name every brand including the NAs when somebody does that. Drives me crazy if I miss one."

"That's bad, man," I said.

"Tell me. But it's okay. I'm in treatment. It's better when I'm busy, though." He plopped some cream and sugar down in front of me and resumed his neutral territory near the cash register, presumably to count some more chair legs.

I waited. The guys at the other end of the bar ordered another round. Nobody came in. Some music was playing — a stereo system, just loud enough to be heard — of all things, an old Lettermen album. Probably the same one they'd been playing in here for thirty years or so: I thought I could even hear the scratches and pops. I looked at the fire some more.

Then she arrived. A wind must have picked up, because when she came in the door a lot of snow came with her. I can still see the way she looked. She stood there stamping her feet a minute, and then turned to survey the place. I got off my stool and walked over.

"Corrie Blake?" I asked her.

"Yeah. You Haggard?"

"That's right. Sam. Let's sit at one of these bar tables; I think the waitresses have gone home, but someone's still cooking."

"Thank God," she said. "I could eat a dead cat."

I followed her into the bar. The baseball caps were giving her a look, one she probably would have gotten even if she hadn't been the only woman in the place. She wasn't tall, five-two at most. And she was trim, not trim like she worked out, but trim as in a gift from God. Her hair was very black and very curly, I guessed naturally so, falling in thick ringlets just below the collar of the bomber jacket she wore. A shopping bag of a purse swung from her right shoulder, banging against her hip as she walked. I saw her shoot a look back at the baseball caps that was brief but downright intimidating in its dismissiveness, and then she selected a table not far from the fireplace and sat. I took the chair opposite.

"Fire feels good," she said. While she drew off a pair of leather gloves, I looked at her more closely. Her face beneath the dark curls was unlined, but something in her expression reflected experience and a lot of it. She certainly conveyed an age well beyond her twenty-four years. Her nose was a little too big, and in the firelight I could see that her face bore a small crescent scar by the right cheekbone. Her eyes were her best feature: big and honest. You immediately had the feeling she'd never look away before you did.

"Bad night," I said.

"A killer. I have a Blazer and it was still hell getting here." I could see a little snow in her hair, dissolving fast. She pulled off her coat and draped it across the back of her chair. I realized that I'd never gotten out of mine, and did the same.

"Sorry for your drive," I said. "There just wasn't anyplace else."

"Yeah," she said noncommittally, and commenced digging in that purse. She came up with a pack of Pall Malls and a Zippo lighter. Seeing the look I gave the cigarette package, she said: "If you're gonna smoke, I say smoke," and then lit one. Bob appeared, bearing menus.

"Just the lady," I said, and he handed her one.

"Something to drink?" Bob inquired.

Corrie Blake exhaled smoke. "What kind of imported beer have you got?" she asked him.

Bob's face fell. "Bring her a Bass," I said.

Visibly relieved, the bartender vanished. "I usually make my own order," Corrie Blake said.

"Trust me on this," I said.

Bob returned with her beer, a glass for it, and more coffee for me. Corrie Blake, who hadn't even looked at the menu, handed it back to him and said: "Bring me a burger. And tell them not to burn it."

After Bob had retreated for the second time, she said, "They're so spooked over that Jack In The Box case that they burn the shit out of burgers any more." She breathed in more smoke, blew it out, and took a long pull on her beer bottle, dismissing the glass altogether.

"Let's talk about your mother," I said.

"You've been doing security work?" she countered.

"Yes. At the university."

"What, Floodwall Tech down there?"

"Yeah," I said. My desire to defend the institution had disappeared with my job.

"And you were a cop?"

"Right. The city police. For eight years."

"Why'd you quit?"

"Got tired of it," I said.

"You from here?"

"Not originally."

"How'd you wind up here?"

"It's where my life stalled out," I said.

She gave me another of those fixed looks of hers. "You sure you can do this work, Haggard?" she asked suddenly. "No offense, but you look like you've been driving all night and getting nowhere."

Maybe I should have worn a tie after all. Then again, maybe I didn't care. "Look," I told her. "Let's get basic. If you want to fire me before you've even told me what you want me to do, I don't see much of a future in this." I stood up.

She gave me another look, took a last drag on her cigarette, and stubbed it out. "Bullshit, Haggard," she said. "You need this job and we both know it. Sit down."

I kept standing. "Are we talking now?" I said.

"We're talking," she said. "Sit down."

The food came. What Bob presented was one of those fern-bar burgers, oversized and open-faced, on a plate piled high with french fries, which at least looked homemade. Corrie Blake accepted the food and I sat down again. The guys doing shots and beers had gone. We were alone, except for Bob and the open fire and, somewhere in the barely audible distance, the Lettermen.

"Have some of these fries," she said, and started dumping them on the empty salad plate in front of me."

"I ate," I said, although I hadn't.

"Eat some more. Let me tell you about dear old Mom." She bit into the burger, and chewed thoughtfully. "Not bad," she said. "I was starved. Crystal is living on tofu and gin out there, near as I can tell."

"She drinks," I said.

Corrie Blake sniffed. "Do pigeons crap?" she said. "Yeah, she drinks. Somebody ought to hand her some Clearlight. She was better off as an acidhead." She chewed some more.

"What is it she thinks she's seen?"

"My dead daddy. Delbert Eugene Jones." She put down her burger, wiped her fingers on her napkin, and dug in her purse again, this time coming up with a photograph. She laid it flat on the table and tapped it. "That's him," she said.

I was seeing the photograph for the second time that day. It was one of those reproduced in Michener's book, one of the Filo shots. It had been taken maybe fifteen minutes before the Guard had climbed the hill to the pagoda on that Monday noon a quarter century before. On the front row was Jeff Miller, soon to be shot dead, his left arm raised in defiance; his index finger thrust at the unseen Guard. It was the picture in which Mac had earlier today claimed you could find a shadowy Mary Vecchio, the high school runaway who had wound up famous when her picture was taken as she crouched in horror over the dead body of Jeff Miller. And under Corrie Blake's fingernail was Lucifer Jones himself, his Mansonish hair a wild tangle; goatish beard barely concealing lips frozen in a shout of anger. In the firelight I could see the S and the Y of his "Sympathy for the Devil" T-shirt, the only part of the logo not concealed by the big Afro atop some other kid's head. Delbert was up the hill a little and standing somewhat away, as if he had not yet committed himself fully to the crowd.

"That's the last time anybody ever saw him," Corrie Blake said.

"Until now," I said.

"Yeah, well," she replied with a shrug. "Crystal sees things that never were and says Why not? She's usually in the bag by this time of day: that's her condition at the moment, in fact. But she wakes up by ten so she can get blotto again, and that's when her best visions seem to occur."

"She says he came to the house?"

"Sort of. She says she saw him in the driveway, two weeks ago. She was looking out the kitchen window, and all of a sudden there he was, just standing there. The garage has one of those lights . . . "

"Mercury vapor," I said.

"Yeah. Well, it had burned out, but there was plenty of moonlight, I guess — and there he was. At least according to Crystal."

"How would she know? It's been over twenty years."

"She knows, she says. Plus she's had some phone calls. Odd times. Nobody says anything, but she thinks it's him."

"Did you have a sense of your father?" I asked her.

"Are you kidding? I wasn't even born when he disappeared. All I know about the bastard is hearsay, and that's nuthin' but bad. Here," she said, cutting off a wedge of her remaining burger. "Eat some of this. You look hungry." She dropped the wedge on my plate.

Her story had a hook to it, I had to admit. Lucifer Jones, clown prince of the revolution, back from the dead and hanging out in his own driveway, like he was getting ready to edge the lawn. The absent father returned: Ulysses, home from the wars. I realized that I had picked up the catsup bottle and was upending it over my plate. Like all catsup bottles, it didn't pour.

"Hit it on the 57," Corrie Blake said.

"What?" I said, my mind still holding the image of Lucifer Jones grown old — old like the rest of us.

"Here," she said, taking the bottle. "See these numbers, five and seven, right on the side here? Like in Heinz 57?"

I looked. They were there.

"Well," she said, "just tap." She did, and catsup poured forth onto my plate as if she had turned on a spigot.

"Amazing," I said.

"Tricks of the trade. I'm paying my law school bills by working in a bar."

"Law school." I was impressed: the way she talked, I was afraid she'd set her career sights on Hate Radio.

"Yeah. My ex, the jerkoff, is a lawyer, so I've got experience, sort of. I used to watch him soak his clients, at least."

"So you want to get your fair share?"

"I want to be a different kind of lawyer," she said, as if that settled that. "Anyway, look. I have got to get back to Columbus. I've got classes and a job. If you want to babysit Mom until she exorcises herself here, that's great. I know you'll do fine. Crystal's got income: my dad's parents left her some and she still gets a little from that book. She can pay."

"Does she know about this?" I asked.

"She will. It'll be fine. What do you charge?"

I had an answer ready for that. "I need three hundred a day, Mrs. Blake," I said. I'd never been paid three hundred a day to do anything, but what the hell.

She didn't blink. "That's fine. I don't expect this will last long. And call me Corrie."

"It's a good name," I offered.

"It's a lucky name. Remember when I was born and who to. I coulda been another Starshine or Moon Unit."

Bob was beside us again. "Anything else?" he asked.

"Just the check," Corrie said. "Here." She produced a twenty. Bob carried it away.

"I would have gotten that," I said.

"No need," she stood up and shrugged on her jacket. Then she picked up the picture, giving it another look before she dropped it in her purse.

"Crystal had this damn thing in a frame, you know," she said. "Is that necrophilia, or what?"

"It was the most important day of her life, as it turned out," I said.

She considered. "Well, I wish I could relate. Always looked to me like some kids in the Guard just got pissed that day and shot some other kids they didn't even know."

A line of Mark Twain's brushed through my mind. "All war must be just the killing of strangers." I stood too and drew on my coat. Bob returned with change. Corrie threw down two ones and we both turned toward the door. As we passed Bob, now back at his cash register post, I said: "Hang in there, man." He raised his fingers slightly in a woeful peace sign. Probably a salute he had to give those who came in looking vaguely like they might have voted for McGovern.

Outside, the snow had let up. A few flakes made their desultory way on the slight wind. The stars had come out. I walked with Corrie to her Blazer. She got in and started it to let it run. Her keyring, I saw, dangled from a big gold *C*.

"Come out tomorrow by noon," she said. "We're on the Hill; the last house up on Gallia Pike."

"I know where it is," I said.

She put out her hand and I took it. "Thanks," she said. "You're helping me out of a jam."

"You'd think the Heinz people would spread it around about tapping the bottle on the 57," I told her, for lack of something better to say.

She smiled, just faintly, and then her eyes fixed me again. "Well, you know," she told me, "Life's better with a little mystery to it." She swung open her door and got into the Blazer. Then she was gone, her headlights cutting wary eyes across the parking lot.

I got into my own car and started it up. During the time it took to warm, I considered going back inside and helping Old Bob count the rest of those chair legs, but I figured it was something he had to do by himself and so I went on home. My heart went out to him, though, and I mean it. About half the time, I feel pretty damn compulsive myself.

FIVE

I awoke around six on Saturday morning. It was a pattern: I'd been waking with the dawn pretty much since the divorce — even if I'd had a night full of insomnia, which was also a pretty common occurrence these days. I'd had a bout with it the night before: my mind kept playing out a movie that was decades old, one filled with scenes I thought I'd never have to see again.

Linc was asleep on the couch. We'd had our dinner, but had gotten to talking about the Sixties and never made it to *Wages of Fear*. Sometime around ten we'd started digging out the music and that went on until maybe one. Linc was mostly tolerant, but a lot of it, especially Neil Young on *Comes a Time,* was sounding pretty damn good to me.

So I let myself out and had a walk along the levee in the dawn, my boots leaving first impressions in the snowscape. It wasn't snowing this morning, but the air was full of ice crystals. They were beautiful in the early light. I went back and showered and put on my only suit: blue wool Corbin's special. I knotted one of my three ties — the paisley one —

around my neck and stood back to look at myself in the bathroom mirror. Not the paisley. I went back to the closet and fished around until I found the red and black stripe and tried that one instead. Subdued but assertive. Good. Into the inside pocket of my coat I tucked the contract I'd typed out the night before and my good Cross pen. I pulled on my wool topcoat I'd bought on sale last July and took myself over to the Ramada for breakfast.

Halfway surprised to find the place open and feeling solvent as hell, what with Corrie Blake's check in my pocket, I started to treat myself to the Deckhand Special: three eggs scrambled with ham and hash browns. Then a wash of Spartanism mysteriously poured over me, and I wound up ordering Eggbeaters and wheat toast. The Eggbeaters were so bad that after I'd taken one bite, I asked the waitress for two real ones over easy. She didn't care: except for two salesmen marooned by the storm, I was the only customer in the place.

Fortified, I went back to my place and picked up the gym bag I'd dumped my extra shorts and socks and my toothbrush into. Underneath the clothing I tucked my gun: it was, after all, a security job. I had no idea whether I could hit anything with it — the only shooting I'd done in years had been on the practice range. I took the bag and some hanging clothes out to the car, went back inside, and stood looking at Linc. He slept on his back, with his head turned slightly away — as if someone had just called his name. I wanted him to be here when I got back, but I knew that wasn't going to happen. I closed the door and locked it and went on down to the car.

I drove up the hill, past the graveyard and on past the medical center. The streets were frozen slick, but there was very little traffic out and I made good time.

Crystal Jones, who, in spite of multiple marriages, was still using that name, lived up on Pill Hill, a realtor's dream so named because most of the doctors in town called it home. Pill Hill did have a view: it overlooked both the town and the river to the south and the rising hills to the north. Houses up there started at around $300,000, which meant that I couldn't have even afforded the green fees on the Hill's own private golf course. It was just after ten in the morning when I pulled my car in behind Corrie Blake's Blazer in the driveway of a two-story Tudor, which now wore a stately coating of snow. The sun had been threatening for about an hour now, but the sky was still overcast.

In the drifts, which had piled up in the front yard, a dog whose black coat contrasted sharply with its surroundings was bounding around: a rottweiler, about medium size for those dogs. Watching the animal from the porch was Corrie Blake. She still wore the bomber jacket. She was smoking, with a thin cloud rising on the slight wind. She offered me a brief wave and came out to meet me. The dog loped along behind her.

"Hiya," she said as I rolled down my window.

"Hi. This is it, huh?"

"This is it. Park over on the other side of me."

I pulled the car over, parked and then got out. "I wonder if even rich people get nosebleeds, being up this high and all," I said.

"You're a smartass, Haggard," she said, flipping her cigarette into the snow. "I noticed that last night."

"Want to fire me?"

"No. I like a smartass, to a point. Let's walk a minute."

The dog and I followed her across the street and toward a little park, its swingset and jungle gym now covered with snow. "Who's this guy?" I asked her. The dog seemed friendly enough.

"One of my two best friends," she told me over her shoulder.

"Rottweiler, huh?"

"Yep. But don't worry. He doesn't eat people unless I tell him to."

"What's his name?"

"Ollie."

"As in . . . "

"Stan and Ollie, yeah," she said, stopping by the swingset. "Stan's at home. He's a Lab. This is where she says she saw him."

"You mean . . . "

"Yeah. Crystal. This is where Delbert did his supper show. From her front window you can see this whole park. It's lit pretty good, but then by nine at night, so is Crystal."

"You don't like her much, do you?"

She looked straight at me. "Crystal earned my contempt," she said. "Every inch of it."

I surveyed the park. It was built on a triangle, and it evidently had been meant to dress up the cul-de-sac which half-circled it. Delbert would have had to have walked at least a half block to get there, assuming he had left a car on the street running back down the hill. Or maybe he had descended straight from the heavens.

"Yeah, I know," Corrie said. "You're thinking that Scotty must have beamed him down. It's a bunch of bullshit." The slight wind flurried her long hair across her face as her words trailed on breath you could see. She pushed her hair back, but not before I saw that the scar I'd noticed the night before was bigger and deeper than the light at the Huckins House had revealed. It ran nearly to her ear. She hunched into her jacket. "Just drunk bullshit," she said.

"Probably," I said.

She looked around. "Playgrounds always look scary in winter," she said. "Like a clown outside your door at midnight."

I looked at her. "Tell me about this lady," I said.

"She's scary, too," Corrie said. "She's almost human until around seven at night. Then she's drunk, and Crystal drunk is bad news."

"That the way you've always known her?" I asked.

"Somewhere back there, it was mostly drugs and not so much booze. Now it's all booze. And gin. I don't know when that changed. I hate the smell of gin."

"Who takes care of her when you're not here?"

"Her father, and a woman who works for him. Grandmother is dead."

"Why don't they handle this?" I asked.

"Crystal's father," she said with distaste, "is nearly ninety. And the secretary broke her foot. Broke her fucking foot. Can you believe it? They're sitting up there in that dump of his taking care of each other, I guess."

"No love lost with your grandfather, huh?"

"Something like that," Corrie said. She tossed her head against the wind. "Let's go meet Crystal. She won't stay sober all day, you know."

I followed her and the dog back across the street and up the stone steps to Crystal Jones' front door. Corrie pushed it open and let the dog in, then gestured to me to follow her. The interior wasn't as large as I would have guessed. The foyer opened onto a sunken living room built around a freestanding fireplace. A circular stair ascended into the upper portion of the house. From what Corrie had said, those were stairs Crystal must have a hell of a time negotiating some nights.

Off to my right was a kitchen, and that was where Corrie led me now. At the counter was Crystal Jones, carving a grapefruit. She looked pretty steady with the knife. "Crystal," Corrie said. "This is Sam Haggard."

She turned to meet me, working hard at a bright smile. It couldn't have been easy, since her thin face had endured one too many lifts: the telltale windows at the cheekbones seemed etched into her skin. She had the drawn quality of a Holocaust survivor, and much of that same sad sweetness. Her hair was the same bright blonde it had been in photographs from the Sixties, except that it came out of a bottle. She wore jeans and a long pullover sweater, and I was surprised to see that she was tall, maybe five-seven. She was bone-thin.

"Thank you for doing this, Mr. Haggard," she said, extending her hand. I had the feeling I was touching a casket handle. "I try to be strong, but I just can't be alone right now."

Her grip continued to hold mine. Her eyes were a pale gray. They fixed me pleadingly, with a cultivated vulnerability. I was at once attracted to her and repelled by her, as one might react to marginal art.

"I'll stick around for a couple of days and see how it goes," I told her. "This is probably just somebody's bad joke."

She freed my hand. "I don't think so," she said. "Let me show you where you'll stay."

I followed her through the kitchen and into a short hall while Corrie stayed behind. Crystal Jones led me to a small guest room which held a double bed and an ancient sewing machine. On the end table by the bed there was a good-sized lamp and a picture of Corrie. The room had no window.

"Bathroom's across the hall," she said.

"This looks fine," I told her. "You sleep upstairs, then?"

"I do. When I sleep. This thing has given me insomnia."

I stepped out of the guest room and she passed by me into the hall.

"But I promise not to keep you up," she said, brushing me lightly. I followed her back to the kitchen.

"So," Corrie said. "Are we set here?"

I pulled my contract out of my coat pocket and offered it to her. "Who wants to sign this?" I asked.

"I will," Corrie said, and took it. She unfolded the paper on the kitchen counter and peered at it.

"I should sign it," Crystal Jones said.

Corrie didn't look up. "You can't," she said shortly.

Her mother's eyes nearly closed. I could see their puffy quality now in the sunlight from the window by which she stood. Crystal Jones said nothing.

Corrie finished her reading. "Got a pen?" she said.

I handed her my Cross pen. She took it and signed the thing. "Not half bad as contracts go," she said, handing it back to me. "Better than my ex used to do."

"Jack is a good man," Crystal Jones said.

"As men go," Corrie said. "But he's a shit lawyer. C'mon, Bud," she said to the dog.

"I'll walk out with you," I said. "I need to get my bag."

The sun was now shining its rear end off and the wind had died. I walked with Corrie to the Blazer. She opened her door and let the dog jump in, then turned back to me.

"Crystal will probably try to get in your pants, if she hasn't already," she told me. "Don't let it go to your head. She'd fuck a roadrunner if she could get it to hold still long enough."

"Sounds like hazardous duty," I said.

"That's why you get the big bucks, Haggard. But there's no hazard: she passes out before she can make it every time." She fished a cigarette out of her coat and stuck it in her mouth. I hoped she wasn't counting on Ollie for much in the way of protection: the damn dog had to be half dead already of secondary smoke.

"And remember who your employer is," she said. "Me. I wasn't kidding about Crystal: her father has her power of attorney." She shook her head. "How screwed would your life have to get to make you hand it over to a senile old fart like him."

Now that we were parting, I found her cynicism irritating. I wanted something else from her, or at least less of this. "Maybe you should cut her some slack," I said. "There's a lot of drunks in the world. Some just happen to be mothers."

She gave a short laugh and then cupped her lighter. "Right," she said, and thumbed the Zippo. She snapped it shut and drew heavily on her Pall Mall. I thought she must be taking the smoke down to her toes. She looked straight at me. "Lemme tell you something, Haggard. There's a lot to be said for my childhood. Think of the life skills imparted, for one thing. Hell, I could roll a joint before I was two. They got pictures of me. And what's better than one daddy? How about seven or eight? How about maybe two or three at once? How about a couple of 'em in a fuckin' drunken brawl right outside your bedroom, if the shithole we happened to be living in that year had bedrooms. And how about cops? Man, I got to the point where I loved those cops. At least they sometimes took the daddies away with 'em when they left."

"I get it," I said.

"You just think you do," she said. She dragged on the cigarette again and looked away, into the sun.

"I'm sorry for your life," I said, and meant it. "I wish it had been different."

She sat resting both forearms on the steering wheel as the car warmed, the cigarette hanging loosely between the first two fingers of her right hand. She smiled. "I wish your suit was different," she said. "Where the hell do you get something like that, Haggard? The Family Dollar? Jesus. Go in there and get your jeans on and hang out. Big Mama needs babysittin'." She put the car in gear and backed into the street. She gave me a wave as she pulled out. She had rolled the back window down so Ollie could hang his head out. I hoped to God she wasn't thinking of driving the eighty miles back to Columbus that way.

I stood looking after her until the Blazer was down the hill and out of sight. Then I got my bag and went back into the house, thinking that Corrie was right: I'd better change clothes. In a high-profile job like this, image is everything.

SIX

Maybe you ought to tell me about it," I said to Crystal Jones. We were sitting in the kitchen. She had taken me on a tour of the house, which turned out to be a lot smaller than it looked. She had made coffee, and we both had a cup in front of us on the small table. I had gotten rid of my tie and jacket. She sat across from me, opening a package of Eve cigarettes. Her hair in the kitchen sunlight seemed to me to be bleached nearly white: there were points at her temples where the hairline was indistinguishable from the pallor of her skin.

"Is it all right to call you Sam?" she asked me, and when I nodded she said: "What did Corrie tell you?" She picked a Bic lighter up from the table and held it in one hand. The cigarette pack lay on the table in front of her as if it were Pandora's box, containing some terrible truth, which would emerge when she opened it.

"That you believe you have seen your husband," I said.

"Due to a particularly bad case of delirium tremens." She clutched the lighter.

"Not exactly."

A ghostly smile played on her thin lips. "Not exactly. I'll bet. I know what she says about me. Well, I saw him all right. Right out that front window." She waved the lighter in the direction of the living room.

"I have to ask. How would you know it was Delbert? I mean, twenty-five years . . ."

"I know," she said. She opened the pack finally and took one out. She tapped it on the table in staccato thumps. Her nails were polished a pale pink which even so stood out in sharp contrast to her skin.

I drank my coffee. She knows. Simple as that.

I tried again. "Where would he have been all this time?" I asked.

"Canada. A lot of them went there. Mexico. Or anywhere."

"And why wouldn't he have made contact in all this time?"

She tossed the cigarette down without lighting it. "We didn't part on the best of terms," she said. She pulled a kitchen napkin out of the holder on the table and started dabbing at her eyes with it.

"When was the last time you saw him?" I asked. If she was about to buckle on me, I wanted to get a couple of more questions in.

She looked at me, sort of. "I just told you," she said. "Out there. Two weeks ago."

"I meant before that."

"On that morning, the morning of the shootings. I was pretty far pregnant with Corrie, but I still had the morning sickness like everything, a long time after it was supposed to quit. The last time I saw him I was throwing up." She blew her nose into the napkin, then wadded it. "Fitting, really. He made me vomit about half the time anyway, pregnant or not."

I got up and went to the counter to pour more coffee. "I thought you two were celebrities at that point," I said.

"Well," she said, "We were on Cavett. For about three minutes." She gave a short laugh, an ugly one. "Big effing deal," she said.

"You were enrolled at Kent?"

"Once upon a time. Not by then. We were living pretty much on the charity of the movement by that time, up there in the haunted house."

I knew what she meant. I'd read about it the night before. "SDS head-quarters," I said.

"Headquarters?" She snorted again. "It was an effing dump. Just a crash pad, that's all. We weren't organized enough to have a headquarters. Ohio State was organized. OU at Athens was organized. We were smoking pot and dropping acid and listening to Buffalo Springfield. Believe me, nobody thought the whole world was about to be watching us."

"Some have greatness thrust upon them," I said.

She turned mildly defensive. "Del and I knew some of the big ones, though. We met Jerry Rubin in New York. And we met Abbie Hoffman. That Vecchio girl stayed at the haunted house, you know. I met her, too."

"Had Del been involved with the trouble down on Water Street?"

"He was down there. I was too sick."

"So what do you think happened to him?" I asked her.

She had picked up the cigarette again. "I think he ran," she said. "What else? He didn't believe that Corrie was his child. Also, he was in some kind of trouble. More than usual, I mean."

"What kind of trouble?"

She shrugged. "I don't know. Police trouble, I guess. Maybe the FBI. He was into so much I couldn't keep up. Anyway, I know he was at the Commons later. Wait." She got up and went into the living room, return-ing with the same picture Corrie had showed me the night before. "There," she said, plopping it down in front of me.

"Corrie showed it to me," I said.

"I guess you think it's stupid to hold on to a black-and-white photo-graph like that," she said. "Corrie does."

I said nothing.

"Before the colors came," she said.

"What?" I asked her.

"Once when Corrie was little I found her looking at this picture. She must have been four or five. And she said: 'Mommy, is this before the colors came?' I guess she'd never seen a black and white picture before."

I smiled. I was trying to picture Corrie that young.

"I guess the world really wasn't black and white then either," Crystal said.

"No."

"We tried to make it that way. 'Don't trust anyone over thirty.' What a G.D. crock that was."

I was getting as impatient with her inability to utter an honest curse word as I was with Mac's penchant for the things. "You and Corrie don't get along," I said.

"Corrie has a lot of resentment. I don't blame her. I dragged her around a lot." She looked briefly like she was going to mist up again, but it passed. "I want to be close with her," she said finally. I couldn't tell if she meant it or not. I couldn't even tell if I had yet seen the real Crystal Jones. Her pallor gave the impression of transparence, as if she were more hologram than real.

"She's very independent," I said.

Crystal finally put the cigarette in her mouth and lit it. "Nobody can tell Corrie anything," she said. "Nobody ever could."

Once again I said nothing.

"She's dumping me, you know. That's all this is about. She wants to get on with her effing life, but she doesn't want to feel any guilt about it."

I felt like the woman was talking more about herself than she was about her daughter. "Look," I told her. "That part is none of my business. Your daughter seemed sincere enough to me, but even if she wasn't, she did hire me to do this job and I'm going to try to earn the money. I'm here, which means I'm here to help you. If the phone rings, you pick up in the living room and I'll get to that one —" I pointed to the wall phone in the kitchen, " —to pick up with you. If you see anything funny out your window, I'll check it out. But I wouldn't be looking out the window: it's the last thing you want to do if somebody's watching you."

She shivered and then ground out her cigarette. She'd held it for a while, but I hadn't seen her actually take a puff, in contrast to Corrie, who seemed to inhale every drag down to her knees. "I don't like to think about somebody out there," she said.

"Then don't. That's what I'm here for." I stood up. "This weather has broken. By tomorrow the sun will be out and this will be a bad dream."

"The police wouldn't do anything, you know," she said.

"They're pretty busy."

"Right," she said.

"I'm going to settle into that room," I said. "I'll check with you later, or just yell if you need me." I left her sitting at the kitchen table and went out to my car.

How do you do a job like this? I wondered. Should I have offered to play board games with her? The woman seemed to have nothing to do except wait for something that wasn't coming. If not Delbert, then some other lost dream. The patchy sunlight felt good. I dreaded going back into the house, but I got my gym bag and my change of clothes and toted them inside. She was sitting where I had left her, tapping on the table with another cigarette.

"I'll want to put my car in your garage," I said.

"Great," she said without looking up.

I went through the kitchen door into the garage and activated the rollup door from the inside. I stowed the Corsica and then came back in and went down the hall to my room, leaving the door open. I dug out my toothbrush and my deodorant and put them in the little bathroom. Then I got one of my books out of the bag and stretched out on the bed, propping myself up on the pillows. I took a crack at reading, but Corrie kept looking at me out of the silver frame. After awhile I looked back and wondered how old she would have been in the picture. Maybe eighteen — a graduation photo? She was wearing a sweater. A small chain hung from her neck. Her hair was a little longer even, and she had that unflinching look in her eyes. A ghost of a smile played at the corners of her mouth. Had she been born looking that savvy?

Presently I heard Crystal Jones get up and go into the small study in the front part of the house. I heard a door shut and then distant music: she must have turned on a radio. I tried to read some more, but I couldn't stick with it. I put the book down and lay back thinking about the bad contract I'd made. How did you know when this job was finished? Corrie had said to give it three days, but would it really work that way? Was Crystal going to pop in and say she was all better? That she'd run that monster out from under her bed all by herself? Would she dipso out on me? I had yet to see her take a drink, but according to all reports that wouldn't last long. Who the hell was I supposed to call then? Gramps? The hospital? The Old Hippies' Home?

The phone rang.

I jumped off the bed and got to the kitchen in time to see Crystal Jones emerging from her bedroom. We looked at each other. I pointed to the cordless which sat in its cradle on the living room coffee table. As she went to it, I backed into the kitchen and got ready to pull the receiver off the wall. More or less together, we picked up the two receivers. We wouldn't have fooled anybody on the other end, but all I was looking to do was establish that she was getting strange calls. Even a hang-up might do that.

"Hello?" said Crystal.

"It's Corrie."

I put my receiver back in its cradle and started back for my room. Then Crystal said: "Wait a minute." I looked back to see her dangling the receiver from one hand. "It's for you," she said.

I went back to the kitchen and picked up there. Crystal hung up and went back to the study, although she did not close the door.

"Yes," I said into the receiver.

"Haggard," she said. "I'm in Columbus."

"Roads okay?"

"Yeah, they're all slop by now. How you doing?"

"Fine."

"Sorry for cutting loose on you." She laughed at little. "And I'm sorry for what I said about your suit."

"Rolled right off. I've got the hide of a rhinoceros."

"Anyway, you can get me if you need me. I work most nights at the Purple Haze in the Brewery District on High."

"Purple Haze. How do Hendrix People tip?"

"Shit," she said. "Hendrix wouldn't be caught dead in the dump. But I'm not a waitress. I'm assistant manager, fuck you very much."

"Just assistant? I'm surprised."

"Kiss my ass, Haggard," she said, but nicely enough.

"There's an extra charge for that service, Ma'am."

She laughed. "How's Mom?"

"She's okay. What's the phone number where you work?"

She told me. I wrote it down on a paper towel I tore from the roll in front of me. "Okay," I told her.

"Okay yourself," she said. "Call me on Monday or before if you need me."

"I will."

We hung up. I went back and lay down. After awhile Crystal emerged and started rattling in the kitchen. I went in.

She looked up. "Hungry?" she asked me.

"Sure. Why don't you let me cook us something?"

"Nonsense," she said, and took down a chopping board. Some tomatoes, lettuce, and an onion already lay on the counter.

I moved beside her. "Then at least let me do some slicing," I said.

That seemed to be all right. Crystal took some deboned chicken breasts out of the refrigerator and threw them in a frying pan with some olive oil. Then she added spices.

"Smells good," I said.

"I can cook," she told me.

The phone rang again. This time I ran for the living room. We picked up again. Crystal spoke.

"Honey?" came a voice that sounded like a flushing toilet.

"Daddy," she replied.

"Is the detective there?" I heard as I took the receiver away from my ear, and I heard Crystal answer that I was. Then I went back to my chopping.

When dinner was on the kitchen table, Crystal asked me to open a bottle of wine. I did and poured her a glass.

"None for you?"

"I'm working," I told her.

"Suit yourself."

We ate — or I did, anyway. Crystal picked. She drank a glass of wine and poured herself another.

"I did see him," she said suddenly. I looked up. She had a little color now, but I had trouble believing she was feeling much effect from one glass of wine. But how did I know? She could have been sloshing it down in the study all day.

"I believe you saw someone," I said.

She went over to the counter and came back with cigarettes. She sat back down and stared at her plate. "Where were you in 1970?" she asked me.

"Waist deep in the Big Muddy," I said.

She looked at me. "What?"

"Viet Nam."

"I never even understood what that was about," she said.

"Neither did I."

She drank more wine. "You were in the army?"

"Yeah. I was drafted."

"So it's probably hard for you to understand people who protested the war."

"Nope," I said. "I did that, too."

"After you came back?"

"Yeah," I said.

"Did you know about Delbert and me before this?" she asked, maybe a little urgently.

"Not at the time. I heard about you when I got back."

She brightened a little. "What did you think about us?"

"I thought you were pretty silly. Shock effect wasn't playing very well for me by that time."

"Serves me right for asking," she said. She pushed back her plate and started fiddling with another cigarette. "I won't get drunk tonight," she said.

"Okay."

She looked at me again. "It's the only drug they left me, you know," she said.

"I can appreciate that. I'll do the dishes."

She got up. "I insist," she said.

We watched some CNN on the living room set, and then Crystal went up to bed. I turned the volume down and flipped channels awhile.

I finally came upon *The Day the Earth Stood Still* and watched that through to the end. Crystal's light had been out for forty-five minutes or so. I flicked off the remote and looked around the room, settling on the bookcase. I got up, stretched, and walked over, curious as usual about what people read. But there wasn't much in the way of reading matter: some new age stuff and a lot of popular novels. The May 4 picture and some scrapbooks were there as well.

I took one out. It was labeled Wedding. Corrie's as it turned out. She was early twenties, looking pretty much like now. The guy she was feeding cake to was blond and handsome, as surfer-looking as a guy from Ohio was likely to get. This must be Blake. They made a damned attractive couple.

"He's there," Crystal Jones said.

I looked up. I hadn't heard her come down. She was wearing a long nightdress and she was standing at the side of the front window, peering through the curtains. I dropped the photo album and went to her. I looked over her shoulder. I could see the little park across the street, bathed in moonlight. A man stood by the swingset. He was medium height and his hands were shoved into the pockets of a dark overcoat. He was hatless and, from this distance, appeared to be balding. He wore glasses.

"There," Crystal said again. "He's there."

"Go upstairs to your room and lock the door," I said. "I have to go out there. I need your keys."

"It's me he wants," she said, almost matter-of-factly. She went into the kitchen and came back with a set of keys. Then she went upstairs again and shut the door. I heard it lock.

I went over to the indoor garage door and opened it very carefully, wishing I'd gotten the gun. But I didn't want to lose the guy. I slipped into the darkness of the garage and shut the door as quietly as I could. Keeping my back to the far wall, I moved forward to the garage door and looked through one of the small windows. He was still there.

I went to the side garage door and very quietly opened it. Outside, the air was frigid. I pushed in the knob lock and closed the door. A fairly stiff wind cut through my shirtsleeves. I made my way around the side of the house, stopping at the driveway.

He was gone.

Somewhere up the street a car started. "Shit," I said aloud.

I walked over to the playground. Most of the houses I could see were dark, but there was plenty of moonlight. I walked to where I'd seen the man standing. There was no trace of him, not a telltale cigarette butt or dropped book of matches bearing some incriminating address or anything. He might as well have never been there.

I realized that I was standing where he had stood, and that I, too, was looking at the house. I didn't know why, but a word I'd read someplace crossed my mind: doppelganger. Double. The cold finger of the night traced a pattern up my spine.

Crystal. Why had she acted so calm about this? Was she zoned? Was she that scared? What the hell was going on?

I went on back across the street and let myself in the front door. When I got to the bottom of the stairs I stopped. Though I'd told her to lock it, Crystal's door was wide open.

SEVEN

Crystal was sitting on the floor by her bed. It was a brass bed, unmade. She was on the left side, in front of the night table. The receiver of a portable phone was in her hands.

We looked at each other. For a moment nothing happened. Then she threw the telephone onto the floor in front of her, flinging it away as if it had been a snake.

"Who was that?" I asked.

"I tried to call my father. The machine was on."

"What about the police?"

"They won't come." She remained sitting on the floor, grasping her arms around her knees. She rocked a little. The room was cold. I looked to the other side of the bed and saw that a window was open. I went over and shut it, then went to Crystal.

"Let me help you," I said. I bent down and got her around the arms, pulling her to her feet. She obeyed listlessly.

"I saw someone out there," I said.

"Yes," she replied.

"Let's go downstairs. Maybe get some coffee."

We went, Crystal allowing herself to be supported most of the way. I got her seated on the living room couch and started for the kitchen.

"Drink," she said.

I turned back.

"Drink. I want a drink. I want a gin. It's above the sink."

I found the bottle in the cabinet over the sink. Seagram's. It was about half full. I poured some on ice.

"Any tonic?" I called back to her.

"Just the gin," she said.

I brought in the glass. She took it from me and pretty well downed what I poured in. Happy days.

I sat down on a hassock. "Who is he, Crystal?" I asked her.

"Who do you think?" She drank again. The glass was nearly empty.

"Delbert's dead."

"Think what you want. Get me another drink." She held out the glass.

I went back to the kitchen and poured Crystal more gin. I took it back and she repeated the same ritual.

"Slow down," I said. "We need to talk about this."

She sat back, clutching the gin as if stitched to it. She seemed to need nothing else. Not a cigarette, nothing. Not even a life. "He wasn't very attractive, you know," she said.

"I saw the pictures. He looked like any other freak did then."

"No. Del was not a pretty boy. There were plenty who were. There were men who looked like angels." She killed the drink.

"If you want any more," I told her, "you'll have to get it yourself."

She looked straight ahead. "Angels," she said.

I moved to an armchair. The seat had a busted spring and I sank into it. "Were there angels at Kent?" I asked her.

"Yes," she said. "There were angels. A lot of them. I knew angels. An angel took me to Yellow Springs, a dark angel."

"What angels, Crystal? What are you talking about?"

"About Yellow Springs. We went there on the bus, right after the shootings."

"Who went there?"

"A lot of people. Me and a lot of people."

I waited. Crystal wasn't a linear thinker, and she wasn't telling the story that way. But at least she was telling me something.

She pulled her bare feet up under her. She still wore the nightdress. If her arms were cold, she showed no sign. "We didn't go to very many classes anymore, any of us. Del wasn't even in school. He said the real education was in the streets." She was looking at something across the room so intently that I turned my head. Nothing. Just the bookcase wall.

"But I remember," she said, "that in a history class at that time we had studied the Triangle Fire." Now she looked at me. "Do you know about that?"

She was very different now. She had lost that coyness, and she had dropped the affectations; no spelled-out swear words, no forced sensuality. Her delivery was dead on. "I know the name," I said. "I don't remember what happened."

"It was right before World War I, in New York. These sweatshop girls got locked in their own factory. The owners locked the exits because they were afraid the girls would take breaks." She picked up her glass and looked at it. "And a fire started, and they burned up in there. Except for the ones who jumped. But they were on the seventh floor and they knew they were jumping to their deaths." She sat the glass down. "They must have thought it was the end of the world."

I said nothing.

"That's what we felt like," she said then. "We had been chased around all weekend, especially after the ROTC building burned. Not me, I mean. I didn't go out. But I saw it. We got up in one of the dorms and saw it all. But when they started shooting on Monday, that was like the end of the world. It was the fire all around." She sighed. "And so they took us to Yellow Springs, and it was all hippies there. All angels."

The woman was quicksilver. I still said nothing. She got up and went into the kitchen. She poured more gin and downed it right there. I stood. She looked at me.

"Might as well just use the bottle," she said. She laughed a little, a forlorn laugh.

"Tell me about that day," I said.

"Since then I never get very far from an exit," she said. "Never. I won't even go in the basement. I've never been in the basement of this house."

"Tell me."

"One day I lost my husband; the next I had a baby."

"Tell me about that."

Crystal returned to the couch, sloshing gin and walking badly now. "Where're my cigarettes?" she asked. She sat.

I fetched them from the kitchen counter where I'd seen them earlier, and I handed her the pack, figuring she'd want to play with them for a while. But she was too drunk for that. She tossed them on the end table beside her.

"My baby was born the next day," she said. "My Corrie."

"I know."

"I made that scar."

I looked at her. "What?" I said.

"Corrie's scar. I did it."

I leaned forward. "What are you talking about, Crystal?"

She spoke matter-of-factly again, not slurring now. "I threw an ashtray. At a man. It hit a wall and broke and then it hit Corrie. She was five. The fight had woken her and she had come down the stairs at the exact right time . . . " She stopped. "Exact wrong time," she continued, and, slur or not, I knew she was drunk. Very drunk.

"It cut her deep, a piece of it did." Crystal took another drink, sloshing it badly. "But I never did . . . I didn't understand . . . The doctor said that when she was sixteen he could fix that, but he wanted to see how it came in. You know, as she grew. But then Corrie wouldn't have it fixed. She wouldn't do it. Daddy would have paid for it. I mean, I didn't personally have any insurance or anything."

"Corrie's a beautiful woman," I said. "She must know that."

"Corrie knows everything," she said.

The story sickened me. A familiar feeling of powerlessness swept over me, the same one I have always had in those moments when life has shown me how badly it is possible for us to treat our children: hostages to our thousand broken dreams. "What man were you fighting with, Crystal?" I asked her.

"Wasn't John," she said. Her head lolled against the back of the couch. Four tumblers of gin had done their work, but I tried anyway:

"Who's John?" I asked.

Crystal said nothing.

I carried her up and put her to bed, sort of. Of course it hadn't been just four gins, even of that size. Crystal had been drinking all day. I covered her up and turned out the bed-table light. I looked at her in the moonlight and tried to feel better toward her, but couldn't. I went back downstairs.

It was ten after two. I got my gun, loaded it, picked up the key to the house, and went out through the garage again, locking the door behind me. I stood in the darkness at the side of the house, listening. I could see part of the driveway. It was very quiet. The temperature had warmed a lot: it could have been in the thirties. The snow still glistened, but if this weather held it was going to melt quickly. I let myself back inside.

I went to the kitchen and put on some coffee. Then I went to my room and picked up my book. But that wasn't what I wanted to read. I put it down and dug in my pack for the Kent State books. I took them back into the living room and sat down.

I was partway through the first chapter of *Four Dead in Ohio* when the coffee perked. I made myself a cup and sat back down. I read until just before six, skipping around some in both my books. They had very different theses. One said that the shooting occurred because Richard Nixon had chosen to make an example at Kent State, a relatively small venue, easily contained. The other said that the Guard had finally had enough taunts and threats by the time it got to the football practice field, and that then and there it had collectively decided to start shooting. The first came down on the side of conspiracy; the other on the side of spontaneous action.

I thought for a while about the nature of violent behavior. Every detective story I'd ever read began with the premise that there is always a reason. I wondered what you were writing when you went from the presumption that there doesn't need to be. Maybe True Crime. I suddenly became aware that I was staring at the bookcase. Something had caught my eye, the spine of a book. I went over and pulled it out. *Getting Out Alive,* by Crystal Jones. With Selena Blair, whoever she was. The cover bore a butterfly design, badly done. I'd never heard of the publishing company. Flipping the book over, I found myself looking at Crystal, maybe fifteen years ago. Her hair was long and pinned back in a clip. She wore a simple dress and looked almost virginal. A snow queen; an ice goddess. I studied her features for something of Corrie, but it wasn't there.

Somebody was stirring in the kitchen. I had lain down with my clothes on. I got up. Something, a glass probably, crashed on the kitchen floor. Around the corner of the living room I could see her. Her back was to me. She still wore the night dress. There was a fresh bottle of gin on the counter in front of her, and broken glass around her bare feet.

"You'll cut yourself," I said.

She turned around. Her eyes were hard and her downturned lip made her mouth ugly. "Fuck off," she said.

"You need sleep. Let me help you back upstairs."

She picked another glass out of the sink and threw it on the floor. It shattered. I watched a shard carom across the floor and come to rest by the dishwasher. "Keep away from me," she said.

"Crystal. I'm here to help you."

She picked up another glass and threw it at me. Her aim wasn't bad, and I had to sidestep. It landed on the living room carpet and, amazingly, didn't break. I went to Crystal and caught her by the arms. She tried to wrestle away, but I held her elbows to her side. "Stop it," I ordered.

The thought came to me that we must make a fine pair, standing there in the kitchen at six in the morning fighting over a bottle of gin. By any measure we would look ridiculous. The dog was us. All my life I had been around alcohol-induced behavior. Twice I had almost become a drunk myself: right after I came back from Vietnam, and the second year I was a cop. I saved myself the first time by realizing I was blaming things on the war that were really my fault. The second time I didn't know what had saved me. Linc, I guess.

Crystal wrenched her arms away. "Stop that!" she hissed. She pushed away hard, backing up until she was against the stove. "All my life," she said, "men have held me down."

"Crystal . . . "

She tore open the drawer beside her and came up with a butcher knife. She held it overhand, as if she were going to attack. Then she screamed.

I moved in close and slapped the knife out of her hand. She screamed again. I put my shoulder into her midriff and lifted her, carrying her like a toesack. I didn't know what else to do. I was sure she would scream again, but instead she went limp. I carried her into the living room and sat her down on the coach. She stayed there, rigid. I sat beside her.

"Now, you have to understand this," I told her. "Either you get it together, or I have to call somebody. And if somebody does come here, you will probably get taken away."

I could see in her eyes that this was not an unfamiliar premise. She continued to sit in that rigid posture. She didn't even blink.

"Crystal," I said.

"He's coming for me."

"Who? Who's coming? Is it Delbert?"

"No," she said. "Not him."

"Crystal. Listen to me. Is it the man you called John?"

She laughed, letting her head fall back. Sometime during the night she had tried to put on some lipstick, and aimed badly. A scarlet slash ran down from the corner of her mouth like a scar. She was passing out again.

I knew enough CPR not to be too threatened. Her breathing remained regular and she seemed to be in no danger, just drunk. With Crystal, there was no just anymore. For the second time that night I carried her up and put her to bed in the blue gray of first morning light

I cleaned up the glass, and then went back to my reading. I thought I'd doze, but I didn't. So I got up and made coffee and was pouring myself a cup when I heard a car in the drive. Then two doors slammed, one after the other. I went to the front window and saw that it was a police car. An uniformed officer and an older man wearing a well-cut black overcoat were making their way to the door. I waited, letting them ring. Then I went to the door.

The sunlight outside hurt my eyes. "Morning," I said.

The cop was black, late twenties. "You Haggard?" he asked. He wore aviator sunglasses whose frames glinted in the sun. The older man stood back a distance.

"Who wants to know?" I said.

"Crystal Jones here?"

"Who wants to know that?"

The cop pulled off his sunglasses and looked me over. "Her father," he said. "This is Mr. Mills."

The older guy stepped forward and handed me a card. I looked at it. Lawyer. "I represent Carl Payton," he said.

I handed the card back and pushed open the door. "I'm Haggard," I said. "Come on in."

They followed me into the kitchen. "Want some coffee?" I asked them.

The young cop, whose nametag read Leasure, shook his head, but Mills said he'd like some. I saw that the cop kept staring at the floor, and I wished I'd done a better job on the glass. Probably little pieces all over hell. I poured the lawyer a cup and pointed at the half-and-half and sugar I'd set out for myself.

"Where is Mrs. Jones?" Mills asked me. He took a tentative sip of his coffee.

"She's sleeping."

"That's fine," Mills said. He set down his cup and reached into his inside topcoat pocket, drawing out an envelope. "This is for you," he said.

It was unsealed. I opened it and shook out a check. It was from Carl Payton, in the amount of seven hundred dollars. "What's this?" I asked.

The cop was looking out the window. "You're paid," Mills said. "In full. You are free to leave now."

"I think I should talk to Ms. Blake. She hired me."

"Only directly. Indirectly her grandfather did, and it is he who is now terminating your services. Mrs. Jones will be fine. We have dealt with her in these . . . situations before."

"I want to call Ms. Blake."

Mills sniffed. "You are quite welcome to do that. On your own time. But you are off our clock as of now. Thanks very much, Mr. Haggard."

The cop turned now and looked me over again. His eyes were sullen, as if he too had been up all night. I didn't say anything. I took another drink of coffee and then collected my books from the living room, also grabbing Crystal's. I got my clothes from the bedroom. When I passed the bedside table, I got a last look at Corrie's face in the picture. She seemed to be looking at me with reproach, but I didn't know what the hell to do except get out of there and call her.

I went back into the kitchen. "I think that's my old uniform," I told the cop.

"Could be," he said. No expression.

"Thanks again, Mr. Haggard," Mills said. He was pouring more coffee.

"I think I should tell you," I said, "that there was someone outside last night."

Mills stirred coffee. He didn't look at me. "Crystal said that?" He asked. It was strange to hear him use her first name.

"I saw a man. There was someone out there." There was a short sound from the cop, who was standing behind me. Mills leaned against the counter and stared at me.

"Do you have anything to say about that?" I asked him.

His hair was very thin and combed back. He wore steel-rimmed glasses, which he now took off, as if to polish the lenses. He looked at them, and then at me again. "I say you were the right man for this job, Haggard," he said. The cop behind me snorted again.

I got out of there. The dog was Haggard. I drove down the hill and as far as the first Stop and Go on the Scioto Trial. The phone was outside, and I shivered into my jacket while I held the napkin in one hand and punched in Corrie's number in Columbus with the other. The "ding" sounded and I punched in my calling card number.

The machine picked up. "Hi," her voice came. "This is Corrie. Leave a message." Then the buzz.

I hung up. I couldn't figure out how to sum this up. I looked at my watch. It read ten till nine. I drove home to try to put this mess together. The sun was bright and much of the snow was turning to slush. By tomorrow most of it would be a memory.

My apartment looked the same. I started some coffee and then broke out a skillet, working with the portable phone wedged in my neck. I called Corrie several times, but kept getting the service. I fried myself a couple of eggs and made some toast, then sat down in the breakfast nook to eat. I had thought I was hungry, but I wasn't.

I had been bought off. From what, I didn't know. Finally I called back and left a message on Corrie's service to call me, then scraped my breakfast into the trash and washed up my dishes. I took a shower, put on pajamas and stretched out on the couch. After awhile I heard church bells. Maybe that's where Corrie was. Maybe not. Maybe she'd spent the night somewhere.

I dozed, but couldn't really sleep. There were vivid pictures waiting for me when I closed my eyes — sometimes of the pagoda and of soldiers; sometimes of the figure I'd seen in the little park last night. Sometimes of Crystal, her mouth a scar. Sometimes of Corrie.

I read more about Kent State. I thought about going to the library and sifting through old newspapers for the kind of background I'd need if I — if what?

By four o'clock Corrie still wasn't answering. I showered again, shaved, got dressed, and went down to the car. I guess I thought I was going out to dinner. I drove around awhile, and wound up heading north on 23, toward Columbus.

EIGHT

The eastern jag of Whittier — Corrie's street, according to the address I'd copied off the check she'd given me — was in a mostly black neighborhood which was also mostly poor. The few stores had bars on their windows, as did many of the homes. The house with Corrie Blake's address sat by an alley. It was small and needed paint. I could see a driveway off the alley, and in the driveway sat the Blazer.

I rang the bell. First barking, and a lot of it. Stan and Ollie. Then Corrie. Her hair was loose over her shoulders. She wore a man's work-shirt and jeans. On her nose was a pair of dark-rimmed glasses. On her left was Ollie. On her right a tan Labrador who stood past Corrie's knees.

"Shush," she said, and both dogs did. I immediately became aware of Janis Joplin in the background. "Summertime." Corrie fixed me with that look I was getting to know very well. "Haggard," she said. "You're off your turf."

"Sorry to bother you at home," I said.

She pulled off the glasses. "What the hell?" she said. "C'mon in."

I followed her into a living room, the dogs pacing me every step of the way. The little house was strictly World War II issue: a longish living room which opened onto a tiny dining room and, at the back of the house, a kitchen. Somewhere off the dining room there would be a bedroom and bath. I'd been in a lot of houses like it over the years: the people I'd known seemed to favor them. The living room had a long couch against one wall with a couple of guest chairs facing it. The furniture was old but not shabby — probably the result of careful shopping in the junk shops above the Short North. The opposite wall was filled with stereo equipment — even a turntable. All this sat in a large bookcase, and CDs were piled high in the shelves below the big speakers, which perched on top of the entire thing. And everywhere there were candles. There must have been ten or twelve of those small vases that a votive candle fits in, and every one bore a lighted candle. The table lamps on each end of the couch were on, and so was the kitchen light. But the candles blazed away nonetheless. Corrie went to the stereo and turned down Janis. Not off, just down. Then she returned.

"What's up?" she said.

"I got fired."

"By Crystal?"

"By Grandpa."

"Shit," she said. "The asshole." She pointed toward a chair for me and deposited herself on the couch, crossing her legs beneath her. She was shoeless, wearing white socks. The dogs sprawled on the rug under the coffee table. Candles: on the mantle above the fake fireplace, and on the end table near the window, and at each end of the table between us. We were maybe five feet apart. She plucked her Pall Malls off the coffee table, sat back and shook one out. She reached in the pocket of her flannel shirt and pulled out the Zippo. "You get paid?" she asked me as she tapped down the cigarette against the lighter.

"Yeah," I said.

"All of it?"

"Seven hundred bucks."

She lit the cigarette, dragged in, and then exhaled. "Crystal go psycho on you?" she asked.

"Only mildly. I'm not here to get paid, Corrie. I came to tell you that your mother really is in danger."

"You talk to the old man?" she said.

"No. He sent his lawyer."

"Him," Corrie said with an eyeroll. "What reason did he give?"

"He said their own people would handle it now."

She snorted. "What people?" she said.

"I don't know. Look, something's funny here. I told you about seeing the guy and about Crystal being on the phone. Well, like I also told you, later on she really did get pretty hammered and she unloaded on me. Lots of guilt; lots of memory. She rambled about Yellow Springs a lot . . . "

"Yellow Springs?" Corrie said.

"Yeah. She talked about getting bussed there after the shootings and about living there for a few weeks. I guess you were born there."

Corrie ashed, then sat back again. "That's what it says on the birth certificate."

I shifted in my seat, feeling a strange urgency. "You must have heard her talk about this before," I said.

Corrie got up. "Want a beer?" she asked, and padded into the kitchen.

"No, I don't. Corrie — I'm serious about this."

I heard the fridge open and close. She reappeared, applying an opener to a Corona. She held the bottle up to me. "Sure?" she said.

"I'm sure." I waited while Corrie sat again. She held the bottle by the neck, dangling it over the arm of the sofa.

"Okay, Haggard," she said. "You have to understand something. I've been on my own a long time, and I've kinda done my best to avoid Crystal."

"But you must have—"

"No. I didn't. I haven't. Not even holidays. She was at my wedding. That was the last time I saw her before this, and that was ten years ago. I have no idea what her demons are, and I don't much care."

"So why did you call me? Why bother?"

Corrie shrugged. "You called me," she replied, and drank some more beer.

"Look," I said. "I'm telling you that the woman may really be in danger. Somebody called her — someone she believes she can trust. But I think she's wrong. It's connected somehow to something that happened in Yellow Springs, maybe right after the shootings and right about the time you were born."

"I don't remember anything about that time. How could I?"

"I understand that. I want to know if she ever talked to you about any of this, drunk or sober."

"No. We went down there once, though. I was maybe twelve."

At last, something that sounded like information. "What happened?" I demanded.

"Nothing. We ate lunch, went to a junk shop. It was one of Crystal's periods where she was making a stab at mothering." She drank again, nearly emptying the bottle. In three swigs.

"Anything else?"

"Seems like she met a guy, but that happened a lot."

"Remember anything about him?"

Janis quit singing. Taking that as a cue, Corrie drank again and set the empty bottle on the coffee table. She got up and started blowing out candles. Both dogs bounded up, nearly knocking each other over. "Not a damn thing," she said. "I'm surprised I remember that. Seems like we went to a big park, though." She walked across the room and blew out the rest of the candles. For a minute I thought I was being dismissed, but then she went into the little dining room and shoved her feet into some scuffed brown loafers which had been sitting under the table. "Come on, Haggard, if you want to keep this going," she said. "I gotta run these dogs."

I followed as she headed through the kitchen to the back door, the dogs bounding around her legs. She snared her bomber jacket off a hook on the kitchen wall and opened the back door, motioning me to follow. The steps outside led to a small back yard, completely enclosed by hedge. I trailed Corrie and the dogs through a back gate which opened onto the driveway I'd seen. Corrie opened the driver's door of the Blazer and pulled down the seat. The dogs jumped in, Ollie first, to the back seat. As I got in the other side, she said: "Gotta leave the windows open. These guys like to hang their heads out."

I dutifully rolled down my window. It was almost mild outside, but not quite. Corrie backed out into the alley and drove toward the street. Ollie panted in my ear. Once on Whittier, she picked up speed. Some young black males stood on the opposite side of the street from Corrie's house, hunching into their coats.

"Crack deal going down," Corrie said and shoved a Pall Mall into her mouth. She lit it and glanced at me. "Don't smoke, huh, Haggard?" she demanded, as if this were the first time she had noticed it.

"I might as well. Everybody I care about does."

She laughed a little. We drove a few blocks, then turned off in the direction of the 270 outerbelt. Out here there was still melting snow, gathered in forlorn clumps at the side of the road. I thought we were going to get on the loop, but Corrie, who was driving well, but too fast to suit me, turned off instead and pulled into an industrial park. The buildings, mostly one-story, stood like sentinels around us. She stopped the car.

"Here we go, boys," she said, and let the dogs out on her side. They knew where they were and took off immediately into the thicket lining the road. Corrie puffed on the cigarette and drove ahead slowly.

"Ollie comes back, but sometimes Stan doesn't," she said. "That's why Stan never gets to go on trips. He hates the kennel, but what can I do?"

"It's got me, Corrie," I told her. "I tried not to let it, but the damn thing's got me."

The dogs emerged from the brush and took off running like hell, Stan in the lead. "Rabbit," Corrie said and gunned the Blazer in order to pace them. Suddenly we really were going fast. I shot a glance at the speedometer and saw we were creeping on sixty. I cranked my window, but Corrie left hers down. We left the dogs behind quickly. I looked up and saw we were heading for a dead end.

"Jesus, Corrie," I said.

She hit the brakes about a half block from the end of the street and spun us around easily. We came to a stop. She let out breath and turned to me. "Jacques Tati," she said. She jammed her cigarette in her mouth and then got out of the car. I did, too. The dogs, both of them, came loping up.

"Jacques who?" I said.

"Tati. Jacques Tati. He's like Charlie Chaplin, only French." She bent and hugged the dogs to her, then looked up at me. For the first time she seemed small to me. There in the moonlight, I could almost see her as a child. " I saw one of his movies that day," she said "at a little dump there in town. Crystal left me in the movie for a couple of hours. First time I ever had to read subtitles."

"While your mother did what?"

"How the hell should I know?" She got up as Stan raced off again. "There he goes," she said. "Ollie, go get your brother." The rottweiler took off obediently.

"When was this?"

"I told you. I was maybe twelve, so it was early Eighties."

"What time of year?"

"Summer. I remember being cold because that movie had the air conditioning cranked up so high and I was just wearing, you know, shorts." She flicked away the rest of her cigarette and jammed her hands into the pockets of her jacket. She looked around, and for the first time that night I was aware of her scar. After Crystal's story, I'd thought I would have noticed it immediately, but I hadn't. There was something about Corrie that made you forget it.

"You do this every night?" I asked her.

"Three hundred and sixty-five a year," she said, "Including Christmas. Drunk or sober."

"I thought your mother was the drinker."

"I like my beer," she said. She looked off at the far buildings. "Sometimes when I'm here I pretend the world has ended and we're the only ones left. Just the dogs and me."

She came about to my chin. I liked looking at her. I liked the way the mild wind stirred her long hair, fanning it a little.

"What were all the candles for back there?" I asked her.

She shrugged. "Nightly ritual." Ollie returned, without Stan. "Shit," Corrie said. "C'mon."

We piled back in the car, all three of us. Corrie proceeded at a slower pace, honking the horn every now and then. "C'mon, ya dumb dog," she yelled out the window. "You're gonna get left."

Jacques Tati. Summer of maybe '81 or '82. A kid and her mom, out together for the day. What was this about? Anything? And why did it haunt me? Stan finally showed up, and Corrie braked and let him in. "Dumbass," she said, and drove on.

Back at her house, the phone was ringing away. "I want to catch this," she said. "If I don't he'll just call back. He knows what time I run the dogs." She crossed to the phone and picked up before the answering machine could get it. "Hi," she said, and listened. She shifted the receiver to her other ear and dug another Pall Mall and her Zippo out of her pocket. She lit it, said, "Yeah," and kicked off her loafers. I tried not to look at her, focusing instead on her stereo equipment. Those were Jensen speakers up there on top of the bookcase, the big kind that I'd have given my ass for.

"Yeah," she said. "I'm back. Look, I got somebody here." She listened again, then said impatiently: "No. It's the guy who stayed with Crystal, okay? He's just filling me in on what happened down there." She stuck the cigarette in her mouth and shrugged out of the jacket, tossing it on a dining room chair. "Sorry, Jack," she said more kindly. "No. I appreciate it; I do. No shit. Call me tomorrow if you want." She listened a moment and hung up. She went to the fridge, this time bringing back two Coronas. She opened both with the bottle opener and handed one to me. I took it. "Sorry," she said. "I'm fresh outa limes." She sat. "That was Jack," she said. "A year later, and he's still having a hell of a time letting go. He calls me to make sure I didn't get raped, as if the dogs would let that happen." She drank. "It's just a damn good thing we didn't have any kids," she said, then eyed me. "You got any?"

"What?"

"Kids," she said and sat her beer on the coffee table.

"One. Well, halfway. He's my stepson, but the marriage didn't last."

She processed this. "How old?"

"He's fourteen," I said.

She took another drag on her cigarette and leaned to put it out. "What's his name?" she asked.

"Lincoln. He likes Linc."

"And how long were you with him?"

"Eight years. From the time he was three until he was eleven."

She picked up her beer again, but didn't drink from it. "Yeah, well," she said, looking somewhere past me. "Daddies come and go."

"I didn't want to go," I said.

She spoke as if she hadn't heard me. "I must've had five or six daddies in all," she said. "To this day I can't keep 'em straight."

"We do crazy things to our children."

She shook her head, not in disagreement, but as if she were trying to shake something away. "I was home-schooled, you know, which basically meant that I could roll a J by the time I was two. Finally the welfare folks came and had a talk with Crystal, and of course I wound up in Public School Number Some-sorta-shit."

"Here in Columbus?"

"God, no. We were back in Two Rivers by then. Crystal had pretty well bottomed out. Which meant she had come crawling back to the biggest daddy of 'em all, Ol' Gramps." She drank. "Tough times, Haggard," she said.

"I can imagine," I said.

"Tough times for Crystal, anyway. I sorta liked having running water on a regular basis."

I tried shifting the focus. "Suppose Delbert were alive," I said. "After all, I did see somebody out there the other night."

"He's not," Corrie said. Once again, she was knocking back her beer at an alarming rate, not that it seemed to faze her.

"But just suppose. Why would he want to show up in Two Rivers anyway? Crystal says they hated each other's guts by the time he disappeared."

"Beats me," Corrie said. "How about revenge?"

"Revenge for what?"

The dogs, who had resumed their places on the floor by Corrie, suddenly became restless.

"Somebody walking down the alley," she said.

I walked to the back door and looked out on the dark yard beyond. I saw nothing. I went back into the living room. Corrie hadn't moved. The dogs were still again.

"Why do you live here?" I asked her. "It's dangerous."

"It's cheap," she said. "I got doo-dah from the divorce, you know. Old Jack is in hock to his ass. I work every night except Sunday when the place is closed, and I live cheap." She held up her beer bottle. "Corona's about my only luxury, Haggard. But, hell: I hate shit beer."

"No wonder Jack is worried."

"Jack's in denial. Like I said, he won't let go."

"I went through it. Time does wonders. He'll get over it."

"I wish to God he'd hurry up," she said. "Sometimes I think I'll go back with him just to get off the fuckin' telephone."

I put my beer bottle down and stood up. I'd drank about half of it. Corrie hadn't really been hinting for me to leave, but I didn't want to take a chance on that happening. "You need the rest of your night," I told her, "and I need to get out of here. I wish you'd think about what I said."

She got up, too, and put out her hand. "I will. And don't think I don't appreciate it, Haggard. Even though it didn't work out, like I said, you saved me some hassles."

I took her hand. "From what I saw this week," I said, "I'd say you still have them."

She let go. "No doubt," she said, and led the way to the door. The dogs followed along.

"So long, boys," I said.

"They would know you if you came back," Corrie said.

I was standing in the door looking down at her. She looked like an orphan in a Chaplin movie, standing there in her man's shirt and her sock feet. She looked defenseless to me right then, and what I remember now is wanting to touch her again.

But then those eyes caught mine and held them and I knew she didn't need much of anyone, much less me. "Maybe I'll see you again," she said. "Someplace down the pike."

"I hope so," I said. "The world's a better place now that I can pour my own ketchup."

She smiled. "G'night, Haggard," she said, and closed the door.

I sat in the car a moment looking back at the little house. Through the curtains I could see the candles burning. I tried to imagine how she would spend the rest of the evening. It was pretty early. She could still go out. Or maybe Jack would come over. Then I saw the window candle wink out. And another. She was turning in. I started my car feeling irritable and uneasy, the way I feel in summer when I see heat lightning on the horizon.

I caught the 270 outerbelt out by where we had run the dogs. But by the time I saw the 23 South exit, I knew I was going to pass it up. I continued on to 71, where I took the turn that said East to Cincinnati. Yellow Springs was just over an hour away. I looked at the dash clock: 11:05. I pushed Search on the radio dial looking for something good, and sure enough I found a Cincinnati station tracking some Delbert McClinton. Fine by me. There were few cars on the road, and somewhere out there I rolled down my window and let the wind hit me. Turned the radio up, too. That felt good, and then I realized that I was starting to feel better, a little better. I didn't know why. Maybe it was because what I was doing felt a little like working.

NINE

Yellow Springs had rolled up its sidewalks hours ago by the time I pulled in, just after one. I'd only been there once before and it was pretty much as I remembered it: small. So small that there wasn't a motel in sight. I drove south on 68 and eight miles later found the relative metropolis of Xenia, one of the few towns I know of whose name actually starts with an *X*. After I finally woke up the desk clerk at the Motel 6 he didn't seem to be such a bad guy: he even found me a toothbrush and a little tube of Crest.

I woke up at eight and lay for a while, listening to Monday morning traffic outside. I thought about everything that had happened since Friday morning in the snow. I thought about Crystal and about Corrie, but mostly about Corrie. How had she gotten through the hell of her childhood to become— What? Self-sufficient? What the hell else was self-sufficiency ever born of but hard times?

After awhile I got up and showered and wet-combed my hair. Then I looked hard at myself in the bathroom mirror and decided that if I was going to be meeting people, I couldn't get away without a shave. I pulled on my jeans and last night's shirt and went off in quest of a razor, which I found, along with a travel-size shaving cream, at a 7-Eleven about a block away. By nine I was shaved and reasonably presentable. I'd draped my jacket over the seat on the drive last night, so it wasn't even wrinkled at the butt.

The drive back to Yellow Springs was a quiet one. A bike path ran along my side of the highway, and every mile or so I'd see someone, pressing in against the wind. There seemed too many for a Monday morning, especially since the weather hadn't really turned. About two miles before Yellow Springs the path curved very close to the highway, and that was where two of them, a couple, their wind-reddened faces visible beneath their protective helmets, came very near to me. They were early twenties, college kids, I guessed, at Antioch. We gave each other a wave, stranger ships passing in the brilliance of a sunburst morning at the end of winter.

I came in past residential streets, the low, red-brick buildings of Antioch visible off to my right. Suddenly I was in town, and would have been out and northbound just as suddenly if I hadn't quickly turned in. I found myself in a designated town parking lot, looking back over my shoulder at a scene that should have been titled "The Grateful Dead Go to Brigadoon." Two forking streets were lined with what appeared to be a countless number of organic foods restaurants, bookstores, and funky bars. And even this early the streets were filled with a few possible tourists, but mostly old freaks: guys my age who hadn't cut their hair, looking like *Easy Rider*-era Dennis Hoppers grown older, but still wearing the fringed vests and fatigue jackets and Levi's that had always been the uniform of hippie culture. There were women, too, some with long, straight hair glistening in the sun; others with Janis Joplin mops. And there were younger counterparts: eighteen and nineteen year olds who clearly emulated their parents — mere kids who nonetheless wore tie-dyes and granny glasses and even bellbottoms. I rolled down my car window and felt like I could damn near smell the reefer.

It was amazing, like looking at Amish people. A woman who had to be my age, lines crinkling about her eyes, glanced over at me as she passed in front of the Corsica, favoring me with a brief smile. Then she bent and scooped up a child, a boy of five or six, whose arms had been out-stretched. He seemed too much for her, too large, and she shot me a look, which seemed apologetic. I smiled back, and something, the past maybe, clutched inside me.

I just sat and watched; I couldn't help it. Then I pulled the car into one of the parking slots and got out. The day was going to be almost warm. I was standing not far from the entrance to a bird sanctuary. It was densely wooded, and the entrance crossed a wooden bridge. "Seems like we went to a big park, though," Corrie had said. I turned the other direction and walked up the closest street, coming after about a block to an honest-to-God head shop. Its window was filled with old Fillmore posters, but inside against one entire wall I could see the bongs and hash-pipes on display. Imagine that. "Open at eleven," the sign on the door read. Made sense to me. I crossed the street and found a little bakery, which advertised a build-your-own croissant breakfast. Be still, my heart. I went in.

The girl behind the counter was maybe twenty and she looked like Heidi. Her long blonde hair was braided and her face was as fresh as the morning. She wore overalls, God bless her.

"Good morning," I said.

"Good morning. The coffee's fresh."

There was a nice bit of Appalachian in her accent. "Please," I told her.

She poured and handed me a cup, pointing to the cream and sugar on the counter. "Are you hungry?" she asked.

The place smelled wonderful. "I am now."

She gave me a paper plate with an open croissant and gestured at the display of meats and cheeses before me. "It's all there for you," she said. "Just take what you want."

I accepted this information as if it were the Gospel in our century, and did as instructed. I piled that croissant indecently high with meat and cheese and sat at the little counter, munching and reflecting on the inordinate number of times in life that the condition the girl had described actually does hold true. It had all been there once or twice for me, I knew that. Maybe more times. Then I realized that this was classic stoned logic. Maybe I was getting a contact high from the place.

For a few minutes I was the only customer in the place. Then a couple of locals came in: a big man with a gunfighter's moustache, also about my age, dressed in chinos and a jean jacket, and a bearded guy a little younger who exuded College Professor. They picked up cups of coffee and then went on beyond the counter to a door that I now saw opened on to a glassed-in porch. I finished my sandwich and went back for more coffee.

"Got a local paper?" I asked the girl.

"What passes for it," she said, and reached under the counter. She came up with a tabloid-size newspaper, maybe eight pages. "Keep it," she told me "It's free, anyway."

I took the paper and the coffee back to my seat. *Talk of the Town*, the banner said. I scanned a front-page story about a travel writer who had just moved to town, and then riffled through the pages, looking for a movie ad. I was starting there because I had no place else to start and, sure enough, there was one. The Celluloid Dreams Theater was showing a movie named *Crumb*. I'd read about it, and I knew it was a documentary about the Sixties artist Robert Crumb. That was at night. In the daytime it still had a matinee of *Braveheart*.

"Where's this?" I asked the girl when she arrived to refill my coffee.

"Two blocks, straight over. Right between the grocery and the greasy spoon. But no movies this time of day."

It was hard for me to believe this gingerbread town had a greasy spoon, but I thanked her and paid my tab, taking the paper with me. For a minute I thought I saw Jerry Garcia applying a garden hose to the sidewalk outside the head shop, and then I realized it was only a lookalike. I went over.

"Anybody ever tell you— " I began.

"Yeah," he replied, spattering water off the curb. "Look out. Don't wanta get you wet." He was way overweight and sported a massive gray beard. He wore overalls, sunglasses, and a headband fashioned from a red bandanna. I couldn't tell how much hair he had left under the bandanna, but very little showed.

I sidestepped. "This your place?"

"Yeah." He turned off the water at a spigot in the bricks and then looked me over. "You a narc?"

"Not me," I said. "Honest."

"Because if you're a narc, all you need to do is read that sign in there. You know what it says, and you know it makes me a hundred percent legal. I been through this shit before."

In fact I did know what the sign would say. It would claim that every piece of paraphernalia in the place was sold for recreational use only and not for any illegal activity. The doper's dodge.

"I'm a travel writer for *Ohio Monthly*," I told him. I stuck out my hand. "Sam Haggard."

He winced. "Ah, shit, man. That's the last fuckin' thing I need to be in." But he took my hand and didn't really seem much afraid.

"Don't worry about me. It's a historical piece."

"Thank Christ," he said. "I'm Jake." We mutually pumped. "History about what?" He demanded.

"About the Sixties. About the hippie movement, really. Let me ask you: were you here at the time of Kent State?"

"Oh, hell yes. Bad scene, man. Bad, bad scene."

"You must have been in school."

"I was. Came to Antioch as a freshman and never left. Never fuckin' graduated, either." He leaned back against the door of his shop and hooked his thumbs in the bid of his overalls.

"Well," I said, "It looks like Yellow Springs is an education in itself. I understand some of the students from Kent got sanctuary here."

"Yeah, they did. Tom Hayden showed up too, man. So did Ravi Shankar. We had a lot of celebrities."

"Sounds like it."

"I got Eldridge Cleaver's wanted poster. Took it off the post office wall."

"You ever know any of those Kent people?"

"Naw, that was all an SDS show. Every bit of it. I was more into the dope thing than I was the peace thing, if you dig."

"Yeah," I said, "I dig. Thanks. You have a theater over here, huh?"

"Yeah — that art movie place. Last damn movie I saw there was *The Hellstrom Chronicles*. You see that?" I shook my head, although I had. "Well, don't see it loaded, man," he said. "It's nothin' but fuckin' bugs; bugs crawlin' all over the screen. I hate that, man. I've hardly been to a flick since."

"That's a shame. There've been some good ones."

"What I hate worse, though, are those shows on TV where they show a guy, like, putting a sandwich on the counter, and then when he picks it up they do a real extreme close-up and there's all kinda little counter vermin crawlin' all over the fuckin' sandwich that you could never see with the naked eye. I mean, how you gonna protect yourself against that?"

"You have a point."

"Hard ta eat when you think about your food swarmin' in maggots. Sometimes I have to get really stoned so the munchies will, you know, set in."

Jake didn't look like he was having any trouble eating to me, but I gave him a sympathetic wave all the same and headed across the street. I felt funny. Here it was the shank of the morning in this nice hippie town, and I was wandering the streets telling lies. It reminded me of what a working cop does every day. I had to admit I missed it.

The Celluloid Dreams Theater was right where the bakery girl had said it would be, a Fifties-vintage neighborhood theatre with its small marquee displaying *Braveheart* 2 P.M. and *Crumb* 8 and 10. The little box office was closed, but the grocery next door was downright bustling with traffic. I went in.

The little market smelled of fresh bread and something simmering, maybe vegetable soup. One entire wall was a wine rack. Near the back there was an old-fashioned meat counter, complete with a slicer and a grinder behind it. A tall man, pale with sandy hair, was working the slicer, neatly sawing lunchmeat. He wore a butcher's apron. A fireplug of a woman in her fifties, wearing a warm-up suit, waited, presumably for the lunchmeat. She drummed her fingers on the counter, flashing several diamond rings. Other customers were milling through the compact aisles. The shelves contained mostly gourmet items.

At the front register another of the fresh-faced young women this town seemed to grow was standing behind a cash register. She smiled at me, a good smile.

"Help you with something?" she asked. Her blonde hair was long and straight, hanging free.

I picked a package of Certs from the display by the register, fishing change out of my pocket. Beside the display rack was a fishbowl partly filled with what looked like torn movie tickets.

"What goes on here?" I asked her, pointing at the bowl.

"Ten stubs get you a free ticket," she told me. "Most folks don't want to fool with collecting ten, so they'll throw them in here after a show. We stay open late."

"Nice idea."

"It's like a penny pot, only for the movies. Anybody can take out ten who wants to. I've done it, what movies cost these days. Besides, they're still sort of a community experience around here."

"You folks look after each other," I said.

She smiled. "Well, you know. Small town."

I paid her and returned to the street. I took my time, basking in the morning and the place. After a half block I came to a used-book store. Looking in the window, I could see that unlike the market this place looked empty. I entered and found a dark-haired woman of middle age, sitting behind the counter reading. A calico cat sunned itself atop a set of medical books. I took in the smell of old pages, the same one that always greeted me when I walked into Mac's. But the inventory here was wonderfully ordered in comparison to Mac's clutter. "Just looking," I told the woman. She smiled and returned to her paperback.

I roamed a little, and found myself in the Mystery section, which was enormous. Browsing a little, I came up with a couple by Fredric Brown, a good but forgotten Cincinnati writer. They were Fifties vintage in good condition, tucked away in plastic baggies. The two of them cost me a ten. The dark-haired woman seemed pleased with my choice.

"Public library?" I asked her.

"Two blocks up," she told me. "It's open now."

The library was old and small, essentially one room. I asked the librarian, a balding guy who wore his fringe of hair very long, about newspapers and he pointed toward Microfilm, asking me for a date.

"I'd just like to look at May of 1970," I said.

"Kent State, huh," he said.

"Among other things," I told him.

"If I were you," he said, "I'd use the Antioch newspaper. Coverage was probably better."

"I need to go to the campus?"

"Nope. We have them. Over here."

He set me up in a corner with one of the two machines the library seemed to own. Before long I was cranking through images of protest. Antioch had been a hot spot indeed. The paper was a biweekly, so there were real gaps. But in the May 6 issue I found something remarkable. There on the inside front page, getting off a bus, was Crystal Jones, big as a house. The cutline read: "K.S. Students Arrive: Twenty-nine students from Kent State sought sanctuary here after Monday's shootings. Pictured is Crystal Jones, wife of campus radical Delmore 'Lucifer' Jones."

I studied the grainy image. Crystal was quite pretty. She wore John Lennon sunglasses, the square kind, and her hair must have been down to her ass. It was just as blonde as now, close to the color of the two young women I'd talked to this morning. Crystal was being helped off the bus by a man who dwarfed her: he could have gone six-four. He was older-looking, although it was hard to tell in the photograph, wearing a sweater with Kent State lettered on the front. He and Crystal might have been together; he might have been simply helping her off the bus. Although he was prominent in the picture, his name was not mentioned in the cutline. There was no accompanying story: the rest of the Kent State news was the report on the first page and an angry editorial. I turned back to the picture and looked at it again. Then I shoved in coins for a printout.

I went through the rest of May. No other mention of Crystal. I put the microfilm back in its envelope and returned it to the librarian.

"Anything else?" he asked.

"You weren't here then, were you?" I asked.

"Me? Nah. I was twelve and lived in Toledo. Anything else?"

Twelve. "Let me see summer, '82," I said.

He went away and returned with another envelope. "Here you are."

I took the new envelope back to the machine and started working my way through June, looking at the movie listings. The Celluloid Dreams Theater had been going strong, showing the likes of *Zabriskie Point* and *Little Big Man.* No Jacques Tati. Then I saw another listing— this one at a theater named Le Flick. I looked back. No Flick listing before Friday. I looked forward: Friday, Saturday, Sunday. This one was open on weekends, and it showed foreign films, mostly classics. Here was an Antonioni double feature. The next weekend had *Seven Samuri* doubled billed with the *American Magnificent Seven*. Cute idea. And then, on the last weekend in June, a Jacques Tati double feature. Mr. Hulot's *Holiday* and *Mon Oncle. Bingo.*

I sat back. On the table beside me lay the newspaper I'd picked up earlier and the printout of Crystal, 1970. On the screen in front of me was a theater listing from 1982. If this was connected, I couldn't see how. I looked again at the man in the picture with Crystal. His arm was under her elbow, his gaunt face slightly turned, into the sun. I could see that his features were hawklike, but I really couldn't make them out. He seemed to be smiling.

For the hell of it, I also printed out the ad from Le Flick. I stuffed it all into my jacket pocket and went back to the desk to tell the librarian from Toledo that I was finished. He was hunched over some videos to which he was applying an official-looking stamp, his balding pate shiny in the library fluorescence.

"I remember when libraries were just printed matter," I said.

"Pretty soon we'll be all videos," he said glumly as he looked up. "I'll live to see the day."

"I won't welcome it," I said.

"Got that right. Say, I thought of somebody you might want to talk to if you're really interested in Kent State."

"Who's that?"

"His name is Benedict. Loren Benedict. Got a dairy farm just north toward Springfield up there. He was there."

"As a student?"

"Nah. He was in the Guard. He's from here — Springfield, really. But he's been farming that place for maybe twenty years. Somebody found out about him once, I guess, and the alternative campus paper ran a little story. You rarely saw him before that and since then you don't see him at all."

"So what makes you think he'd talk to me?"

"Shoot, man," he replied, turning back to his stamping. "What I said was that you might want to talk to him. I didn't say anything about him talking back."

I RECLAIMED MY CAR FROM THE PUBLIC LOT and, just under two miles north of town, I found the Benedict farm, a drowsy little spread that was fronted by a tiny store where you could buy the milk the Benedict cows were putting out. Neither the farm nor the store looked prosperous, but the store was at least open. I parked in the deserted gravel lot and went in. There was a black man of maybe fifty behind the counter, and he seemed glad to see me.

"A good day to you, sir," he said with enviable enthusiasm. He wore tinted glasses and sported a small goatee and an ancient-looking afro the size of the rest of his head. "How many gallons can I fetch you?"

"I'm not here for milk," I said. "I'm looking for Mr. Benedict."

"He'd be up at the house. May I ask the nature of your business?"

"Just wanted to talk. I think we might have a mutual friend."

He considered. "I can buzz him up there. What was your name?"

"Haggard," I said. "He wouldn't know it."

He dug an old dial phone out from under the counter and called the house. Somebody, evidently Benedict, answered, because in a moment the black guy pulled the phone away from his ear and said: "He wants to know who the mutual friend is."

"Crystal Jones," I said, on a wing and a prayer.

They spoke again. Then the black guy hung up the phone. "He's coming down," he told me.

"Thanks," I said. "You been working here long?"

"Yeah," he said. "Long time; long time."

Loren Benedict was my age but a lot better kept. He was wearing jeans and a sleeveless T-shirt, and you could see the clear lines of his farmer tan — hands, face, and neck. He wore a full beard which was mostly silver, and his curly hair was similarly flecked. His eyes had something boyish about him, as if the rest of him had grown up and left the eyes behind.

"Hi," I said. "Sam Haggard."

"What's this about Crystal Jones?" he demanded. He sounded angry.
"You know her?"

"I know who she is. Who the hell around here doesn't? What's this about?"

I just had to throw out some bullshit and hope it worked. "I've been doing some work for her this past week," I said. "And we got to talking about Kent State . . . "

He flared, and then he flexed. Whatever he did he worked hard at it, because a wall of muscle rippled pretty much from neck to abdomen. "I thought so," he said with fury. "You the press?"

"Hell, no. In fact I'm unemployed."

"Bullshit." He turned on the black guy. "Dale," he said. "You got to watch out for these creeps." He turned back. "I want to forget Kent State," he said. "I've wanted to forget it for twenty-five years. But now it's this goddamn anniversary and every maggot who thinks he has a fucking angle is crawling out of the woodwork. You're the third this week. And you're going to be the last. Now, get the hell out of here."

I opted for good old-fashioned chauvinism. "I was military myself at the time," I told him. "I know how you must feel. Hell, it was a bad break, but it's still a good country."

"You don't know shit about it. You know nothing." He advanced on me, glaring. In the face of so many muscles, I reflexively backed a step. "Lemme tell you something, asshole," he said. "You want to talk about country? Well, I used to have a country. Now I got a dairy farm." He turned and stomped out, never looking back. Dale and I watched him.

"Well," I said. "Thanks."

"You guys want to write about that time," he said. "Why don't you write about Jackson State?"

I knew where this was going. Jackson State College, a mostly black school in Mississippi, had exploded a little over a week after Kent when police had fired into a crowd of students, killing two of them. I'd just read the account two nights ago. I'd known about it, of course, but like the rest of white America I'd ignored it.

"You're right," I told him. "Nobody's ever given that one the attention it deserved. But your friend has it wrong. I'm not a writer."

Dale pulled down his tinted glasses and looked at me. "Lemme ask you something," he said. "You know the names of the kids got shot at Kent?"

"Yes," I said. "I do."

"You know the names of the dead at Jackson State?"

"No," I admitted, though I had recently read them.

"Phil Gibbs and Jimmy Earl Green, that's who. They had lives, too, you know. Just like your Kent State folk did."

"I know that. Were they friends of yours?"

"Never knew 'em," he told me. "Never been to Jackson State. But dig: I know the names."

I'd spent most of my American life half-ashamed of being born white, and some days all the way ashamed. Dale was turning this into one of those days. "You're right," I said again.

"Damn straight," he replied. "Sure you don't want some milk? It's good milk. Good cows, you know."

"How'd you and Benedict get together?" I asked him.

He laughed shortly. "Coupla survivors," he said.

"I don't suppose you know Crystal Jones," I said.

He laughed again. "Who the hell around here doesn't?"

I left him there and drove away, feeling the sting of their collective charges. They were right: I was nothing but an interloper in significant events, a trespasser in lives that had come to far more than my own had.

I FELT A NEED TO BE BACK ON THE ROAD. My journey to Oz, save the last part, had been pleasant enough, but it also seemed superfluous, as if my real work was elsewhere. Pushed by a sudden urgency, I drove back through the town. It was just after eleven. The head shop sign said OPEN. I drove on, heading south.

I took 64 to 125, and stopped for a quick lunch at a cafe outside West Union. The drive was two-lane and pretty, especially the part through the Shawnee Forest, but the winding road kept me from moving as fast as I wanted to. I pulled into my own parking space at about two-fifteen. The phone was ringing when I opened my apartment door and I caught it before the machine picked up.

"Where the fuck you been?" Mac's voice.

"What's up?"

"You've had visitors. Cops."

"About what?"

"You haven't seen a paper?"

"I've been looking at papers all morning. On the microfiche."

"Wrong papers, Bud. Try today's. Your acid queen is dead."

The receiver was cold in my hand. I looked up, around the room. "Crystal?"

"Fuckin' A, Crystal. Burned herself up. Torched the whole house."

"When?" I said.

"Last night, man. Where you been?"

"Thanks, Mac," I said and hung up. I went back down the stairs and fetched my own newspaper, unrolling it as I hurried back up to the apartment. I shut the door and stared at the front page. Crystal was the headline and she was dead, all right: just as dead as she could be.

TEN

Corrie was home this time. In fact, she answered on the first ring.
"This is Sam," I said.

"Where the fuck have you been?" she demanded.

"Yellow Springs."

"Crystal's dead."

"I know. It's in the paper."

"It's all over the goddamn paper," she said. "It's all over the fuckin' TV." She laughed shortly. "She's never had it so good."

"The cops have been there?"

"Yeah, they've been here. Two Columbus cops. What the hell were you doing in Yellow Springs?"

"Not enough," I said. "She's dead, isn't she?"

She let out her breath. "Easy, Haggard," she said. "You're not responsible here."

"I told you this thing had me. Are you okay?"

"Yeah. I'm okay. They say she burned herself up with a cigarette."

"I doubt that. She barely got around to lighting them."

"Wait," Corrie said, "there's precedent. Crystal tried to light a candle when that Pope died and burned down a whole apartment complex. Shit, she wasn't even Catholic. A hundred and forty-three units up in smoke. She was drunk, of course. They know about that. It happened right here in fuckin' Columbus."

"Why did they leave her alone, I wonder?"

"Who knows, Haggard. The funeral's Tuesday afternoon, down there. Old Carl isn't screwing around. He wants her in the ground."

"Fairlawn?"

"Yeah."

"I'll take you," I said.

"I said I'd go with Jack," she said.

I put my head against the wall of the breakfast nook. "That what you want to do?" I asked her.

"What I want to do is not go at all," she said. "Jack liked Crystal. Don't ask me why."

"Sorry," I said. "That was a stupid question."

"Forget it."

"What time?" I said.

"Three. It's graveside. But you don't need to go, Haggard. It'll be just family, or what's left of it."

"No," I said. "I do need to go."

"Suit yourself," she said.

"In this case, I will."

"I didn't think I'd see you again," she said.

"I'm here if you need me. You have the number."

"Thanks, Haggard," she said, and hung up.

I kept holding the receiver as if I expected her to speak again. I hung it up at last and went into the kitchen. I had a bottle of Absolut in the cabinet above the fridge, and I took it down and poured half a tumbler over ice. Then I sat down on the sofa and read the account of Crystal's death, waiting for the cops to arrive.

Not that there was a hell of a lot to it. The story, in fact, wasn't much bigger than the size of the picture they used: the very same picture that appeared on the jacket of Crystal's ghostwritten book. Well, at least she'd made the front page. Corrie was right: she'd have liked that. The headline read: LOCAL WRITER IS FIRE VICTIM

I had to smile a little. "Writer" was the last description most people would have used to sum up Crystal's broken life. The story, which was really an obit, read:

> Crystal Jones, Sixties radical and author of *Getting Out Alive,* is dead as a result of a fire in her home at 45 Gallia Pike early Monday. Jones, 47, was in the house alone at the time of the blaze. Officials believe that the fire, which gutted the first floor of the residence, may have been started by a forgotten cigarette. Crystal Jones was the daughter of Carl and the late Lorraine Payton. During the late '60s she became well known as wife and fellow activist to Delbert Jones. Delbert, nicknamed "Lucifer," was known nationally for his dramatic and often humorous counter-culture pranks. The pair first gained attention when they were arrested for trying to disrobe on the floor of the 1968 National Democratic Convention in Chicago. They became minor Merry Pranksters, even appearing on *The Dick Cavett Show.* Stranger episodes would follow. Delbert Jones disappeared on the day of the shooting at Kent State University, May 4, 1970. He is presumed dead.
>
> Ms. Jones returned to her home here a decade ago, and in recent years had lived in near seclusion in the Gallia Pike house. She is survived by her father, Carl Payton, and a daughter, Corrie Blake, of Columbus. Arrangements are pending at the Hempill Funeral Home.

I put down the paper and picked up the autobiography, which I had left on the coffee table, and found Crystal's picture. The doorbell downstairs rang. I went over to the window and looked down. It was full dark outside, but the light over my door showed me a familiar shape, even from this angle. It was Harvey Smoltz, come to fetch me. I went down to let him in.

"Want a drink?" I asked him at the door. "I'm having one."

"You expect me to climb those stairs?" Harvey said, "you're fuckin' crazy. Not for ten drinks. C'mon, I gotta take you down and ask the questions, do the report. You been there before, and I been here twice already."

"I'll follow you down," I said. "I've got questions of my own."

"THINGS HAVE CHANGED," I TOLD HARVEY as we entered the squadroom.

"Yeah," Harvey said. "We even cleaned out your locker finally."

I looked around. "Everybody's got a computer," I noticed.

"Yeah." He shrugged. "Well, what can I tell ya? Use them or they use you. I sorta like mine. Got the MacPlaymate on it, y'know."

At least some of the same people were left. Gus Evans waved at me over his computer, looking as hangdog as he used to. "Thought we retired you, Sam."

"I spent the retirement check. Gotta come back and work some more."

Carla Dobbs was there, too, and I gave her a wave. Harvey took me into the break room, which was empty, and shut the door. He motioned for me to sit down and went to the coffee pot.

"You can fix this," he said, pouring me a cup. He sat it in front of me and pointed to sugar and creamer in the middle of the table.

I stirred in some of both. "What do you want to know, Harvey?"

He brought his own cup to the table and sat wearily, carrying too many pounds and too many problems. "Just what happened," he said.

I told him, starting from last Friday morning and working forward. I laid it out like a cop would want it, working it through to Sunday morning when I had gotten bounced. "The uniformed cop's name was Leasure," I told him. "He had a bad case of attitude."

Harvey put his pen on his notepad. He hadn't made many notes. He sat back and drank some coffee, dripping a little on his gut. "He's young," Harvey said. "He'll be all right."

"Mills isn't young. What's his problem?"

"Beats me. Sounds like they weren't taking Crystal very seriously."

"They weren't the only ones, as I remember."

Harvey gave me a look. "All right," he said. "Somebody should have gotten her with a shrink, that's for sure."

"You think she was a suicide."

"Naw, I think she got drunk and set herself on fire. Isn't that what you think?"

"Maybe." I drank coffee.

The door opened and in came a guy who looked like he ought to be in graduate school. He was in shirtsleeves, a tie askew at his neck. He wore horn rims, and his curly brown hair was cut very close. There was a pencil clamped sideways between his teeth. He shut the door and flipped open a file he held in his hand. He took the pencil out of his mouth and scribbled something, then looked up at Harvey.

"This Haggard?" he demanded. Funny he didn't just ask me.

"Yeah," Harvey said. "Sam, this is Barry Askew. He's captain now."

I was well aware of that. Roy Marcum had retired three years ago. I saw him at the Kroger sometimes.

Askew stuck out his hand, and I took it. He sat down at the end of the table. "Mess, huh?" he said.

"Crystal? Yeah. A bad one."

"Harvey says you believe you saw someone up there."

"I don't believe it. I know it."

"Okay. We believe you."

"I didn't know I had a credibility problem around here."

Askew put out a hand. "Take it easy, Sam. Nobody's saying that."

"Harvey's got my description. You're going to want to check this guy out. And what does Mills say? When did he see her last?"

"Nobody saw her after noon on that day. Some doctor Payton's got on his payroll came out there and gave her a shot."

"And left her?"

"He swears she was all right."

"What's the doctor's name?"

Askew leaned forward. His loosened collar was stained with something, maybe cheap aftershave. He took off his glasses. "Let's understand something, Sam. You're not investigating this matter. We are."

"Well, if you leave it at this you're doing a shit job of it. That house had more traffic than the outerbelt this weekend, and you're— "

"Sam," Harvey said.

Askew stood up. "Do we have his statement?" he asked Harvey.

"Yeah," Harvey said. "I got it."

"We'll be in touch," he told me. "Thanks for coming in." He left.

"Couldn't you have gotten somebody younger?" I said.

"Time and change," Harvey said. "They happen. Listen, Sam. I'm pretty sure Askew's been told to shitcan this one. Nobody is going to get too lathered about Crystal. You know that."

"Maybe he was told to shitcan it for some other reason," I suggested.

"Don't go *X-Files* on me," Harvey said. "You know that bitch was delusional."

"Doesn't mean she wasn't right for once."

Harvey sat back and laced his fingers over his pauch. He waited a beat, then said: "Sam, I'll tell you again what I told you in the beginning. Forget this. Go get a nice job someplace and forget it. There's nuttin' here for any of us."

"What's the doctor's name?" I asked him.

"Sam . . . "

"What's the name, Harvey?"

He sighed. "Kearney. He's seventy if he's a day. Probably delivered Crystal."

"Thanks," I said. "How about I see the file on this?"

"How 'bout you shit and fall back in it," Harvey countered.

"You through with me?"

Harvey shut his notebook. "Yeah. And I advise you to be through with this, too."

"Good advice," I told him.

I claimed my car from the city lot and headed in the direction of Gallia Pike. I passed the Huckins House, its parking area almost as empty as it had been during the snow. I drove on up the hill and turned up Gallia Pike. I parked on the other side of the little park and walked to just about where I'd stood on Saturday night. The house wasn't as bad as the newspaper had indicated, but it wasn't pretty. The big front window had exploded outward. In the shadows I could see that the front porch was seared and crumbled; the brick scorched. The police had sealed the house off, but left no one to guard it. Windows in distant houses glowed cozy and yellow, as if Crystal had burned and died and gone unnoticed by her neighbors. But I guessed that most of them had stopped paying attention to her years ago.

I had worked fire scenes before, and I could imagine the situation inside. Glasses and medicine vials would have popped in the heat upstairs. Downstairs the fire hoses would have made a river of the living room and kitchen — and the bedroom where I had tried to sleep. I wondered about Corrie's picture; about the scrapbooks, too. Then I went back to my car and started for home.

About the time I got back to the Huckins, I realized I was hungry. *What the hell,* I thought, and pulled in. Bob was behind the bar, likely counting something. The dining room was closed, but a handful of trucker types sat at the bar, drinking in a morose manner. I squinted at the clock as I sat down at the bar. Nine fifty. Bob came up.

"Hello again," I said.

"Hi," he told me.

"Probably too late to get anything to eat."

"We got cold sandwiches. You want a turkey and Swiss?"

"Sounds good," I said. "And a Bass."

He brought me the beer and went to the kitchen. I realized that Bob would be making my sandwich. Presently he brought it, complete with chips and a pickle. He sat it down in front of me.

"I'm glad you didn't say club," he told me. "Trying to get all that shit on there just right drives me crazy."

I picked up a sandwich half. "How's your . . . "

"My OCD. It's fixing to be worse. They cut me to half time today, and I won't be able to afford the medication." He fixed me with an apocalyptic stare. "It's gonna get bad. I know it."

I chewed. "Maybe they'll up your hours again."

"I doubt it. Most of the time this place might as well not open. Hotel doesn't do any business anymore, unless they get a convention. And the word is sort of out on the place, I guess, because only the weird ones book us. We got an identical twins convention coming in here next week, I swear."

"My name's Sam Haggard, Bob," I said. I wiped my hand and offered it to him.

He took it. "Bob," he said. Maybe he didn't have a last name. "You came in the other night with a woman." He nodded at the bar. "We don't get too many women any more."

"Too bad."

"A lot of the identical twins are women, though." He retrieved my beer glass and drew me another Bass. "On me," he said.

"Thanks."

"Somebody followed her the other night," Bob said.

I looked at him. "Followed the woman I was with?"

"Yeah. It was a guy. Brown Honda Civic. A new one. I saw him when he pulled out. He was parked over there where we park, the cook and me, I mean, and he waited until you left and then took out in her direction. I mean, I'm pretty sure he was following her. It looked like it, anyway."

"Maybe he was just going that way."

"Why would he sit out there all that time? It was bitter out there that night, man. Seemed like it to me."

I didn't want the other half of my sandwich any more, but I didn't want to hurt Bob's feelings either. I picked it up. "See what the guy looked like?" I asked.

"He was bald. Wore glasses."

"That it?"

"That's it." He went off down the bar to check on his truckers. I put down the sandwich and finished my beer. I could feel the nerves prickling against my skin.

"Thanks," I said when Bob came back. I handed him a ten.

"Hope I didn't speak outa turn there, man."

"Not at all. Keep the change, Bob."

I got out of there. Halfway home I was looking over my shoulder. I needed sleep, but I knew I wasn't going to get it now.

At home I checked my messages. Mac and Linc had called. And somebody else had called and left no message. The phone rang as soon as I put it down.

"Sam. It's Alison Schwartz. This too late?"

"No. Hi, Alison." A longtime friend, Alison worked the city desk at *The Two Rivers Times*. I'd hoisted beers with her many nights at the Royal, and I'd never beat her at darts.

"You're in the paper tomorrow, Sam. I thought you'd want to know."

If I'd thought about it, I could have guessed. "Because I got questioned?"

"Yeah. And that's all it says. You gave your statement; you're not connected. I just wanted to tell you."

"Thanks, Alison."

"So what do you know about this thing?"

"Ah, shit. I should have seen that coming."

Alison was small and wiry in person, filled with energy. She knew how to bulldog, and so I was surprised when she immediately backed off.

"Okay, Sam," she said, "Call me tomorrow if you want to talk about it. Or whenever. I'm buying the beers."

"Great. Unless I go with the deal *The National Enquirer* offered me."

"In that case," she said, "You can buy your own beer."

I still don't know what got into me at that point, and I have had reason to wonder many times since. She was ready to hang up, but something about the news and the day and even something about my conversation with Corrie came together at that moment in Unharmonic Convergence. Hell, I let loose.

"Listen," I told her. "If you really want to get at a story here you'll follow the Delbert part of it. She thinks she saw him, as in back from the dead. And I'm not so damn sure she didn't. It might be that Delbert is alive and maybe somebody doesn't want us to know it."

"Jesus, Sam."

"Yeah."

"But who would cover this up? Are you saying the government?"

"I'm saying I don't know. But the CIA has done worse, you know. They arranged the hit on Diem in Vietnam and I know that for a fact. I talked to guys who were there."

"Is this an interview, Sam?"

"I don't give a damn what it is. Somebody needs to start looking at this thing, and it's not likely to be Two Rivers' Finest. They'll do what they're told." I slammed the phone down and thought, *Oh shit.*

I started to call Alison back. I even picked up the phone. But I didn't dial. I don't know why. Maybe my outburst was the only way I could think of to get myself back into the damned thing.

Feeling like a fool, I sought diversion. To that end I stretched out on the couch and read some of Crystal's book, hoping to hell that Alison would call back. Crystal's miserable saga was terrible: a poor pistache of brushes with greatness, which never amounted to anything. Delbert might as well not have even been in the book, a figure so shadowy as Crystal told it that he came off as bit player rather than romantic lead. The disappearance rated three paragraphs before Crystal was into her post-Delbert commune period. She did mention being bussed out to Yellow Springs, but that story, like the rest of the book, went nowhere.

I flipped over to the dust jacket and looked at the other name. Selena Blair. The blurb said she had lived in San Diego. That's where the vanity house that had printed the book had been located, too. Evanruh Books, San Diego. It would be seven-thirty there now. I got the phone book and checked the area code. Then I dialed San Diego information.

Evanruh Books had a phone number. I dialed it. A woman's voice answered. No Evanruh Books; just Hello.

"Is this Evanruh?" I asked.

"Yes," the woman said. "This is Joy Evanruh. I have the phone forwarded. Did you need information about the company?"

"I need information about an author," I said. "My name is Sam Haggard. I'm calling from Ohio. You published an autobiography of Crystal Jones."

"Yes. We did."

"Are you aware that she is dead?"

"No," the woman said. "No, I wasn't. Are you with the police?"

"No. I was employed by the family. I wanted to ask about Selena Blair. I understand she also is no longer living."

"I'm not sure I should be talking to you," she said.

"You could call Detective Smoltz here at the Two Rivers Police Department if you need to confirm my credentials." I hoped to God she didn't. "But this isn't really a police matter. We are trying to contact some people about the funeral and I needed to know if any of Ms. Blair's family might have been close to Ms. Jones." It was lame, but it was the best I could come up with.

"Oh, I would doubt that. Selena Blair took that project strictly as a job. She had done magazine work and she was hired by the father, there where you live. They were not close."

"I see," I said. "How long ago did Ms. Blair die?"

"Three years ago, something like that. Here in San Diego. She died in a house fire."

I gripped the phone. "We have a little bit of a bad connection. What did you say?"

"She died in a house fire. She burned to death. Who did you say this was?"

My choices were to hang up or come clean. I had to hope she might be taken off guard enough to talk to me. "Ms. Evanruh," I said, "I'm a former policeman who was hired to watch Crystal Jones just before she died. You're going to learn that she also died in a house fire."

"My God," she said.

"Did you know Crystal Jones?"

"I never met her. We dealt with her father."

"What about Ms. Blair?"

"I talked to her many times by phone, of course, and she was in the office twice, I guess. No, I didn't know her."

"But you met her."

"Yes. She was in her thirties, I would say. Nice girl, pretty. She didn't care for Crystal Jones, I can tell you that."

"What do you mean?"

"She said she was dishonest and a liar. She handed in the book and said she never wanted to see or talk to her again."

"Anything else?"

"Not really. She was paid directly by the father, just as we were. The royalties, such as they were, went to Crystal. Selena got a flat ghosting fee."

"The police will want to talk to you."

"Well, I can't tell them anything but what I told you."

"They like to hear it for themselves," I said. "Thanks for talking to me." I hung up the phone, acutely aware that I was alone. I looked at the time: eleven. I dialed Harvey Smoltz at home. He was cranky when he came on.

"I had enough of you at the office," he said.

"Selena Blair died in a house fire," I told him.

"Who's Selena Blair?"

"The woman who ghosted Crystal's book. She died the same way Crystal did."

"That's funny," Harvey said.

"Yeah."

"Better come by tomorrow," he said after a moment. "How about two, something like that?"

"How about one. I have to go to a funeral." I hung up again. I looked at my watch. Too late to call Linc. And Mac would be in the zone by now. I sat and listened to the silence, but I already knew what it would say. Crystal had been murdered. Ditto, in all likelihood, Selena Blair. At least one killer: maybe two. But I figured one—out there somewhere, maybe not far away.

ELEVEN

I t was the first funeral I'd ever attended on April Fool's Day, and I hoped to God it was the last. We stood there, all seven of us, on this sunswept Tuesday afternoon and waited for Carl Payton to arrive. Nobody had even thought he was coming until the little Presbyterian minister with the shock-white hair and the patient smile told us he would be. For my part I wouldn't have been surprised to hear we were waiting for the Pope: the day been just that bizarre to this point, starting with calls from both *The Columbus Dispatch* and the Cincinnati *Enquirer* this morning, thanks to the story about me in the local paper, and progressing to another round with Harvey and Barry Askew down at the bullpen. This time Askew had hauled in a stenographer to take down my whole statement. By the time they finished I was glad to be anywhere but there, even the graveyard.

Corrie Blake wore black wonderfully. For the occasion she had put on what looked like a black trenchcoat, but made of something high dollar. I could see from the collar of her dress that it was black, too. A single strand of pearls hung from her neck. I wondered if they were the ones in the picture. She wore black pumps and dark stockings. It was the first time I had ever seen her legs and they were pretty high dollar, too.

Jack Blake looked almost as good as she did. His dark topcoat set off his surfer blond hair, which fluttered in Robert Redford disarray all over his forehead. He was my height but muscular. He had the neck of a one-time football player. The two of them stood together close to the little minister, braced against the wind. I stood on the other side of the casket, which bore too many flowers for such a dismal turnout. An older couple stood beside me. The rest of our party were gravediggers.

"We need to wait a few minutes for Mr. Payton," the minister, a Reverend Fisher, cautioned us. He clutched his Bible and squinted around him, as if seeking support from the dead. We were on the Kinney's Lane side of Fairlawn Cemetery, which was big and old. The man who founded Two Rivers was buried here. So was the first white baby born here, an infant death. I looked at Corrie. She touched Jack Blake's coat and they came over to me.

"Jack, this is Sam Haggard."

Blake produced a gloved hand. I shook it, feeling shabby and out of place. This guy could have been an Armani model, and here I was in my blue suit. "Thanks for helping out, Mr. Haggard," he said to me. He conveyed the impression that he was speaking to a senior citizen.

"Corrie," I said, "There've been some new developments. I need to talk to you after the service. Can you meet me somewhere?" I looked at Jack Blake. "Both of you."

Corrie shook her head. She wore small pearl earrings which matched her necklace. It looked very much like the one she had been wearing in the picture. "I'm due at work tonight. But you can call me. Call me at work if you want."

I hesitated. "Corrie," I said. "You may be in danger."

Jack Blake took a step in toward me. "I'm sticking pretty close to Corrie," he said. "I think she'll be all right."

"You need to hear what I have to say. After the service."

Corrie looked at Blake and then back at me. "Okay," she said.

Blake started to say something, but then we heard the crunch of tires on the dirt road. Here came a Lincoln Continental with Mills, the attorney, driving. He parked and got out and went around to the passenger door. "All hail," Corrie muttered. Carl Payton got out of the car.

He was certainly old, but quite able to walk on his own. He had kept his hair, and it ruffled in the wind as handsomely as Jack's. He took Mills' arm and they came around the car together. Payton was a big man, and he moved in a clipped manner which suggested a military background. He wore a tan trenchcoat and a silk muffler. He was telling the lawyer something in a low but animated tone.

They entered our circle. The Rev. Fisher shook hands with both of them and motioned them to stand beside Corrie and Blake. Corrie and her grandfather looked at each other but didn't speak. Blake shook hands.

"He's holding up," the older woman next to me whispered. I turned to her.

"We're the Washburns. We live next door to Crystal. I mean, we did." Her rouged cheeks glowed. Her husband wore a hearing aid. They were both small people: he couldn't have been more than five-eight, and she was several inches shorter. Age had stooped them as well, giving them the appearance of Keebler elves.

"You know Payton?" I asked her.

"Everybody knows Mr. Payton, if you've lived here long enough." Her husband nodded enthusiastically, but I couldn't tell if he had heard a word.

The Rev. Fisher asked us to pray. We did, for Crystal and for all those untimely taken from us. Then the minister read scripture, Ecclesiastes — "For everything there is a season." The last time Crystal heard that, The Byrds were singing it. I stood with the older couple, Mr. Washburn's head bobbing up and down in silent agreement with the words of the scripture that Melville once called "The Fine Hammered Steel of Woe." I looked at Corrie. She stared straight ahead.

Presently the two morticians went about their work, lowering the coffin into the ground. We all watched. Mrs. Washburn came close to my ear and whispered: "Mrs. Payton is at the bird sanctuary, you know."

I looked at her. "I thought she was dead."

"She is dead. Her ashes were scattered there. It was her wish, as she founded the sanctuary, you know. We attended that one, too."

Mr. Washburn broke in, talking too loud. "Big wind like this one came up that time, too. Just as we were getting ready to scatter our hand-fuls." He shook his head. "Always was afraid that I took some part of Lorraine to the One-Hour Martinizing."

"She blew all over us, you know," added Mrs. Washburn. And to her husband: "Shush, dear."

When Crystal was under we prayed again, then began to file away. Corrie and Jack Blake were going in one direction and Payton in another. I wanted to talk to the old man, but I could tell my possibilities were slim: the young cop, Leasure, had now arrived and was lounging against his cruiser. Must be moonlighting for the old fart. It was just as well. If I went in his direction, I'd lose Corrie.

I caught up with them at what I took to be Blake's car, a black Grand Prix. Too nice a ride for a guy who was supposed to be ass deep in debt. They had seen me coming and were standing by the passenger side of the car.

"Let's get in," Corrie said. "It's cold as hell."

The late afternoon sunlight had grown weak, and the wind was definitely up. Corrie got in and hit the power lock. I got in the back seat, and Blake went around to his side. He got in and started the car. His heater kicked in a lot quicker than mine did.

Corrie got a cigarette going and then turned in her seat to face me. The heavy tobacco smell filled the car. Blake made a face and cracked a window. Corrie ignored him. "What's up?" she said.

"You were followed when you left the restaurant on Friday night," I said.

Blake lifted an eyebrow. Corrie looked straight at me. "By who?" she demanded.

"I wish I knew. The bartender saw him, but not very well. He could have been the man I saw in the park."

Blake turned to face me as well, doing his best to stay out of Corrie's smoke. Must have been hell when he was living with her. "If you ask me, Haggard," he said, "I think you're stirring this thing up."

"There's something else," I said, speaking directly to Corrie. "Selena Blair. The woman who ghostwrote Crystal's book. She also died in a house fire. In San Diego."

"No shit," Corrie said. She gave a low whistle, shrugged her curls back and drew on her cigarette. Blake turned back and gripped the wheel, looking disgusted. I could feel Corrie's closeness in the small space, her warmth.

"Corrie," I said, "I think you're in danger."

"She'll be fine," Blake said, without turning around. He drummed his fingers on the wheel.

"Maybe she'll be fine," I said, "and maybe she won't. Two women are dead."

He snapped around. "Get out of this car," he said. "Now."

"Stop it, Jack," Corrie said.

He jerked his head toward her, seething now with old wounds. "Or what?" he said.

"Or I'll get out with him."

Blake faced forward again. Corrie turned back to me, her smoke curling around her. "Haggard," she said, "I have to go back. To work. I can't fuck up my life any more over this today. Call me at the work number. Tonight. We'll talk about this."

"Sure," I said. "I'll call you." I pulled on the door handle. I looked at the back of Blake's head. "Sorry for the trouble," I said. He made no reply. My eyes met Corrie's again. Nice suit, she mouthed, smiling. I smiled back and got out. Blake put the car in gear and pulled out. I stood looking. Harvey walked up, his unbuttoned London Fog slapping at his thighs.

"What the fuck you doing out here, Sam?"

"You know."

He gathered the raincoat and went to work on the buttons. "You need to forget this one, Sam. They want us to bury it."

I looked at him. "Bury it? Who wants you to bury it?"

He buttoned the top button and stuck his hands in his pockets. He looked off. "The feds, maybe," he said. "I didn't say that, though."

"So you doing it? Just like that?"

"Wait a minute, bro. You got a bad memory? You think we never buried nuttin' together?"

"Not for the feds," I said.

"Buryin's buryin'. Besides — all that means is, they're handling it."

"Right," I said. "Like they handled the whole Kent State thing in the first place."

Harvey shook his head. "You reverting to your angry young stud days, Sam? You don't even know that any of this is related. Why shouldn't the feds be interested? They were looking for Delbert for questioning once upon a time."

"Who told you this?" I asked. "Askew?"

Harvey shrugged again. "He's the boss."

"And what if I tell you there's a case here? That cuts no ice at all?"

His lips pursed. He made a little popping sound, and then said: "You ain't the boss, Sam. You're a beat cop who got out before you ever made detective. Personally, I like you. But I don't answer to you."

I started walking, talking over my shoulder. "You can forget it if you want to, Harvey. Not me." I felt righteous and full of piss. I was also pretty much sleepless. My parting shot felt good right then, even though I knew already that later, when I rethought it all, the dog would be me. But at the moment I didn't care. I left Harvey standing there and walked to my car. Drove right past him. He watched me all the way. April Fool's Day in the bone orchard. Jesus.

NOTHING ON THE MACHINE EXCEPT another hang-up. I got out of my blue suit and put on some jeans. The phone rang.

"Haggard."

"This is Delbert Jones," a voice said.

I froze. "Bad joke," I told the caller.

"No joke. It's me." There was something metallic in the tone. It was a measured voice, very much in control. But its timbre was hollow, hollow with the echo of a thousand hopeless hopes. "Who are you?" I demanded.

"Jones. Delbert Jones. I saw you at the house the other night. And now I read about you in the paper. Nice interview. Very perceptive on your part. Keep it up, Sam, and you'll be as famous as I am."

"What the hell is this?"

"It's me. Delbert Jones. And I want to talk to you, Sam. Face to face."

"Me too," I said. "Where?"

"How about Kent? Wouldn't that be appropriate?"

"What's wrong with here?"

"What's wrong with here is that it's time for me to go. If you come to Kent, stay at the University Inn. I'll be in touch. Oh, let's keep this our little secret, shall we?"

I was going to lose him. "Wait a minute," I said. "I need to know what this is about."

"All right, Sam," he said. "I'll make it simple for you. There are two of us. Only one's a killer." He hung up.

Two of us.

There was no point in trying a trace. There was also no point in calling the Two Rivers cops. Maybe the state cops, but the best bet I had, I knew, was to go to Kent. If I talked to anybody else, what were my chances of getting to him? Our little secret. And then, why should I trust him at all? He was probably a killer.

I put the machine back on and went over to Mac's. He and Rita were cooking supper, something that required lots of veggies and a boiling pot. Mac sat dicing carrots. Rita was cutting up squash. She was a big woman with red hair that always managed to be both fiery and frizzy. She had enough love in her to put up with Mac, but enough Irish to give him pretty much what he dished out. I liked Rita a lot and for many reasons, not the least of which was her ability to play dobro.

"It's the celebrity," Mac said. "Looks like your fifteen minutes have arrived."

"How you doing?" Rita asked me. "We got gumbo going here."

"I have to leave," I told them. "I got a call from a guy says he's Lucifer Jones."

Even Mac looked surprised. "Well, shit," he said. "Lucifer was welcome to come to supper, too."

"I have to go meet this guy," I said. "I know it sounds crazy. And I can't tell you anything else right now. I want Linc to stay away from the apartment. And don't tell the cops about this, if they show up."

Mac blinked at me. "Sure," he said.

"They probably will."

"No problem. Call us when you get there, wherever it is."

"Thanks," I said. I kissed Rita on the cheek and waved to Mac. I walked back through the arcade, feeling for my wallet. I'd have to hit an ATM. Just outside, I stopped. In the glow from the streetlight in front of my door I could see two men. They wore heavy flannel coats and hiking boots and they looked like they meant business. They stamped their feet in the cold and looked at each other. The taller one pushed the bell again. They waited, and then turned to leave. I stayed in shadow, watching them down the street. They got into a gray LTD, a new one, and drove slowly past my front door.

I ran to my own car in the lot behind the apartment. I fumbled my keys into the lock and got the thing started, screeching the wheels as I jerked it through the alley. There was little traffic, and I could see the LTD a little over a block away. They must have missed a light. I pulled into the same lane they were using and followed.

We were going to Columbus. It was a Tuesday night and traffic was very light. The only problem was staying far enough back in the inter-mittent small towns, but I managed to. Once at Waverly I thought they were going to pull into a McDonald's, but they changed their minds.

I fought sleep. I wanted coffee something terrible. And hunger and fear and something else I couldn't name gnawed at my stomach and threatened to make me sick. Around Circleville I started pinching myself hard to stay awake, but when I saw the Columbus skyline the adrenaline kicked in again.

When I saw them turn off on 71North, I figured they were heading for Corrie's. I decided to count on the dogs to take care of things there and headed for the Brewery District instead. That move depended on Corrie's having gone to work like she said she was. I had no time to call.

The district was surprisingly alive for a Tuesday night. The micro-breweries up and down High Street were doing good business and even the hot dog wagons were out. I found a parking space on a side street leading into German Village and ran back to the strip. I looked up and down, then spotted it a block away.

The place was big. I threw three ones down for the cover charge rather than argue, and while I was waiting for the guy to stamp my hand I looked over my shoulder. I froze. They were coming, not twenty yards away. They walked side by side but a bit apart, as if each had taken responsibility for one side of the street. I'd been wrong: they'd never gone to her place at all.

I jerked my head around before they could make me, presuming they could at all, and ran up the walkway. A girl wearing very little stood inside the door selling beer out of an iced-down horse trough. "Corrie Blake," I said.

"I can page her." The girl's eyes had widened. I was scaring her.

"Which way?" I said, but about then Corrie came walking out of an office to my left. Her job must not have called for her to take her clothes off: she wore slacks and a blazer. Her glasses perched on her nose. I took her arm.

"Haggard," she said.

"There's two guys," I told her. "They're already in the building."

I took her hand and pulled her into the bar area. It was large, a ringed room in whose center sat matching pianos. Pumping away on them were a couple of women singing Motown. I looked around, lost.

"This way," Corrie said, and pulled me right. We pushed past a small crowd at one bar and into a lighted hallway. There was an EXIT door at the end of it. We pounded down the hallway, not looking back. Just as Corrie hit the exit bar I heard footsteps in the corridor. I looked back. Here they came.

We pushed out into a small parking lot. I saw the Blazer ten feet away. "You got the keys?" I said. She pulled them from her blazer pocket. "Start the car," I told her.

"Haggard, haven't you got a gun or something?"

"I didn't have time to pack. Start the car." I grabbed an aluminum trash can from beside the door and let its contents fly. Shit went streaming everywhere. I was aware of Corrie behind me, trying to open the car door. I heard the keys hit the pavement. *Pick them up, Corrie. Pick them up.*

The EXIT door flew open. I saw him for just a minute, the tall one, silhouetted against the harsh light. He had a gun, something with a silencer, something ugly. I threw the empty garbage can as hard as I could. It hit the door with some force, nearly closing it. Then it banged open again, as if kicked with great force.

"Behind me," Corrie shouted. "Come on, dammit!"

The Blazer, running, was right beside me. I threw open the passenger door and dived in. "Punch it," I told Corrie. The Blazer leapt ahead. We took a two-wheel turn onto High and ran the first red light we came to. "Maybe I should—" I began.

"Drive?" she shot back. Her window was open and her hair was blowing wild. "Bullshit, Haggard. Driving's my thing." I looked back and, as she turned onto the 71 ramp, I saw the LTD turn the corner.

"They're coming," I told her.

"Get some music," Corrie said.

"What?"

"Get some fuckin' music. I drive faster to music. Ah, hell, I'll do it." She flipped on the radio. *Jumpin' Jack Flash.* Whoa, shit.

We hit 71 North doing fifty, taking a good bounce off the ramp. Corrie pushed the speedometer past sixty. I buckled my seat belt and kept looking back. It was nearly twelve and cars were sparse. The moon was full; the highway looked like glass. I spotted the LTD as soon as it came off the ramp. "Maybe a half block back," I said.

Corrie hit the gas again. We were cranked up to eighty. The wind whistled in loud through Corrie's window, but I could still hear Mick and Keith and Charlie. I wondered where I'd been the last time I'd heard this song. Someplace other than Dead Man's Curve.

They were closing. This far north there was almost no traffic. No cops either, evidently. Out the left rear window I could see the nose of the LTD, then the face of the tall guy. I saw his gun.

"They've got us," I yelled to Corrie.

"See that exit?" she shouted back. I looked. The Polaris Amphitheater exit was coming up.

"I see it."

"Hang on," she yelled. She gunned the car and veered toward the exit. She'd never take it at this speed. We were dead. And the LTD was right behind us.

But just as the concrete abutment on the driver's side loomed up before us, Corrie jerked the wheel left. We couldn't have missed the abutment by more than five feet. She almost lost control then as the Blazer started to skid, but she got it back by coming hard right. Our right side screeched against the guard rail, leaving a shower of sparks behind us. I got turned back around just in time to see the LTD, unable to stop, roar through the Polaris exit pretty much airborne. I heard a crash, but didn't look back.

Instead, I looked at Corrie. She brought the speed down slowly, taking the next exit. In the distance I could hear sirens. Corrie stopped the car, letting it idle. Mick stopped singing. Corrie and I looked at each other.

"Nice driving," I said. I was shaking like hell. So was she.

"Better than theirs," she said, nodding back at the road.

Both of us exploded in laughter. Hard for a moment, and then we stopped. We looked at each other again. Corrie put the car in gear and took the overpass, heading back toward Columbus. To our left we could see the Polaris exit. Two Highway Patrol cars were already turning off there.

"Who the fuck were those guys?" Corrie said after awhile. She was fumbling for a cigarette. I took her purse, found her Pall Malls and her lighter, and, still shaking, lit one for her. I passed it over.

"I don't know, Corrie. They were looking for me first."

"Feels strange to drive the speed limit," she said. She pulled off on the Alum Creek exit. I knew where we were going. We drove through the vacant lots and the boarded up houses, and then we entered the industrial park. Corrie pulled the Blazer up beside a curve and at last turned it off.

"What now?" she asked me. She threw her half-finished cigarette out the window. Her eyes were very large in the moonlight. She pushed back her wind-whipped hair and looked at me, waiting.

"Same answer," I said. "I don't know." I looked out the window. The moon was very full and, despite the city's reflected light, you could see the Milky Way.

"What about my dogs?" Corrie said.

"We'll get them," I said. "I promise." Then I reached out for her hand. She let me take it and we sat like that for a while, waiting, homeless now among the stars.

TWELVE

We waited for a while. I filled Corrie in on the phone call I had received, taking her up to the point where the two guys had showed up at my place. She listened, sitting with one leg tucked under her and the other hiked up on the seat. She smoked another cigarette, her big eyes fixed on my face. When I finished, she said:

"We gotta call the police."

"The Two Rivers cops don't want anything to do with this. The Feds may have come down on them."

"I mean the Columbus cops."

"I know that. And I also know that if we call them, I don't get to Kent."

"They've already been to where I work, wouldn't you say?"

"Yeah. I would. And when they put it together they'll find us. So I need to get you to a safe place and take my own chances."

She swung her legs down, but didn't turn away from me. "Let me get this straight," she said. "You're going to meet somebody who could be my father — we're talking about the one I've never seen — and I'm not invited?"

"Corrie . . . "

"Fuck that," she said. "I'm calling Jack. He's a lawyer. He'll figure something out. But I go with you, Bud, and that's that."

I wanted her with me. It was dangerous, but it beat worrying about her while I went on alone. It was also wrong, wrong to put her deliberately in harm's way. I told her that.

"Every way in this mess is harm's way," she said. "I'm going."

"Corrie, I'm dragging you in. I nearly got you killed tonight."

"Bullshit. You saved my ass. And besides, I dragged you in. Come to that, you're still working for me, as far as I'm concerned. And that means do what the fuck I say."

I looked at her. I'd never known anyone like her, not in all my life. "Okay," I said finally. "But it's just because I can't come up with an option I like any better. And don't kid yourself: Jack isn't going to cotton to this."

"Fuck him, too. He says he wants to help me; I'm telling him how. He gets the dogs awhile. He'll like that. What about your car?"

"Cops probably got it."

"They'll be after this one, too. We need a rental."

"They'll trace that."

"Then I have another idea. I gotta dump you awhile, Haggard." She saw my look. "I'll be back," she said. "You came back for me, didn'tcha?"

"I go to fetch the dogs with you. Then you drop me."

She started the car. "Fair enough," she said. "Let's go."

Her place was quiet. Corrie pulled the Blazer into a side street and we walked through the alley. The dogs started up as we opened the back gate. I looked at my watch. It was 3:10. Way past time for their run. Corrie unlocked the back door and Stan and Ollie bounded out. She hugged them both and then herded them back inside.

"Leave the lights off," I told her. "And hurry."

Corrie took less than three minutes. I heard her bang around first in her bedroom and next in the bathroom and then she was back. She carried a B. Dalton bookbag stuffed with some clothes and what looked like a very small makeup bag. She had stuck her toothbrush in the side of her mouth.

"I couldn't see worth a shit," she said around the toothbrush. "God knows what I put in here."

"Your purse," I said.

"At the Haze, man. But tough luck: I ain't going back for it." She grabbed her bomber jacket from the hook by the back door and motioned me out. The dogs bolted past us as she opened the screen. We hustled back down the alley, all four of us, looking like the fugitives we were, no doubt. The dogs, too, seemed to be lurking and why not? I'd even gotten them into it now. I could see our shadows large on the back wall of a garage across the alley, liquid and hallucinatory. We made it to the Blazer, where Stan and Ollie commenced jumping at the door, long since ready for their run. Surprise, boys.

Corrie knew exactly where she was going. Seven blocks from her place, she pulled into the parking lot of an all-night pancake house. Its red neon blinked: *Hotcake Heaven*. She kept the motor running.

"Go have breakfast," she told me. "I've got errands. Be back in an hour."

I must have hesitated, because I got the eyes again. "I do what I say I'll do, Haggard," she said shortly.

I jerked the door handle and got out. "See you in an hour," I said.

"Damn right you will," Corrie said, leaning down to talk through the passenger window. Her glasses glinted neon. "Hang in, Haggard. We're better than these guys."

I watched as she drove off in the direction of downtown. Ollie's head was hanging out the back window. I could see the Zippo flame as she lit a smoke.

Hotcake Heaven was lively for three in the morning. The place was small, and mostly counter. I took a seat where I could watch the street. There were half a dozen other night owls in there, all of them male and of the senior citizen variety, probably living off their Golden Buckeye cards. They seemed to know each other. The waitress who put the menu down in front of me was a golden-ager, too: she looked a little like Marjorie Main. All of them talked to each other, swapping jokes and lies; filling the steamy room with at least as much conviviality as there was cigarette smoke.

I ordered coffee. Directly behind the counter was a long mirror in which I could see my reflection. I was tousled and unshaven. I wore the same clothes I'd started yesterday in. I was a wreck, but I felt very much alive. I felt that my possibilities, however dangerous, were at least ahead of me instead of behind. I hadn't felt that way in a long time. I drank my coffee and listened to the old men and waited for Corrie, who seemed to hold those possibilities in the palm of her hand.

She arrived. I saw her first in the mirror in front of me. I turned around as she came in the door. She now wore the bomber jacket and jeans. Her glasses were still in place. Her hair was a beautiful tangle. Her T-shirt had a picture of Neil Young on it and the words WorldWide Tour '75. She took the stool beside me.

"We're outta here," she said. "But I need coffee."

I motioned Ma Kettle over and ordered two cups to go.

When we got them I left some bills on the table and we went outside. The night was clear and very cold. I wished for a heavier coat than my blazer.

"Take a look at our new ride," Corrie said. She led the way to a blue Ford pickup."

"Where'd this come from?"

"Jack," she said without further elaboration.

I got in the passenger side. I hadn't particularly liked Jack when I'd met him at the funeral, but now I had to admit the guy seemed to be turning into a Christian martyr. I smiled a little at the thought of Corrie waltzing in on him at three in the morning, dumping the dogs and demanding a car. Love can be hell sometimes. We pulled out of the parking lot into the quiet street.

"There's a map on the dash there," Corrie said. "We have to go 71 for a while, but we can get off up by Canton and come into Kent the back way, if you think that's better."

"If Jack can't fix this, the police will be looking for us. They could be even if he does. I'm just hoping we can get to Delbert before they find us." I looked at her. "Then there's the other guys."

"They looked pretty well finished to me," Corrie said.

"Guys like that don't stay finished. They're soldiers, and they'll be along. Don't kid yourself."

Corrie took the 71 ramp. The highway was even more deserted than it had been four hours ago. She set the cruise at fifty-five and took the lid off her coffee. She pushed her glasses back on her nose and drank. "Shit," she said. "Too fuckin' hot." She drove one-armed, holding the coffee in her left hand. "So," she said after a moment. "You think it's really Delbert?"

"I don't know. And I don't know what he meant by 'there are two of us.' It's even a lousy bet that he'll show."

"We gotta go," Corrie said. "What the hell else have we got?"

"Thanks for saying we," I told her. "I was feeling pretty lonely there for a while."

"You made your point last night," Corrie said. "Or those guys made it for you."

We rode a little. "I'm sorry about this, Corrie," I said.

She shot me a look. "Sorry about what?"

"Tearing up your life like this."

She shrugged. "My life was a mess already. Maybe this will sort things out." She handed me her coffee. "Here," she said. "Hold this." And when I did she dug for a Pall Mall. She fired it up, took a long drag, and clenched it between her teeth. She held out her right hand. "Gimme that," she said out of the corner of her mouth.

I handed her the coffee. "What hand you gonna drive with?" I asked her.

"Fuck you," she said. She took the cigarette out of her mouth with her coffee cup hand and steered with her left. I sneaked a look at the speedometer. Sixty.

"When we get there I'll get us a couple of rooms someplace besides the University Inn," I told her.

"How's he gonna get in touch?"

"I'll call and get a room held in my name there. I'll check for messages."

"Would he leave one?"

"Damn if I know. But that's about as far as my options extend. I'm not going to check in there and wait around to get torched, if that's his game."

"Jesus," she said. "You think he killed her?"

"It's all that fits so far."

"Why would he want to kill you?"

"I don't know, Corrie. He says he wants to talk. Let's find out."

The air in the pickup was close and warm. It felt urgently good, like blankets when the alarm goes off in the morning. I looked at Corrie in profile. As I watched she drank coffee, the smoke from her cigarette mingling with the heat rising from her cup. Her hair nearly hid her face. The collar of her bomber jacket had gotten turned half up. Ashes had fallen all over her jeans. I wanted to straighten the jacket collar, but didn't.

"Tell me about that day at Kent State," she said.

"What are they teaching in U.S. history these days?" I said. "May 4 doesn't even get honorable mention?"

She shot me a withering look. "I meant tell me your version," she said. It made me feel stupid as hell.

"Sorry," I said. "In fact, I can give you a pretty good one. It's been my bedtime reading lately."

"Hold this again," she said, handing me the coffee. I took it while she ground out her cigarette in the ashtray. I handed it back. She took a chug and wiped her mouth on the bridge of her thumb. "Thanks," she said.

"The Guard has been patrolling the campus all morning. Nobody thinks to shut down the school. The Guard's pissed; the students are pissed. They yell at each other and throw tear gas. The Guard marches down to the practice field and huddles for a while. Then they march up the hill, turn, and fire, for thirteen seconds, right down into the parking lot below them. Four die. Two women, two guys. Alison Kraus was evidently a campus radical. So was Jeff Miller, the kid in the front row in that picture where you can see Delbert. But Sandy Scheurer was pretty much apolitical, and Bill Schroeder, the other one, was pretty much a scapegoat. He was on his way back from taking an ROTC final. A straight arrow."

"Must have been at least a little anarchy in his soul. He loved the Stones," Corrie said.

"What?"

"He loved the fuckin' Rolling Stones. Knew all their albums and every cut in order. Loved 'em."

"I didn't know that," he said.

"Twenty-five years of Rolling Stones later," Corrie said. "Poor guy missed a shitload of good tunes, didn't he?"

"He did indeed," I said. "You seem to know this story pretty well."

"Jesus, Haggard," she said. "I can read."

I watched her hands rest lightly on the wheel. I looked up at her face again, at the tangle of her hair. "You're very pretty, Corrie," I said, and immediately wished I hadn't.

She gave me her fishy look. "Haggard," she said. "You're not gonna get me up here and pull some kinda sex shit on me, are ya?"

"No," I said. "I shouldn't have said that."

She transferred her coffee to her steering hand and whacked me on the knee with the free one. "Don't apologize, bub," she said. She switched hands with the coffee again. She punched on the radio. More oldies: The Dead, this time: *Truckin'.*" Appropriate. We rode without speaking for a while, but when the song got to the "Long strange trip" line we both sang along, then laughed. "Another generational barrier crumbles," I said.

"Damn sure does," Corrie said.

We drove on. I dozed. Corrie took 76. Somewhere beyond the turnoff she pulled over. We were in a rest area. There wasn't another car in sight. "Your turn," she told me. I got out and went around to the driver's side. Corrie hopped out. "I need to pee," she said, and went off in the direction of the restrooms.

I took my leak right there in the parking lot. On the horizon I could see first light. The trees around me seemed tall. The sky was brilliant with stars and the full moon shone brightly, as if aware of its temporary status before the impending dawn.

"Day is breaking," I told Corrie when she got back in.

"Gotta do it without me," she said, and laid her curls firmly against the back of the seat. "Wake me up at chow time, Haggard."

I started the pickup and pulled out. I found a Fifties station out of Cleveland and played it softly. *Devil or Angel.* A sure singalong, but I didn't. I hit 43 North, leveled off at 57, and drove and listened to the Oldies. Akron went by. The night disappeared. At eight A.M. we pulled into Kent. The first thing I saw was a McDonald's, and that's where we stopped.

There are times — rare ones, but times — at which an Egg McMuffin looks like the very face of salvation.

THIRTEEN

W e ate in the car. "The town across the river is named Ravenna," I told Corrie. "It's close. I think we'll be better off staying over there."

"Okay," she said. She'd already downed a McMuffin and was working on those hashbrowns they have that are shaped like a hockey puck.

"Let's do it. Then we'll call the University Inn and find out if this guy's left word for us."

"And what if he hasn't?"

"We call again later. I'll figure some way to make contact. I've got to."

Corrie wiped her mouth on a napkin and then shrugged. "Don't sound like we got shit else to do, man."

"Good." I started the car.

"But at some point we go to meet him, right?"

"I go. Not we."

"Bullshit."

"Bullshit yourself. We may be talking about a murderer here."

Corrie drank coffee. "You got a gun?" she asked.

"It's back in Two Rivers, with the rest of my life." *Not quite,* I thought, but I didn't say that.

She pointed. "The glove box," she said.

I looked at her. "Jack's got a gun in there?"

"This is America," she said. "Everybody's got a gun." She flipped it open. Among the maps and Kleenex lay a .38 Smith and Wesson, holstered. Corrie pulled it out and checked the clip. "Loaded," she said. She shoved the gun back in its holster.

I reached across and shut the glove box, tight. "Jack really wouldn't like this," I said.

"Best kinda gun to use," Corrie said. "Somebody's else's."

"I don't want to use one at all."

"Yeah," she said. "I know."

JUST ACROSS THE RIVER, RAVENNA LOOKED to be all strip: motels and chicken fried places and some bars. I turned off at one named the Stardust and parked outside a fence which enclosed a forlorn-looking swimming pool. The place had maybe thirty units, and only two that I could see had cars in front of them — older models — battered, like the lives of their drivers probably were.

"Looks like the fuckin' Bates Motel," Corrie said.

"No scary house out back," I said. "See? Nothing but weeds up that rise." I got out and took a long stretch, then walked over to the office. A bell jangled as I opened the door. Behind the counter I could see a clock that read 8:55. A young man I guessed to be Iranian sat behind the counter, reading *Newsweek.* I could see the cover: it was about the baseball strike. "The Neverending Story," the headline read.

"Yes, sir," the guy said, without getting up.

"Two rooms, please. Adjoining."

He pulled a register book from a desk behind him. I could see that the place had an old-fashioned telephone setup, complete with the jacks for the different rooms. He squinted, then looked up. "I can give you connecting," he said.

"Fine. Put them both under the name Lincoln. How much?"

"Sixty-two fifty for two."

It was about what I had. I handed him three twenties and a ten. He stood at last and went to the register, then pushed a registration card in front of me along with my change.

"Thanks," I said. I jotted in some bullshit. "Need the license number?" I asked him.

He shook his head and handed me two keys.

"I want them on the back," I said.

He shrugged and came up with two more. "Two-fifteen and two-seventeen," he said. "On the back."

I took them and thanked him. I could probably have checked in with all the Rockettes in tow if I'd paid in advance. "Rooms clean?" I asked him.

"Rooms clean now," he said, and went back to his *Newsweek*.

We drove round back. The two rooms were on the second floor, right at the east end of the building. There the treeline came right to the balcony, and the branches of a couple of good-sized maples enclosed the railed porch like hands. There were two other cars in the lot on this side. I pulled in the last slot and cut the engine.

"Home," I said.

"Right," Corrie replied. She turned and got up on her knees in the seat, rummaging behind her. She came up with her B. Dalton bookbag and turned back to me. "Let's go," she said.

We got out and found the stairs. The hike up put us amongst the branches. I opened the first door for Corrie, then opened my own. The room had a double bed and the usual motel furniture. It also had a kitchenette, complete with refrigerator. All the comforts. It seemed clean.

A knock came through the connecting door. I opened it and Corrie entered. "Yours looks like mine," she said.

"We won't be here long," I said. "I need to go out and get some stuff, Corrie. I came off with nothing. You need to lock these doors tight."

"Okay," she said. "But hurry up. This has got me a little jumpy."

That surprised me. "I'm going to call that motel first," I said. I went to the phone, sitting down on the bed. I found the small Kent-Ravenna phonebook and looked up the number back in Kent. I dialed, and a female voice answered with "University Inn."

"I need a room held for tomorrow night in the name Haggard. I'll be in late."

"For one person?"

"One."

"Kingsize bed all right?"

"Sure."

"Your rental rate is seventy-one fifty. Care to guarantee this with a credit card, Mr. Haggard?"

"I do." I read her my Visa number and expiration date. What the hell?

"Thanks," she said. "We'll hold it."

"An associate I haven't been able to contact is expecting me tonight. I'll need to call in to see if a message has been left for me."

"That's fine, Mr. Haggard."

"Thanks." I hung up.

Corrie was still standing, looking at me. "Not bad," she said.

"We'll see." I got up. "Lock after me," I told her. I went to the door. She followed me.

"Be careful," she said.

"How much trouble can I get in at Wal-Mart?" I asked her, and left. I heard the door shut and lock behind me. But the other door flew open as I passed it and there she was again. "Bring back some Coronas and some cigs," she said. "And a shake. Chocolate. Hell, just get some food. We got kitchens here."

"You just ate," I said.

"Hidin' out's hungry work," she said. "And if Delbert decides to take his time, I don't want to sit around here and listen to my stomach growl." She flipped her hair back and stood with her hands on her hips, looking at me in the morning sun.

"This door too," I told her. "When I get back I'll knock twice, then twice again. But watch through the window. You'll be able to tell if it's me."

"I'd never have figured that out by myself, fuckin' moron that I am," Corrie said, turning on her heel. She walked back in, gave me a wave, and shut the door. I listened for the lock and then went down to the car and got in, looking back up at the two doors for a few minutes. When I felt better about it, I drove off to find a Wal-Mart.

I did, three blocks away — open twenty-four hours, even. Just inside the front door was an ATM, which I hit for three hundred dollars. That left me a little less than three hundred still in my checking account. I collected my bills and my card and went on into the fluorescent expanse of the place. I picked up new jeans and some socks and shorts and a couple of blue Fruit of the Loom T-shirts. I also picked up a windbreaker and some shaving stuff. I'd been living out of tourist sizes off and on for a week now, and I was getting tired of it. But I paid up — a hundred and three forty — and lugged my new wardrobe out to the car.

The beer and cigarettes I paid for at the 7-Eleven across the street set me back another twelve bucks: I should have gotten more money. But the Dairy Queen shake seemed reasonably priced — How many years since I'd bought one? — and there was a Cleveland morning paper on the counter. I riffled it. Nothing about us, but there probably wouldn't be up in Cleveland.

At the pay phone outside I clung to my purchases and waited for Mac to pick up. Rita did, after six rings.

"What's up?" I asked her.

"What's up with you? The cops think you might be dead."

"I'm not, but let's not disappoint them. Don't tell them I called unless you have to."

"Where the hell are you, Haggard?"

"Better you don't know. How's Linc?"

"Haven't seen him. How about Corrie Blake? They want to know about her, too."

"She's okay. I have to go, Rita. I'll call again." I hung up.

They weren't right behind us, but they were close. I was a short-timer and I knew it. I drove back to the motel, holding Corrie's shake between my legs so it wouldn't spill. I lugged the stuff up in one trip and knocked twice on Corrie's door, then twice more. She opened up right away.

"Thought you'd feel better if you got your knock in," she said. She took one grocery bag and studied its contents, sticking in a hand to move things around. "Where's the cigs?" she demanded.

"In the other bag," I told her. "Give me a hand here."

We locked the door behind us and lugged in the stuff. Corrie had gotten rid of her jacket and her Reeboks and she'd pulled the tail of her Neil Young shirt out. She began taking out the groceries, bending to stuff the little fridge with the lunchmeat and other stuff I'd brought.

"You never saw that tour," I said. "You were too little."

"I search out classic tour shirts," she said over her shoulder. "It's my archeology, sort of. I cruise the Salvation Army for 'em." She straightened. "So. I suppose you saw it, right?"

"Saw it? I worked it. I was a cop by that time. Used to moonlight working rock concerts in Columbus or Cincinnati. Or sometimes a sporting event."

"Probably got called a pig a few times, didn'tcha?"

"This was later than those days. Lots later."

Corrie reached back into the refrigerator and came up with a Corona. She flipped off the top with the bottle opener on the side of the counter, and went over and sat cross-legged on the bed. I flopped into one of the room's two chairs.

"Now we wait," Corrie said, and drank some beer.

"Now we wait," I said.

Corrie leaned back on the pillows and stuck one leg out in front of her. She drank some beer. "This is about half-exciting," she said.

"More thrills than I've had for a while."

"Security work's dull, huh?"

"Yeah, it's dull. But it suits me right now. At least it did. I got shit-canned, if you'll remember."

She kept looking at me. "I remember. But I don't see why. You have a lotta good qualities, Haggard."

She said it so straight-on that I almost laughed. But instead I said: "You have a few yourself. You're not planning to drink that beer and that malt at the same time, are you?" She had the malt sitting on the table beside her.

She looked at the malt, then held up the Corona. "Sure," she said. "Why not?" She took another drink.

"Even your stomach's tough," I said.

"Tough's good," she told me. "Tough helps a lot sometimes."

"That's a fact." I got up. "Naptime for me," I told her.

"Go ahead. I'll probably see what we got on TV."

"Maybe you should smoke cigars, like Bonnie Parker."

"Fuck you, Haggard." She smiled at me. I went into the next room, shutting the connecting door behind me. In the bathroom I peeled off my clothes and took a long shower. I washed my hair with motel shampoo and then just stood there, letting the needles of water beat a tattoo on my skin. I toweled off and shaved, then wetcombed my hair and crawled into bed in a clean pair of Wal-Mart underwear. I lay on my back for a while. I could hear the soft drone of Corrie's television.

What a fucking mess this was. A week ago I hadn't known any of this bunch. Now they had all set up residence in the big middle of my life. No. I was camped in their lives. Before they came along, I hadn't even had one, I told myself.

What a dumb thing to think. But before I could sort it all out, I was asleep.

CORRIE WOKE ME AT FOUR. "Here," she said, putting a cup of coffee on the table beside me. "Place even had cups."

She had showered too. Her hair was damp and close to her head. She wore no makeup at all. She'd changed into a denim shirt and fresh jeans. I lay there looking at her.

"Up and at 'em, bub," she said.

I got up on an elbow and drank some coffee. It was black and bitter, but good. "Were we on TV?" I asked her.

"Nuttin'. Don't you think that's strange?"

"Not necessarily. It could mean they never tied us to the smashup out at Polaris. Nobody at the bar would be able to tell them enough to put it together. And whoever's checking on me in Two Rivers doesn't want this on the news. Or maybe—" I stopped.

"Or maybe what? Maybe it's being covered up all over the place? Maybe the feds are about to disappear us?"

"I didn't say that." I drank some more coffee.

She turned to leave. "Well, anyway," she said. "Get up. We gotta do something or I'll go fuckin' nuts. This dump reminds me of some of Crystal's old haunts." She shut the door behind her.

Haunts. Great. I got up and into a pair of my new jeans, whose stiffness did more than the coffee to get me going. I pulled on a shirt and took a look at myself in the bathroom mirror. What looked back was a middle-aged guy in a cheap T-shirt, badly in need of a shave. I had one while I finished my coffee, then rapped on Corrie's door. When I went in she was toweling her hair dry. Curls were bouncing out all over. Shortly they would be back to their usual tangle.

"Let's do it," I said. I went to the phone and dialed the University Inn number, sitting on the edge of Corrie's bed. A different desk clerk answered, a guy this time.

"This is Mr. Haggard. I have a room there tonight, but I'm still a distance away."

"I see it here. How can I help you, Mr. Haggard?"

"I thought there might have been a message for me."

A wait. "Yes. The party you were expecting called."

I nodded at Corrie, who had been watching me. She came over and sat down on the bed beside me. "What was the name?" I said into the receiver.

"He just said to tell you that this was the party you were expecting. I asked for a name but he didn't give it. He says — I got it right here — that you should meet him at the pagoda at the regular time."

"What time?" I said.

"He just said the regular time. Hey, man. I thought it was a pretty strange message, too."

"Anything else?" I asked him.

"That's it."

"Thanks," I said.

"You want this room held, or not?"

"Sure. Hold it."

"'Cause we're a hotel, you know. We're not just an answering service."

"I understand," I told him. "Hold the room." I hung up.

"What gives?" Corrie said.

I told her the message.

"What the fuck's that mean?" she demanded.

"He's saying he'll be up there on Blanket Hill at noon tomorrow."

"Why noon?"

"Because that's when the shootings took place. That's got to be what he means by the usual time."

Corrie whistled low. She looked at me. "Damn, Haggard," she said. "Daddy's home."

FOURTEEN

I t had started to rain. The first splatters hit the window of Corrie's room, catching us both off guard. She got up and went over to the window and looked through the drapes. Then she opened the door. The storm had hit quickly and it was strengthening fast. There was a wind up too, so that the rain came in sheets across our balcony. Corrie shivered and shut the door.

"Feels like November," she said. She sank into a chair and pulled her knees up under her. "How we doing this, Haggard?"

"I told you. We're not. You could scare him off. Plus I don't want the guy anywhere near you. We don't know what the hell he's done."

She got up and started looking around for a cigarette, patting her shirt pockets first. I picked up the pack from the table next to me and tossed them to her. She caught them, extracted one, and stuck it in her mouth. Then she tossed the pack aside and starting patting again.

"On the bed," I told her.

She looked down and then snagged her Zippo, she lit up and inhaled, then stood with her hands on her hips. "You're taking pretty good care of me here, Haggard," she said.

She didn't sound like she liked it much, but I plunged ahead. "It gets better," I said. "I'm cooking for you."

She looked at me and tossed her head. "Fuck you, Haggard," she said. "You know damn good and well I'm going with you. Hell, I'll fire you and go alone."

"I've already been fired," I said. I got up. "And this scene we're doing is the one I always hate in the movies because you know the girl is going to go. But not in this movie."

"You're a fuckin' sexist asshole. I always knew you were."

"I'm just the cook. How do you like your steak?" I went to the little kitchen and started to rummage. Then I looked at the counter in front of me. An electric skillet. What next? I ran some water and scoured the thing out, dried it and plugged it in.

Corrie brushed past on her way to the fridge. She opened it and extracted a beer. "Rare will do fine," she told me. She perched on the counter. I couldn't help thinking it: only nights before, I'd done something like this with Corrie's mother. I washed the two potatoes I'd bought and set them in the little oven. I got the two sirloins I'd bought out of the fridge and put them on a plate.

"Douse those," I told Corrie.

She poured some of her beer on each and I salt and peppered them and forked around on them. I let them marinate, while the potatoes cooked. Then I threw them in the skillet. While they were cooking I opened the pre-packed salad I'd bought and divvied it onto two plates.

Corrie watched all this with interest. The rain was hitting the windows hard now. She drew her knees up again and sat on the counter clutching her beer, her bare heels locked on the countertop, her toes pointing to the floor. Her toenails were painted. So were her fingernails, a dark red. I tried not to look at her.

"Don't get that thing too damn done," she said.

"I haven't even turned it yet."

"Yeah, well," she said, and drank some beer. "Why does he want to meet there? It's dumb and theatrical."

"Delbert was dumb and theatrical," I said. "He seems to be carrying on the tradition in death."

"So maybe it really is him," she said. She tossed her hair, then tested the ends for wetness.

"You could set the table," I said. Without a word, she hopped off the counter and began doing it. Another surprise. I turned the steaks. Corrie had left her beer and I poured a little more on.

"Check this out, Haggard," Corrie said behind me. I turned. She had one of those fat little scented candles, a green one, stuck in the middle of a saucer and was lighting it. Her hair shone with a little candlelight as she bent over the table.

"Where'd that come from?" I asked her.

"My bag. Never leave home without one."

"You do come prepared."

She snapped her lighter shut. "That ain't even the beginning of what's in there," she said.

We ate by candlelight. "Not bad," Corrie told me after her first bite of steak. "A little chewy, but pretty good."

"We work with what we have."

"It was a Christmas candle," she said.

I looked at her. The candlelight danced in her hair. She held a knife in her left hand and I could see the candle there too, glinting in its blade. It was a second in time I wanted to keep forever, and I tried to freeze it in my mind. But it darted away, lost in candlelight.

She pointed with her knife. "That thing," she said. "I got a bunch on sale last Christmas."

"Happy holidays," I said.

She chewed some more. "Well," she said. "If I'd ever thought last Christmas that I'd be shacked up with you right now I'd of planned ahead a little better."

I drank some of my beer. "What would you have done?"

She shrugged. "I dunno," she said. "You don't cook a bad steak, though."

"It's Linc's favorite," I said.

She looked at me. "So that's why it has to be right?"

"I guess so," I said.

Corrie finished her steak, and I did serious damage to mine. When she'd downed the last bite she pushed the plate away and pulled out a Pall Mall. I picked up the candle holder and she bent to light it in the flame, cupping my hand with hers. The sound of the rain and the touch of her hand intertwined in my senses.

"This place has bad vibes for me," she said as she drew back, puffing.

"This motel?"

"This town. I bet this school doesn't do shit in terms of class reunions for 1970."

"Yeah. Several years thereafter probably, too."

She exhaled smoke, looked out at the rain. "I think the whole thing was set up," she said.

"What? Delbert's disappearance?"

"Maybe that, too. But I mean the shootings. I think Nixon needed a nice, containable situation to make an example of. And the governor bought it, and presto; there you have it."

"Lots of people think that," I said.

"That whole Nixon bunch did shit like that," she said. "The whole generation did."

"You would have fit in well with my generation. That's what we thought, too."

She smiled. "You guys weren't stupid," she said. "Just fuckin' nuts. Nah, you had good reason to hate those turkeys."

"That why you feel the way you do about your grandfather?"

She looked away, then got up. "I need a beer," she said. "You want one?"

"Sure," I said. I watched her go over and open the fridge. She got two beers out and set them on the counter. "You ready?" she asked me. She didn't look around.

"What's up?" I asked her.

She turned then and came back, carrying the beers. She sat one in front of me and left the other by her plate. "Nothin's up," she said. She didn't sit down, but went over to the television and fiddled with the knob. It seemed a hell of a funny time to watch television.

"Remote's over . . . " I started to say, and then realized what she was doing. The television had a built-in radio. She dialed around for a minute and then came up with some old Joan Baez. Really old. She left it there and came back and sat down. She took a pull off her beer. "Must be a campus station," she said. "Decent music."

The song was *Silver Dagger*. A million years since I'd heard that. We listened awhile. The rain fell. Corrie sat in candlelight.

"Why does mention of your grandfather always string you out?" I asked her.

She began to twist a lock of hair, then suddenly stopped, looked at me and smiled a little. "I used to do that when I was little," she said. "Twisted a big hunk out once. I was damn near bald for one whole summer. Crystal used to make me sleep with mittens on."

"How about your grandmother?" I asked.

"She's dead."

"I know she's dead. I meant, how did you get along with her?"

Corrie shrugged. "She wasn't a presence," she said.

"But your grandfather was."

Corrie set her beer bottle on the table slowly and got up. She started piling dishes.

"I'll do that," I said.

She started for the sink, but suddenly set the dishes on the counter and turned back. She stood there in the kitchen, just out of the candle-light.

"You're not quitting on this, Haggard," she said. "My grandfather called the shots in Crystal's life after she tucked her well-used tail and crawled back home. He took her in on one condition, and you can imagine what it was. It didn't make for a very nice setup."

"What do you mean?"

"I mean that what he said went."

"For Crystal or for you?"

"For both of us."

The song playing now was *Four Strong Winds.* Ian and Sylvia, maybe 1963.

"Neil Young does that too," Corrie said.

"I know."

She came back and sat down again. "I don't know why the fuck I'm telling you this, Haggard, except that you want to know so damn bad." She put her face in her hands and she pushed her hair completely back. She sat like that a moment, then said:

"I got pregnant when I was sixteen. The guy was three years older. He was no prince, but he liked me and I liked him. He wanted us to get married, I guess. Shit, I was dumb, but I was smart enough to know that was never gonna work.

"So anyway, Gramps finds out about this and pitches a fuckin' wall-eyed fit. He tells Crystal I'm getting an abortion and that's that."

She paused and lit a cigarette. I watched the smoke curl across her face.

"So Crystal tells me and we have a knock-down drag out that's even worse than usual, and I leave. And the guy comes to get me and we're young and crazy and leaving town. We even get as far as Cincinnati and spend the night."

"What happened then?"

"The cops came. That poor jerk went to jail and I went to a hospital right there in Cincinnati where Gramps had already booked me a room. And a procedure. They cleaned me out, Haggard."

I could see tears on Corrie's face. I reached out for her hand but she motioned me away.

"They kept me there a week and I had to talk to the shrink every day, in case I had anything psychological I had to work out. Shit, they were the fuckin' nuts; not me. I never would have stayed with that guy. I wasn't going to have the baby." She leaned forward again, head down, lacing her hair through her hands. "Hell," Corrie said. "I just wanted a day to run."

We sat awhile. Then I said: "To this day, I don't know how they get away with shit like that. Even money and power shouldn't be enough."

She looked up. "You're in some kinda love child arrested development," she said. "That's all it's ever taken. That's all it took right here at Kent State. You want to solve this mystery, money's the fuckin' answer. It always is."

She got up. I watched her as she went into the little living room. She was listening to the radio. Her body moved a little to the music. It was something important to me in another life of mine . . . old Leonard Cohen — *Ain't No Cure for Love.* I knew it from the first bar, knew what it would be before it began. She turned and stretched out her hands, palms up.

"Dance with me, Haggard," she said.

If it had been any other song. . .

I went to her, took her in my arms.

"I haven't done this in a long time," I said.

We moved to the music, I like a wary boxer. She leaned in to me, taking away most of my awkwardness and some of my fear. There was more to her that I thought there would be, but she still seemed very small: a precious gift, like grace unearned. "You're doin' fine," she told me.

Her cheek was against my shoulder, her soft hair on my neck. We danced through the candlelight while rain streaked the windows and our closeness seared my soul. She turned her mouth to me and we kissed. She moved her arms down and locked them around my waist. She bent her forehead into my chest. Then she looked up at me.

"You can stay in my room if you want," she said.

I could feel what was left of my life sliding out from under me, off the side of the world. Val and Mac and Crystal and all of them, Linc too, seemed to be there with us in the room, close enough to touch. I took her face in my palms and looked at her.

"Corrie," I said. "You know I'd die for that."

It was a stupid thing to say, but she saved it for me, meeting my eyes. "Dying's not what I had in mind," she told me.

"There's too many reasons not to tonight, Corrie," I said.

She stayed where she was. "Even if tonight's all there is?" she said.

"Even then. Especially then."

She looked hard at me, then shrugged and reached up to kiss me lightly. We danced the rest of our dance. Then we did the dishes. I went back to my own room about ten. I heard Corrie's radio for a while as I sat propped on my bed, two pillows under me. After awhile it was quiet in Corrie's room.

I sat there listening to the rain, wanting at once everything and nothing. After awhile I got up and very quietly opened the door to Corrie's room. She was asleep, lying on her back with one arm tossed back on the pillow, hand outstretched, as if lifted in a tentative greeting. I looked at her a minute, then went back into my room, closing the door quietly. I sat again, thinking about Corrie, about her life. I thought some really stupid things, like how, if I could, I would take away every faithless trick and every Judas kiss from Corrie's life. And I thought things even dumber than that. I just couldn't fall asleep.

Around one the rain stopped. I finally fooled around with my radio and found that same damn station. The late-night guy was on by then, playing blues. Luther Allison, maybe: I wasn't sure. Shadows played on the wall and I watched them for some time, looking for something lost long ago.

FIFTEEN

The day dawned bright and clear. I got up around six and made some coffee in the kitchenette pot. I watched the news. Then I took a shower. While I was toweling off I heard Corrie.

"Hiya," I said through the door. "I have coffee."

She didn't answer. I went back into the kitchenette and poured myself another cup and waited. Presently the door opened. She was wearing a green sweatshirt that said Stratford Shakespeare Festival on it and black jeans. Her Pall Mall pack and her lighter were in her right hand. She was barefoot and tousled and sleep clung to her like a lover spurned. She made her way to the coffee pot and poured a big shot into one of the Styrofoam cups on the counter.

"Sleep well?" I asked her.

"Pretty good," she said. She took a chug of the coffee and made a face. Then she got a cigarette going.

"Corrie," I said. "Last night—"

"Don't worry about it," she interrupted. She sat on one of the counter stools and flicked ash into the sink. "What's the plan?" she demanded.

She seemed to be in the all0business mode, which was fine with me. "We need to scout this meeting place out," I said, "and now is the time to do it. I want to run up there and take a look. Then we wait. I want to meet the guy by myself, presuming he shows. But I've thought about this, and I don't see why you couldn't be close. You deserve a look at him."

A corner of her mouth went up, then down. "Thanks," she said.

"Corrie, it's dangerous. But it's also dangerous for us to separate. I'm trying to work this the best way I can for both of us."

She shrugged. "Okay," she said. She drank more coffee.

"Is there a problem here?" I asked her. "Last I heard, we were still friends."

"Sure," she said. "I'm just not awake yet." She got up and carried her coffee into the next room, leaving the door open. When she returned in a few moments she'd put on socks and her Reeboks and she was carrying the bomber jacket over her shoulder. She had a pic in her other hand, and was making perfunctory jabs at her hair. She'd put on a little lipstick, but nothing else in the way of makeup. She looked like a student, and that was good.

"You look just right," I said.

She glanced at me. "Right for what?"

"To blend in."

She gave me a fishy look, but made no comment. I collected my jacket and the gun. I also picked up the little tape recorder I'd bought the night before.

"Think you'll get to use it?" she asked me.

"What's he going to do?" I said. "Frisk me?"

She shrugged again. We locked the place up tight and went out into the morning sun. I could see some clouds scuttling in the western horizon, but they seemed very far away. We went down the stairs and I opened the passenger door for Corrie. She got in. I shut the door and stood looking at her. She rolled down the window.

"What?" she said.

"Maybe you should stay here."

"Get in the fuckin' truck, Haggard, or I'm going alone."

We drove back through Ravenna and across the bridge into Kent. The Cuyahoga looked dark and choppy, despite the bright sunlight. Nobody followed us; nobody paid us the slightest attention. We turned onto Water Street and drove a couple of blocks south to Main, passing through the bar district. All the shutters were closed against the morning. A few empty beer bottles sat on trashcans and ledges, sentinels whose shift had ended. It was 8 A.M. on what for everybody else seemed to be a normal Thursday morning.

We parked on a leafy side street, two blocks away from the campus. "You know where you're going?" Corrie said.

"Sort of. I was here not too long after the shootings. We've got a hike; I can tell you that."

Corrie and I crossed onto the campus and started walking up the hill toward the Administration Building. Nobody was around, and I began to wonder if this could be spring break. Kent State is all hills, big ones. Things had already greened up some, and the new grass glistened around us with last night's rain. I felt at once tired and wired: my nerve-ends were raw, but in spite of it I continued to feel very much alive and somehow ready for what came.

At the top of the hill we crossed behind the Administration Building and found ourselves in the middle of a tight complex of older buildings. I stopped, unsure of which way to go.

"There's a map," Corrie said. She crossed the street and I followed her. Sure enough, posted inside a kiosk we found a campus map, complete with a red arrow which said: "You Are Here."

"Taylor Hall," I said. "It's here. So we go— "

"There," Corrie said, pointing at the winding street which headed down the other side of the hill we'd just climbed. We went in that direction. Coming up the hill toward us were two students, male, maybe twenty. They wore Levis and warm-up jackets and one wore a baseball hat turned around backward. This one had longish hair; the other a buzzcut. They looked sleepier than I felt.

"Hi," I said as we came abreast.

Both looked at us. "How's it goin'?" the buzzcut said. His eyes were on Corrie. In fact, both of them were looking at her. She turned heads, even at this hour in the morning.

Some irritation ran through me, but I didn't sort it out. "Taylor Hall this way?" I asked the kid.

He looked back down the hill and pointed. "Top of the next hill," he said. He was still looking at Corrie, who was looking in the direction he'd pointed.

"Thanks," I said.

"Sure, man," he said. "Nothing opens here 'til eight, no offices or anything. But the Union's open if you and your daughter want to get breakfast."

Corrie looked back but said nothing. "We might do that," I said. The two of them walked on.

"C'mon, Pops," Corrie said.

"That's another reason," I said.

"Another reason for what?" She was already walking.

"For what I said last night."

She didn't look back. "Haggard," she said, "Shove a cork in it."

We walked. I could see the high clouds in sharper relief now. It would probably rain again today. We passed a one-story structure whose windows revealed drafting tables. On our right we saw the incinerator building, its twin smokestacks very familiar to me from the dozens of pictures of Kent I'd studied in the past two weeks. The smokestacks had stood like indifferent, omniscient gods framed against the horizon in most of those shots, uncaring observers of the scene below them. Symbols out of Stephen Crane. I put my hand on Corrie's arm. "There," I said and pointed ahead of us.

"What?"

"Down there. This is The Commons. That's where the ROTC building was. And see up that hill? The building at the top of it is Taylor Hall. Now, look just to the right."

She squinted. "The pagoda," she said.

"Yeah."

We went that way, down into The Commons, and then up. "This is Blanket Hill," I told Corrie. "It's where students used to make out before curfew. This is what the Guard marched up." I stopped and pointed behind us. "Right there by that bell is where your dad got into that picture you have."

Corrie looked back too. Her hair ruffled in the slight breeze. The view was very good, and we still saw no one. The campus was incredibly still, as if waiting. Birds chirped; from a distance the sound of an engine.

"Come on," I said, but Corrie stood another moment, looking back. Then she turned and followed.

The memorial stood directly at the top of the hill. It was abstract and discrete, a little plaza, really, done mostly in granite. A long bench ran through the middle. We read the words engraved on the threshold: "Inquire, Learn, Reflect." Corrie pointed out the four pylons up the hill.

"There's another one, too," I said. "See it?"

Corrie shaded her eyes. "Yeah," she said. "For the wounded, huh?"

"For all of us, I think. For you, too."

Corrie reached into her jacket pocket and extracted a pair of John Lennon sunglasses, which she stuck on her nose. She sat down on the end of the bench and fished for a cigarette. "I never asked anybody for a memorial," she said.

I crossed to the other side of the plaza, from which you could see all the way down Blanket Hill. I read the plaque about the daffodils: 59,000 plus of them planted down the hill, one supposedly for every life lost in Vietnam. Mac could have been a daffodil on that hill, or I could have. I looked back at Corrie, who still sat there. Her cigarette smoke trailed on the morning air. I thought about how the two students had looked at her. I thought about the jumble of events that had brought us here. I walked back to her.

"Finish your smoke and let's take a look inside Taylor Hall."

She tossed the butt down and ground it out, then stood. "Let's go," she said.

I missed her earlier excitement about this mission: it seemed to have evaporated, and I didn't know how to get it back. We went into Taylor, which looked like the classroom building on my campus back in Two Rivers. The student newspaper office was open and almost bustling: I could see several students through the window, bent over computers or talking with each other, drinking coffee. Down the hall, the door of the men's john was propped open and I could see a mop bucket just inside. Janitors were fine; what I feared meeting up with was my own counterpart — some campus cop in his last hour of duty before going off work at nine; some other misfit who'd just worked all night because he'd never found the right day job. Or any job, for that matter. I had a gun in my belt and trouble in every pocket, and I didn't want to screw up the day for some poor bastard who wanted nothing more than breakfast and some sleep.

"Let's take a look upstairs," I told Corrie.

"For what?"

"For someplace you can watch from." I started toward the stairs.

"That's dumb, Haggard," she said.

I turned back.

"The bastard's going to try to walk you out of here. I can't do you any good stuck up there like fuckin' Rapunzel."

She had a point. We went back outside. The trouble with the pagoda was that it stood utterly in the open. Down the walk about thirty yards, though, were some stone benches. I pointed. "Down there," I said. "Stick your head in a book and hope it doesn't rain."

She considered, then walked down to the benches and back. "Okay," she said. "And if you leave with the guy . . . "

"I'll do my damndest not to," I said. "But if that happens, just go to the police. We're pretty close to done for anyway. And you can't get close. We have to assume he knows who you are. Now let's get breakfast," I said.

We hiked on down to the Student Union where the morning traffic had picked up considerably. Inside we found one of those labyrinth cafeteria setups where you pick your poison, the choices ranging from McDonald's to Pizza Hut to Taco Bell. There was also a Dunkin' Donuts in residence. We got coffee and a couple of muffins and found a table along the back wall. The place was about a third filled with students and a few professor-types nursing coffee and juice and scanning morning newspapers.

"My life seems to be moving from campus to campus," I told Corrie.

"Not the worst place in the world to be," she said. She took a bite of her muffin, then pushed it aside. She drank coffee. I could tell she was wishing for a cigarette.

"I liked Antioch," I said.

She shrugged. "All I ever saw of Antioch was the movies." She cradled her cup in her hands. " But I read someplace that Yellow Springs is where old Charlie Manson says he wants to settle just as soon as he gets out of the slam," she said. "Says it seems like a friendly place."

I thought of Jerry Garcia, the Yellow Springs head shop owner. "Ought to do wonders for tourism there," I said.

"Hell," Corrie said. "It probably will."

I picked up a campus newspaper someone had left on the table. In a corner of the front page there was a blurb about May 4 preparations. The gist of it was that a big crowd was expected, it being the twenty-fifth commemoration. A month away. I pushed the paper over to Corrie and pointed out the article.

"Delbert's early," I said. "He could have pulled down a hell of a speaker's fee for showing up next month."

Corrie glanced at the paper and then away. "Let's get out of here," she said. "I need a cigarette."

Before we went back outside, Corrie stopped at the book store and bought a Cleveland newspaper. "Camouflage," she explained. We left the building. I could see now that it would rain again before the morning was over: the clouds had moved in. The air here in the north was still crisp, still not free of winter's grip. The campus itself seemed done up in some elaborate color scheme of grays and very tentative greens. Students were everywhere now, and Corrie and I walked with no particular direction. She pointed out the library.

"You know they have a May 4 room," she said.

"God knows what we'd have to show to get in," I told her. "I'd like to see it, though."

"Let's get past noon," Corrie said, and we walked on.

That's the way the morning went. Around ten we got the car and drove around awhile. By the time we parked again — two blocks farther away, thanks to the school traffic — it was 11:30. I checked the gun and shoved it back in my belt. I checked the tape recorder, too, and tucked it in my inside coat pocket. I looked at Corrie. "You go first," I told her. "I'm going to trail you a little."

She was watching me closely. "Watch your ass on this, Haggard," she said.

"Same to you. And I mean it. Don't do anything crazy. Just call the cops if we move out. It will mean he has a gun on me."

She was still watching me. "Don't you think this is already way over our heads?"

"What do you mean?" I asked, although I already knew.

"We're not that good at this, Haggard. We could have been busted a hundred times already, and we haven't been. Nobody's touched us."

I exhaled. "Yeah," I said.

"We're bait," Corrie said.

"Probably. But what the hell else can we do but play this out?"

She said nothing for a moment, as if deciding. Then she gave me one of those quirky smiles of hers. "Okay," she said. She squeezed my hand with hers. "Balls out, Bud."

We got out. Corrie led off and I followed about a quarter of a block behind. We were in the middle of a class session, so the sidewalks were not as congested as they could have been. I dropped back from Corrie a little as she crossed the open space of the Commons, but I didn't take my eyes off her. She walked with that purposeful stride I'd seen the first time that night she entered the Huckins House, walking out of the snowy night. Her hands were thrust in her jacket pockets. The folded newspaper was tucked into the crook of her right arm. I could see that she'd pushed her sunglasses up on her head.

She climbed the hill, the pagoda standing rigid far above her. I followed.

Corrie topped the hill and started down the other side. It was the only point at which I had been unable to keep her view so far, and I started walking more quickly. There was no one near the pagoda in any direction. I reached it and kept walking. I could see that Corrie was down the walk where she was supposed to be, already seated, her newspaper opened in front of her. It was 11:42.

I walked a little distance into a small grove of spruce trees, stopped, and turned back toward the pagoda. I waited there. I could see Corrie, her back to me, and I could see the hill. The clouds hung low now, but the rain was still holding off. Fifty-nine thousand daffodils. Four dead. Nine wounded. Twenty-five years.

Bait.

I looked again at Corrie. What did she have to do with all this anyway? Students passed her back and forth, talking, animated, full of life and promise. She looked like one of them, and her life at that moment seemed a universe away from mine.

"You're early, Sam," a voice behind me said. "By a quarter of an hour."

SIXTEEN

The first thing that came to me was that I'd never even turned on the tape recorder, and now it was too late. I started to turn, and then I felt something hard being shoved against my back, right at the base of the spine.

"Don't turn around just yet," he said. "Let's walk a little, okay?"

"Okay," I said. "Where to?"

"Just toward that building right below us. Right down the hill. Let's walk together." The voice sounded like the one I'd heard on the telephone, but I couldn't be sure. It was almost a whisper and very much a monotone. It could have been the mechanical voice you hear when you call to get your bank balance. I started walking down the hill. He moved in beside me, keeping the gun shoved up against my spine. I couldn't think about anything else but Corrie. I prayed she wouldn't turn around because I couldn't be sure what she would do, let alone what the maniac behind me might do.

"Just down there," he said. We were coming to an empty doorway. I had no idea what this building was, the damn thing looked so nondescript. The sky had darkened a lot. I wished I had made Corrie stay at the motel, as if I could have made Corrie do anything.

"That's fine," he said. I stopped just outside the doorway. It was a side entrance, and there was a sign in the window. Funny the things you remember, and I remember that sign. It had been generated on somebody's computer, and it said: "Closed For Renovation." Beside the words was a cartoon of a little guy in a hardhat, going at pavement with a jackhammer.

The pressure on my back went away. I started to turn, and then suddenly felt myself being shoved with incredible force. I hit the door behind me, hard, struggling to stay on my feet. That was when I got my first look at him.

He was tall, maybe three inches above my six feet. He wore a brown trenchcoat, beneath which I could see a starched white shirt collar and a blue paisley tie. His face might or might not have been Delbert's: it had undergone some work. His skin was a pale white, and I could see tiny marks, like thin worms, criss-crossing his cheeks. He was thin, particularly in the face, and his gray hair swept into a heavily receded widow's peak. He looked a little like an actor whose name I couldn't remember; the one in *Deer Hunter:* not DeNiro, the other one. But most of all he looked like fucking death warmed over, complete with a .45 Auto Rim, which he now was pointing at my heart.

"Give me the gun," he said. "One hand, the left, very slow."

I did.

"Now the tape recorder."

"I don't have one," I said.

He rammed the Auto Rim into my stomach and dug his other hand inside my coat, extracting the little recorder. He pocketed it.

"Not a very firm foundation for a lasting relationship," he said. His nostrils flared a little; then he seemed to relax.

"Pull up your shirt," he said.

"My ass. It's cold out here."

He shoved the gun into me again and pulled it up himself.

"No wire," I told him.

"Good for you." He dropped his wad of shirt and backed up a little. "Haggard," he said. "Good to meet you at last." His thin lips turned in what I took to be a smile, or the ghost of it.

I was trying to see Corrie, back up the hill, maybe catch her out of the corner of my eye so he wouldn't know what I was doing. I couldn't, and that made me feel all the more disoriented. I was having a hell of a time believing this was happening to me, right in the middle of a campus of what? Fifteen thousand? — here on this April noon. A dead man and me, doing our dance of death.

"You're Delbert Jones?" I said.

The smile still played at the corners of his mouth. "That would seem to be a reasonable assumption," he told me. "Let's go inside here."

"Closed for repairs," I said.

"Not to us," he told me. "Turn around and try the knob."

I did. It opened. He gave me a tap in the back and I went in. We were in a hallway, dark and a little musty, but the light from the door window showed me a set of steps leading down. I heard him lock the door behind us.

"Down there," he told me, and nudged me again.

We went down. At the bottom of the stairs was a hallway that seemed to run the length of the place. We were in the basement of an empty building. Great.

"This will do," he said.

We stood there in the semidarkness. There was just enough light from the door in the window above to be able to make him out. I could see the gun. One side of the hall was lined with a long wooden bench. He motioned with the gun for me to sit down. I did. He handled the gun in an offhand way, as if he had to keep reminding himself that he was holding it. Here in the shadows he seemed to have found his element. He paced a little, never taking his eyes off me.

"You're a rank amateur, you know that?" he said.

"Maybe just out of practice."

"Maybe just old," he said.

This guy was irritating the hell out of me. "That would go for both of us, wouldn't it?" I said.

I felt rather than saw his smile. He was a shape to me, a shroud. "Yes," he said. "It would."

"What's this about?"

"What do you think it's about?"

He was standing quite still now. "I think it's about murder," I said. "Crystal Jones is dead. You told me on the phone you knew something about it."

He said nothing. He was standing very still, watching me.

"You said you might know who killed her," I said.

"I'm going to put away this gun," he said. "And then we're going to have a talk. What do you think about that?"

"I think it's fine," I said.

In the darkness I saw him push the gun into the right side pocket of his trenchcoat. He left his hand in there as well. It looked as if his other hand was buried in his left pocket. *Where was Corrie?* I thought. *Where the hell was she?*

"Let me tell you a story," he said. "Back story, the movies would call it, okay?"

I said nothing.

"Return if you will to a more turbulent time, if such a thought is conceivable. The world was on fire. What's the thing the physicists set?"

"The Doomsday Clock," I said.

"The Doomsday Clock. It was set at one minute to midnight. I remember that very well. I can remember lying on my bed and getting that news from a relic of a Philco radio. The thing was older than I was. And I remember being told that based on the current potential for nuclear disaster, the Doomsday Clock had been set up to one minute before midnight."

I waited.

"It was right here in this city. I lived up there above Water Street. In the Haunted House."

"SDS headquarters." I said.

For the first time he laughed. It was joyless, and cold as the grave. "If you want. I heard that bulletin and I lay there and I thought: Well, how to respond to such a thing? How should one reply to the notification that one has been placed sixty seconds from the Apocalypse? I say 'has been placed' because you see, Haggard, I didn't put myself there, did I?"

"No," I said.

"I was placed there."

"We all were."

"Yes," he said. "We all were."

"I thought I had made a woman pregnant, don't you see. In such a world, I thought I had made a woman pregnant."

"I understand."

"No, you don't. We had entered into a course, a method of response, really, that said we would reply to the absurdity of the world and the time with a series of even more outrageous actions. Not that such a course was particularly original. You had, after all, the Merry Pranksters. And you had Abbie Hoffman. And the Chicago Eight."

I said nothing.

"Hoffman was going to levitate the Pentagon, you know."

"I know that."

"This was a popular and some would even say viable response. At the time of the Chicago convention, it seemed the only response."

"We even tried our hand at it in Vietnam."

I could feel his smile on me again. "Don't pull rank on me, Haggard. I was just as much a soldier as you were."

"I believe that," I said.

"You must believe that," he told me.

Outside, it had started to rain. The drops splattered the door above us and, somewhere, windows I could not see. Corrie.

"I was very young," he said.

"Yes."

"So were you, although I would imagine, Haggard, that you have always been an old soul."

"How do you know so much about me?"

"I am surmising, don't you see." A pause, then: "In a way I was an old soul myself. But I was still impressionable. And I could still be manipulated at that age. And of course John Rood was a very persuasive individual."

A silence. "Who is John Rood?" I said.

"John Rood is the man you are looking for. He killed my wife and he will kill you too. He will kill the young woman you brought with you if he feels he must."

"If you're who you say you are, you're talking about your own daughter."

"Am I?" he said.

Jesus Christ. This was turning into the Titicut Follies. "Are you Delbert Jones?" I said again, trying to keep my voice even. I wanted to scream. I wanted to break the fucker's neck. I wanted to get out of there and find Corrie.

"John was in their employ even then, don't you see. He was older, by five years anyway. And of course when he finally told me about being part of the team that went down to Memphis and killed King I believed him."

"King?" I said. "You mean Martin Luther King? Dr. Martin Luther King?"

"That's correct. I believed him. I still do."

"You know somebody who helped assassinate Martin Luther King?"

"So do you. You just don't know it yet."

The rain was coming in violent waves now, nothing like the steady hammer of last night. I shut my eyes for a moment and could see Corrie in the light from the rainstreaked motel window, beckoning me to dance with her.

"What is this about?" I said.

"John Rood asked for my help. He didn't ask, really. He just told me. And when he told you to do something, you did it. They called me Lucifer, don't you see, but John Rood was the devil. And he had the devil's power."

"What did he tell you to do?"

"To start a fire."

To start a fire. This fucker was talking about the ROTC building. In two minutes, he had claimed intimate knowledge of two crimes of the century, Sixties style. I almost wished I could believe him. There in the gloom and the rain he sounded damned convincing. And I had to admire the sheer guts of the bastard: he had scouted this situation thoroughly. He knew this building would be empty. He knew how to get in. He even knew, I was certain, exactly how long we could stay here.

"So this Rood told you to start a fire," I said.

"Yes."

"What kind of a fire?"

He laughed shortly. "You know damn well what kind of fire. What do you think we're doing here, Haggard? This is where my life ended, for all practical purposes. Twenty-five years ago. Right here. Do you understand me?"

"I think so."

"I told you that John was very forceful. He made me see, or at least think I saw, that nothing was worth doing any more. That this really was the end, the end of it all. Last days, just like in Revelation. You know about last days, don't you?"

"Yeah," I said. "I know."

"The end of the world, Haggard."

"Maybe it was just the drugs," I said. And immediately wished I hadn't. The gun came out again, and then he was close, very close.

"Open your mouth," he said.

I sat very still. The barrel of the Gold Cup flicked across my face.

"Open your mouth," he told me.

Well, before I'd only thought I was scared. Now I really was. "What the hell are you talking about?" I said.

His voice was ice. "You know very well what I mean. I intend to place the barrel of this weapon inside your mouth and leave it there. Then we won't have any more smart talk."

"Fuck you," I said. "You sick son of a bitch."

He hit me, a quick backhand with the barrel. I felt skin tear, but I managed to stay in my seat. He backed off a little and stood there in the darkness. I could hear his breath, coming in short little spurts. I could taste blood: he must have split my lip.

"Feel better?" I said.

"Do you?" he snapped. He extended something. A handkerchief. I took it, dabbing at my face.

"I sought you out for a reason," he told me. "We're not that much different, you and I."

"Bullshit," I said.

"No, Haggard. It's true. I could tell by what you said in the newspaper. You never got over the Sixties, either. You know that."

I said nothing.

"It took a long time for me to come back here. Twenty-five years."

"Why did you?" I said. My lip was swelling badly, but the bleeding didn't seem as bad as I'd first thought.

"I came back because it was time. Long past time, really. Are you following me?"

"I think what you're telling me is that this guy Rood got you to help him set fire to the ROTC building on the Saturday night before the shootings here. And then you disappeared. You've been running from that ever since."

"I didn't set fire to the building," he said.

I waited.

"I set fire to Rood."

My eyes had long ago adjusted to the dark. He loomed above me, the gun still drawn. He was bone white, his face an ivory grimace in the shadows. "You killed Rood?" I said.

"No. He's alive. And he's close. He killed my wife."

"He killed Crystal?"

"You know he did."

"How do I know you didn't?"

He shook his head slowly. "You know I didn't."

"How do I know that?" I said. "How do I know you didn't have a score to settle with Crystal after all this time, and—"

He cut me off. "I didn't kill her."

"This doesn't make a hell of a lot of sense," I said. "You get overcome with Sixties angst and you let some Svengali convince you of the nothingness of it all and suddenly you're the human torch? Sounds more like you OD'd on Camus or some shit to me. We all saw the Big Nothing back then. Why was yours so much worse?"

The short laugh again. "You left a girl back up there on the hill, Haggard."

The hair along my neck rose. Suddenly the dark and the rain outside seemed a terrible net, a black snare. "What do you mean?" I said.

"She's his daughter," he said. "Not mine. She's Rood's daughter. And I'm telling you the truth: he'll kill her, too."

"Delbert," I said. "Or whoever the hell you are. I don't know what you did here and I don't care. But I want to tell you something. I do care about that girl. About Corrie. I care about her. And if you or any of your psycho buddies hurt her, I'll come after you."

"Impressive," he said, "for someone at your obvious disadvantage." He waved the gun, a short, choppy motion. "Get down on your knees."

"I'm not bluffing, man."

"Neither am I. On your knees."

I went to the floor. "There's another day, Delbert."

"Another day has been my stock in trade. Hands clasped behind your neck."

I did. I was facing the faint light from the window in the door. He was somewhere behind me.

"Now stay there. I'll be in touch. Or I won't be. Goodbye, Haggard."

I waited. A minute. Two. And then I unclasped my hands and turned around. He was gone. The luminous dial on my watch read 12:22. Thirty minutes had passed.

I took the stairs in maybe two jumps and hit the door, expecting all kinds of alarms to go off. They didn't. I was outside again, in the rain, bounding back up the hill toward the pagoda. The walk by the memorial was pretty well deserted now, students having sought noontime shelter from the rain. A pretty girl in a red mac passed me, her hood up. A kid came by on a dirt bike, jumping puddles. The bench where Corrie had been sitting was empty. They had her. Shit, they had her.

"Haggard."

I turned. She was there, behind me, her wild, lovely hair soaked with the rain.

"Haggard," she said again.

I went to her, pulling her to me. She came in close, her breath against my neck. I felt as if I couldn't let go of her, didn't dare to, ever again.

"What's going on?" she said. "What happened to your face?"

I wrapped an arm around her shoulders and began to lead her down the hill on the other side of Taylor Hall, away from the pagoda, away from this place of memory and death. She didn't resist. God knows what the people we passed made of us. I didn't care. I just wanted her away from there.

The rain didn't let up. By the time we got to the truck we were both soaked through. Once we were in the cab I got the motor running, then put the heater on low. I was shaking badly.

SEVENTEEN

The motel parking lot was deserted on the back side. I pulled the pickup into a space under our rooms and we sat there, watching the rain pound the windshield.

"Did you ever hear the name John Rood?" I asked Corrie.

"Never," she said. "Who's he?"

"Someone Delbert — if this is Delbert — is obsessed about. In his version Rood tried to get him to burn down the ROTC building. Delbert chickened out or thought better of it or something. Anyway, Rood's had a hard-on about it ever since. Delbert claims to have been smuggled away, laying low for all this time." I shook my head. "I dunno," I said.

Corrie was watching me. "So the movement got these guys to—"

"Not the movement. The feds. Or the CIA, or some similar pit of snakes."

"Shit," Corrie said.

"Yeah, well," I said. "It's not exactly like this hadn't occurred to anybody before."

"It's still news, if it's true. And you know it."

"I guess I do," I said. I laid the story I'd been told out for Corrie, leaving out the part about her parentage. She took it all in. "Anyway," I finished, "he thinks this Rood killed your mother, I guess because she knew who he is. As he describes him, Rood's a nut case paramilitary type. A stone killer, and then some."

"Wow," Corrie said.

"Yeah," I said. "But our boy's a nut case too, so don't get your hopes up that we're onto anything here. Rood may not even exist."

"Can't he be traced?"

"I'm going to make a call about that, but I have a bad feeling my favors are already used up back at Two Rivers PD."

The rain continued to drum. Corrie's dark hair hung in wet ringlets. I wanted to do something for her very badly. I wanted this to work out.

"How do you get at the truth of this?" she said.

"Hell if I know. Maybe in Nixon's unreleased tapes. I read where there's supposed to be about four thousand hours of them."

"This Rood does seem like a Nixon kinda guy," Corrie said.

"Come on," I told her. "Let's make a run for it."

We got out. When Corrie started to break for the stairs I said: "Hang on while I lock this and let's go together."

She said nothing. I locked the pickup and grabbed Corrie's hand. We dodged puddles across the parking lot and clomped up the stairs. The iron rungs echoed against the backdrop of the rain. At the top of the stairs I stuck out my hand and Corrie produced her room key. I stuck it in the lock and pushed the door back as softly as I could. The room was as we had left it.

We went in. I checked the bathroom and then motioned for Corrie to stay by the door while I opened the door to my room and checked that side. When I came back and gave her the nod Corrie threw off her jacket and went to the bathroom. She came back immediately, rubbing her hair with a towel. She sat on the side of the bed and pulled off her tennis shoes without even unlacing them, and then scooted backward to sit in her usual cross-legged fashion on the bed. She rubbed some more. I pulled off my own coat and sat in the guest chair, watching her. I wanted time to stop there, in this moment with Corrie and the rain, stop before things went bad.

"Corrie," I said.

"Huh?" she replied, still rubbing. Then, when I said nothing, she stopped and looked at me. "What's up?" she said.

Her hair was dryer, but matted now and wild. "I'd like to have a picture of you right now," I said.

"Shit, Haggard," she said, starting to towel again. "It might surprise you to know that I'm actually quite photogenic. I really am."

The door to the room flew open and two guys came in. No knock; no anything. One of them must have kicked the thing open. Corrie said, "What the—" and I came out of my chair at the same time. The one closest to me thrust a badge in my face.

"Feds," he told me. "Sit down, Haggard."

He was about my age and balding. He looked like an astronaut who hadn't made the cut. He wore a London Fog over a business suit. His tie bore a pattern of small clocks. The other one was quite tall and bony with a shock of sandy hair. He looked very young, but tired, very tired, around the eyes.

"Let me see that badge again," I said.

"Sit down, dammit." The astronaut sank into the chair opposite mine and plopped an arm on the glass table between us. The tall one hung back by the door. I looked at Corrie, who sat where she had been. She looked more bewildered than scared.

I sat down. "Who are you guys?" I said.

The astronaut squinted at me. "I'm Higgins. That's Marks over there."

"A guy named Marx working for the feds? Good thing J. Edgar's dead."

"Spelled different," Higgins said. "We came to see you two safely back home. This thing's pretty much over."

"What thing's that?"

"Your run at Delbert Jones."

"Run?"

"Shit," Higgins said. "Is there an echo in here? We know you were on the campus today. We know you talked to Jones."

"If that's so, why didn't you pick him up?"

"How do you know we didn't?"

"Did you?"

Higgins said nothing.

"He slipped you, didn't he?" I said.

"Haggard," Corrie said.

"You can believe that if it pleases you," Higgins said. "It doesn't matter. This is finished." He turned to the door but didn't get up. "Joanne," he said. "Come in."

A tall woman with iron-gray hair, cut short but permed into frizzy ringlets, came into the room. She looked at least fifty. She wore dark slacks and a brown blazer over a cream-colored silk shirt. She squinted, as if her contacts were a bad fit. She wasn't pretty and wasn't ugly: nondescript would be the word that fit. She stood beside Marx, saying nothing.

"Now, here's the lay of it," Higgins told me. "No charges are going to be filed against either of you. This never happened, do you understand? Never. Joanne and Marks are going to see Ms. Blake back to Columbus—"

"Just a fuckin' minute," Corrie exclaimed.

Higgins didn't even look around. "—And I will see you home, Haggard. That's the way it's going to be. We're ready when you are, and we need to make it quickly."

"I want to see your ID again," I said. "And I want to make a call."

"What you want and what you need, Haggard," Higgins said, "are two different things."

Corrie had swung her legs over the side of the bed. I caught her eyes and held them. "I didn't come this far with her to split up now," I said.

"That," Higgins told me, "is melodramatic bullshit." He looked down, then looked up. It was one motion, no pause. "As you very well know," he said, "there is the easy way to do this and the hard way. I suggest the easy way."

I held Corrie's eyes. I didn't know what to do. I was ninety-nine percent sure they were the real thing, but that didn't make me any less wary of them. I couldn't see any reason to split us up, either.

"We go together," I said.

But by that time Higgins already had his gun out, and ugly little Lugar. I stood and he did too. If I rushed him, he'd shoot me. But I knew I was going to rush him anyway.

The woman named Joanne had a hand on Corrie's arm. Marks was behind her. Corrie's eyes were filled with fear, but her voice was steady.

"You're no good to me dead, Haggard," she said.

Pretty much like that, they were gone. I remember watching Corrie put on her shoes, standing on one foot and then the other and wondering how she could do that without even untying the laces. And I remember that she looked back at me once, just before she went through the door. I remember I started to speak, but by then I was looking at the back of Marks' coat and the rain through the open door and I couldn't see Corrie anymore.

"We'll sit awhile," Higgins said, motioning with the Lugar toward my chair. "Have a chaw and a talk. Maybe I'll tell you a little story."

The rain stopped just after Higgins began to talk, but the sun didn't come out. And a wind came up, an angry one. "Let's say that a couple of guys got together a long time ago," Higgins said. He was speaking very quietly. His balding head glistened a little in the light from the table lamp. He still held the gun. "This would have been twenty-something years, nearing thirty now, really, during Vietnam. And in fact one, the older of the two was a vet. Special forces, in fact."

I said nothing. I hadn't felt real hate in a long time, but I felt it now.

Now Higgins brought his left hand up and across his forehead, as if he were sweeping back a forelock that was no longer there. In his right hand he held the gun.

"And let's say," he continued, "that the younger guy kind of became the older one's . . . pupil."

I said nothing.

"An apt pupil," Higgins said. He looked down at the gun as if he had forgotten it was there, then at me. "We surely don't have to worry about this anymore, do we?" he asked. "Miss Blake is gone, after all, and I know damn good and well you want to hear this story."

"Where are they taking her?" I asked.

Higgins raised his brows in mild surprise. "Exactly where I said," he told me. "Home."

"Bullshit. You take her home and you're going to get her killed."

Higgins smiled faintly. "And what were you going to do? Run for the rest of your life with her? Is that what?"

"If I had to," I said. *Stupid. Stupid thing to say.*

"Everything is being done for Ms. Blake that needs to be done. She'll be fine. May I put away this pistol?"

I said nothing. He unbuttoned his coat and holstered the thing.

"Do you want to hear this?" he asked.

"Keep talking," I told him. He began to speak again and I watched his face. In the lamplight I could see the bone moving beneath the skin. He looked skulllike, a death's head.

"The younger guy—" he began.

"Delbert. Why the fuck don't you just say Delbert?"

The faint smile again, a skeleton grimace. "As you wish. Delbert. Delbert Jones even, if you want."

"Bullshit again. These guys were student radicals."

"They were terrorists. The older one was, anyway."

"Would his name be John Rood?"

"As good a name as another," Higgins said. "Let's use it."

I watched him. Which astronaut? John Glenn, maybe. Ohio's own.

"Mr. Rood was indeed a skilled terrorist. Recruited right out of Operation Phoenix in '65 or '66. Jumped at the chance, too. I'd guess he was tired of pushing slopes out of Hueys by then, or maybe he had no choice; I don't know. But suddenly he was back here in the States. By 1970 he'd turned up in a number of places."

"Any assassinations?" I asked.

"Why not? He did what he was paid for."

"And who was paying him? You guys?"

"Not us. We're not the ones who run the flakes."

"You mean the CIA."

"Do I? You think that's the only espionage organization that works off this government's payroll? Is that what you think?"

"I think you bastards are capable of anything."

Higgins took another tug at his imaginary forelock, then looked at me reprovingly. "You're not a naïve man, Haggard," he said. "You're not an inexperienced one. You didn't come out of your own Vietnam experience, for example, ignorant of the fact that sometimes our country has need of a man like the one we're calling Rood. And you know what things were like on the campuses. You saw a newspaper, didn't you? Can't you look back and see that there was an argument to be made that this thing had to stop before it was out of control?"

"Are you telling me that Kent State was the example?"

"I'm not telling you anything. We're just supposing. But suppose someone were needed to make sure the Guard had . . . sufficient provocation."

"Like torching the ROTC building."

"Perhaps like that. And let's say that this particular operative rather foolishly enlisted the aid of his young friend—for it would have taken at least two, although one of them certainly shouldn't have been Delbert— and let's say there was some kind of trouble, something acrimonious, something that made the plan not come off as it should have. Something like that."

"All right," I said.

"Well," Higgins told me, "that's pretty much it. I mean, maybe one of these guys tries to kill the other one over something and they both disappear. And we know good and well that whatever is between them is strong, very strong, and it won't die. And the one guy, the older one, goes right on working—-but not for the government any more. Now he's working for mercenary groups, militiaheads, has an ad in *Soldier of Fortune,* the works. And he's in and does the job and he's out, like a cat. Better. Because he likes it; he likes the work. He likes the killing. The only thing he likes better is the sure knowledge that one of these day Delbert Jones will surface again, and then he can kill him too."

"And what do you think was this thing between them?" I asked.

"I think it was the woman," Higgins said. "And I've thought about this a lot."

"You think Rood was screwing Crystal?"

"I think somebody was screwing somebody."

I waited. Then I said: "What is it that you know for sure that makes Rood so dangerous?"

He leaned forward. In the lamplight the shadow of his head on the wall grew larger. "Do you remember the Lavender case?" He asked me.

"No," I responded. But I wasn't even thinking about what he was saying. I was thinking about Corrie.

"Well, this judge down in Atlanta, named Lavender, has a coke dealer coming to trial. Big time coke dealer, tight with Noriega, the works. The guy really has it made because he just sits back and runs mules, and if one of them gets busted he's sitting in an office in downtown Atlanta a million miles away, or might as well be." Higgins rubbed his head, a quick gesture. "And like a lot of those guys, he fucks up anyway. He's got a pilot's license and one weekend he gets his main squeeze and they take off in this little Tomahawk. I mean the thing's maybe the size of that pickup you drove here, and they go down to the Islands and start fucking around. Then on Sunday they fly back, and in the plane is not only the two of them but all this cash the dealer thinks he just has to have, and a shitload of Charlotte Amalie primo grass, the same shit Bob Marley used to smoke. Our boy's a coke dealer, right, but he's bringing back this good grass just as a personal stash. So guess what?"

"What's this got to do with anything?" I asked.

"I'm getting there. The dealer goes to sleep, the both of them do, him and the squeeze, and the plane crashed, just outside Opa Locka. Nearly hits a barn. The farmer comes running and there's dope and small bills lying all over the farmyard. And two half-dead party animals, of course. She's got an eye out and he's waking up, still loaded. Next thing, he's in jail."

"And up before Lavender," I said.

"Eventually. It took long enough and got enough headlines for Lavender to make a pronouncement or two. No buyoffs. No deals with the dealer. Incorruptible."

I waited.

"He walked into his office one morning and switched on the light. Blew himself and two secretaries to hell."

"This was Rood's work?"

"It was," Higgins said. "That much we know."

I said nothing.

"He likes explosives," Higgins said. "Fires. Incendiary shit. That's his thing. Good at it, too."

"How old? He'd have to be. . ." I said.

"Fifty. Just fifty, in January. He's got years in him yet. He works for any side, anybody who pays him his price. He's the real thing, Haggard."

"I believe you," I said. He was right: in Vietnam, I'd known guys who could have turned into John Roods. Known some since, too.

"So you believe Rood killed Crystal Jones?"

"We do, yes," I answered. "What about the writer who did Crystal's book? Selena Blair, out on the coast?"

"It's possible, of course."

"Why do you have the lid on this? If the fucker is this dangerous, why isn't he all over the post office wall?"

Higgins sat back. He had the start of a paunch, which he now placed his hands upon. "First, because Rood's very success is an embarrassment," he said.

"No doubt."

"And second because in many of my circles," he said, "Kent State is still considered an embarrassment."

"So what? There's no guarantee Rood would spill the beans about Kent, even if he were caught."

"There's no guarantee he wouldn't."

"If it's that much of an embarrassment, why not just kill him outright?"

Higgins sat up and stared straight at me. The lamplight played on his features in streaks of yellow: parchment skin on skull and bones. "We would," he told me. "If we could find him. We'd kill him in a minute. Who would not?"

"What about the other one? How can you be so sure that's Delbert?"

Higgins shook his head slowly. "Delbert's out," Higgins said. "Bought and paid for. Or so we thought. He was never supposed to return to this country. It wasn't in the bargain. Not ever." He surveyed me sadly, looking for an answer he wasn't going to find. "But here it is the Kent State 25th. What is there about anniversaries," he said, "that makes people hop their tracks? Jones had a perfectly good deal. All he had to do was never return to this country."

I stood up. Higgins watched me, warily. "Stiff," I told him. I walked around a little to prove it. Then I turned back to him and said: "He doesn't think Corrie's his daughter. He thinks she's Rood's."

"Interesting," Higgins said. "If incidental."

"There's nothing incidental about it," I said. "Those guys in Columbus went after Corrie when they couldn't find me. They knew where she worked. How are you going to guarantee her safety now?"

"By smoking out Rood at long last, if you'll be good enough to stay out of our way for a while."

"Who the hell were those guys?"

"*Were* only applies in one case. The other one got away."

"Shit," I said. "He's out there right now. Is it Rood? Was one of those fuckers John Rood?"

"Take it easy," Higgins said. "It wasn't Rood. We don't know the connection for certain, but it's easy enough to surmise. Those two came special delivery from a group named Shays' Army. Ever hear of it?"

"No," I answered, although the name did reverberate somehow.

"It's a militia group out of Northern Ohio, west of Toledo. They live on a farm together and won't pay taxes. God and guns; you know the shit. Call themselves Shays' Army after the Revolutionary War vet who led a lot of other vets in a riot to get the army bonuses the new republic was too broke to pay. Fanatics."

I waited. Higgins was quiet a moment. Then he said: "We think Rood's got a contract with them right now. We think maybe he sent them, probably threatened to book on the contract unless they helped him out. Or maybe they just did it because they love him. He's got to be a charismatic kind of guy, wouldn't you say?"

I sat on the edge of the bed. "So she's got a squad of paramilitary nuts after her and Rood to boot."

"I don't think so. They fucked up; they blew their cover. We came down hard on them, and fast. They don't need the headlines that would come from pulling something like that stunt the other night again."

"You don't know that."

Higgins sighed. "Haggard," he said. "We will do everything we can. What's the alternative here? Protective custody?"

"Why not?" I asked.

"We'd have to move the two of you in with Salmon Rushdie. At a distance, we'll give you both protection around the clock, just as long as we think you need it. We're trying to wrap this fast. The survivalists are boxed in. What else can we give you?"

I looked at Higgins and realized that, in more ways than one, I had gotten all I was going to get from him. All I wanted to do now was find out about Corrie.

"Hell," I said. "How about a ride home?"

EIGHTEEN

The five hours back to Two Rivers passed more like five years. The sun was out but it was already after five, so we weren't going to see much of it. I wanted the darkness anyway, because I was seriously thinking about jumping when we hit Columbus. But Higgins on the back seat beside me and the missing inside door handles pretty well deep-sixed that plan. We stopped once for coffee and a piss, but Higgins and the driver, a morose asshole named Velie, were on me the whole time.

"What about my car?" I demanded as we piled back into the Suburban the feds were driving.

"Already taken care of," Higgins told me.

We pulled out onto the highway again. I had a lot to sort out, but my mind wouldn't kick in. I kept seeing Corrie going through that door. Shit, I'd fucked this up. Every turn had been the wrong one.

Higgins and I talked a little more, but he wasn't giving out much: maybe this was all news to old Velie up in front. We mostly sat in silence.

I could have slept, but didn't want to. I watched the dark April fields slide by in that flat section just south of the city and thought about Corrie.

An hour later we passed the A-plant, its carcinogenic billow rising white against the night sky. "What the hell's that?" Higgins improbably demanded.

"Your government at work," I told him. "It's the gaseous diffusion plant. Processes uranium."

"Jesus," Higgins said, looking out his window. "Looks like Chernobyl."

Two Rivers looked like it had when I left it, right from the first McDonald's, the one by the Chevrolet dealer. It didn't seem right: I had changed, in ways from which there was no going back. But my little drama had gone unnoticed in the eyes of the Atomic City. Two Rivers used to call itself that in the Fifties, back when it was still proud of harboring an A-plant. The Fifties. Somewhere in my memory the picture came of me at twelve or so, pulling into another town at two A.M. with the baseball team, everyone on the bus asleep or near it, the spring mist on my window like spun smoke. I felt as lonely now as I had then, and still just as far from anything I could call home.

My car was in the lot by the White Stallion club, right where I usually parked it. "Keys are in your place," Higgins said apologetically. "We had to check that too, of course."

"Of course," I said.

Higgins even walked me up and insisted on coming in for a nose-around. I didn't protest. All I wanted at that point was rid of him. When he was satisfied that all of the Seven Samurai weren't lurking in my closet, he retreated to the door. I stood watching him, praying he wouldn't say: "We'll be in touch."

"We'll be in touch," Higgins said. "And here's my card. Just use that number when you need me."

He held it out, but I didn't take it. He looked around once more, shrugged, threw the card on the coffee table, and departed. I watched him descend, his pitiful pate glinting in the light from my stairs. I shut and locked the door and then dropped on my couch, punching on my answering machine. Linc. Linc again. A hang-up. Harvey. Harvey again.

A call about my Visa, two weeks past due. *Corrie.*

"It's me," she said. "Listen, I'm okay. Don't worry. I'll try again." Disconnect. But at least she'd said she was all right.

I called her number in Columbus. The recording. Shit. I hung up. Where the hell was she? Was Higgins as good as his word? I wanted a cigarette, first time in maybe fifteen years. I sat there wanting a cigarette, without the first idea what to do.

The phone rang. I picked up. "Hey," Linc said.

"Hey yourself. I'm here."

"I thought you'd been X-Filed. Where you been?"

"Kent State, believe it or not." I wondered what made me think this phone wasn't being monitored.

"So I was coming to see you Saturday," Linc said.

"That should be great," I told him. "But I have to let you know for sure."

A little silence. "Oh," Linc said. "Okay."

I couldn't remember ever telling him that. "Let me call you back," I said.

"You know the commotion that causes," he said.

"It won't."

Another pause. "All right," he said.

"I'll call you."

"Sure." He hung up.

That had gone badly. But I didn't want Linc over here until this thing was settled. And I had to find out about Corrie. She'd said she'd call back, but I couldn't wait; I didn't have the patience for it. I dug in the desk drawer for the phone book and searched through it for the call forward directions. I found them and punched in the code, hoping it worked. Then I locked the place up and went down the stairs, into the street.

I saw nobody who looked like a shadow. Maybe they were that good, although I doubted it. I walked over through the arcade doors and down to Mac's. It was just before nine, and he was closing up the book store.

He surveyed me. "The Wandering Gentile returns," he said. "Somewhat the worse for wear. Come on back for a beer."

I waited while Mac locked up the front, and then we went through the back to his place. Rita, dressed in overalls and a T-shirt, was on the couch with her feet up, watching CNN. "Sam," she said. "We thought you'd expatriated."

"It occurred to me," I said. I leaned down and kissed her. "My phone's forwarded here. At least, I hope. I only used that once before, and I can't even remember if I got any calls."

"That," Mac said as he wheeled back from the refrigerator, "is a portrait of a man in existential hell." He handed me a Corona. "Sorry," he said. "No limes."

"Somebody else told me that recently," I said. I sat down beside Rita. Mac wheeled up to the coffee table and produced a nickel bag, from which he began rolling a joint. I looked around at the familiar room: the Navajo rug and the faded Fillmore poster; Rita's plants. Not a hell of a lot more, really. Three rooms behind a musty used book store. But these people were happy together, most of the time. They'd worked something out in their lives that I never had. Mac sealed the joint with spit and ignited a kitchen match with his thumb. He lit the thing and passed it to Rita, who took a hit and passed it on.

"None for me," I said. "Lent, and all."

Mac retrieved the joint and took a massive hit. "Lent's over," he said. "Where you been, Haggard? Where the fuck you been?"

"Hell and back. While there, I met the devil."

Mac sat forward a little, the smoke from the joint curling above his head like a low hanging cloud. He'd only pass it once more: Rita never took more than a couple of hits. "You met Delbert," Mac said.

"Yeah. At least I think I did."

"Amazing. The bastard's alive. He still has my Electric Flag record. The first one; the really good one, with Buddy Miles."

"Shit," I said. "I forgot to ask him about it."

Mac took another short hit and cupped the roach in his fingers. "So what did Lucifer allow?"

"He's a wronged man."

"He always was," Rita said. "I can hear the asshole right now."

I had their attention. Lucifer Jones coming back from the dead was nothing less than the return of an icon, although a shitty one, to Mac and Rita. And so I told my story, all of it, glad as hell to let it loose. By the end I must have talked too long about Corrie, because Mac, who never gets less sardonic when he's stoned, broke in:

"You got the hots for this girl, Haggard?"

"I don't know," I said.

"Come on. You know or you don't."

"It's more like—"

"More like what?"

"More like she's somebody I should have—"

"What? Saved a long time ago? How 'bout that? Don't build this into some big-ass lament for what our generation didn't do, okay? Spare my ass. I was in country, Bud."

"So was I."

"Oh, Jesus," exclaimed Rita. "Spare my ass."

Both of us looked at her. We'd broken an old rule. Rita held out her hand for the joint. Mac passed it.

"It means cross," Mac said.

"What does?" I asked him. Mac also does a lot of free associating when he's loaded.

"Rood. That's what the name means. Old English. There's a poem: 'Dream of the Rood.' It's about the crucifixion."

"It's a strange name," Rita said.

"Maybe too strange," Mac told me, reclaiming the roach. "Like it was invented for this occasion."

"You mean—" I started, and the phone rang.

"Mule barn," Mac said into the receiver. "Which jackass do ya want?" He looked at me. "Hang on," he said. He passed me the phone.

"Hello?" I said.

"Hi. It's me." *Corrie. Thank Jesus.*

"Where are you?"

"I'm in Columbus." A pause. "At Jack's."

Relief turned cold. "I'm coming up," I said.

"No. You don't need to. The dogs are here and I'm not going to try to move this operation again tonight."

"You don't have to stay there."

"Haggard," she said. "It's all right."

"You could stay at my place. I'll pick you up. You're in danger, Corrie." I could tell how nuts I sounded and didn't even care. I could see her. I could see her eyes and her hair. I could see her lopsided smile, the one that always came with a question mark. I could see her juggling a cigarette and her coffee while she drove that damn pickup through the night.

"I have to start putting a life back together, Haggard. I gotta go to work or I lose that job."

"Screw the job," I said.

"Look," she said. "A lot's happened. I have a bunch to sort out, and so do you. I'll be here a couple of days and then I'll be home. We'll sort it out together."

She's alive, I told myself. *She's alive and she's all right. Just be thankful for that. You don't have to know more than that.* I took a breath.

Okay," I said. A pause.

"Listen," she said. "I'm sleeping in the guest room."

"I don't have to know about that," I said.

"I want you to. I want you to know it. Here's the number." She gave it to me. I grabbed at the pen in Mac's pocket and wrote the thing on the back of a *High Times* on the coffee table in front of me.

"You okay?" she asked me.

"Yeah."

"We have a lot to talk about."

"Yeah."

"I'll call you tomorrow," she said, and hung up. I took the receiver away from my ear and sat staring at it.

"You gonna eat that thing, or you want me to hang it up?" Mac said.

I handed it to him.

"That was her?" He asked me.

"Yeah," I said. "That was Corrie."

"Where is she?"

"With her husband. Sort of."

"Jesus, Sam," Rita said. "You do get yourself into some shit."

"Yeah," I said. "I know. Listen, what's the chances I can get another beer?"

"IT'S NOT SUCH A GREAT IDEA FOR ME to be trotting over here," I told them an hour later, as I got up to leave. Four beers and a contact high had done much to mellow my mood, but the sense of anxiety about Corrie was still there. I was beginning to wonder if it would ever go away, or if it had settled in forever, like a phantom limb.

"Well," Rita said, "We're not gonna fall out with you just because you could get us killed, you know."

"Sure," Mac said. "What the fuck are friends for?"

"I'm not sure you want to take this too lightly," I told them. "These guys don't dance."

Rita stood up and hugged me. "We're not," she said. "But what are we supposed to do? Cross you off our Existence Roster?"

"Besides," Mac said, "I'm armed."

"You mean that blunderbuss you showed me? You sure it fires?"

"It fires, all right," he said.

I still had my arm around Rita. "I want to drive up and see Corrie tomorrow," I told her. "Call you guys when I get back."

Mac gave me a look, a glazed one, since he was good and loaded by then, even for Mac. "Just be sure," he told me, "you keep your little one in your britches and the big one outta ditches."

"Haven't heard that one since my last pass to Saigon," I began.

"Yeah, we know," Rita told me. "Go home and get some sleep, Sam. You look like you've been up since Woodstock."

"Yeah, well," I said. "I didn't want to miss anything."

NINETEEN

I have to admit that I slept once around the clock. I awoke trying to snatch back the thread of a dream by then long gone, one which, it seemed in that first daylit moment, would have explained everything.

It was nearly eleven. I brewed some coffee and then picked up the phone to call Harvey, willing to settle for an explanation of anything at all. I heard a faint click: they had a bug on me. But Harvey was at his desk, and I talked anyway.

"You shitass," I said in greeting.

"Nothing like getting to the point," he told me.

"You handed me over to those feds."

"They pulled rank on us. Not much else to be done. Besides, you two left a trail the size of the river out there. They didn't need squat from me."

"Higgins is on the level?"

"Checks out real enough to be scary. Look, don't go crying, Sam. You knew to stay out of this."

"Well, I'm in it now, and I need some help. Run a check for me, will you? You owe me."

"Those guys are all over this place, Sam."

"You can figure a way. Just do it."

A pause on his end. Then: "When would you be calling back?"

"Any time convenient to you. Myself, I'm sort of at loose ends these days. Between positions, you might say."

"What's the name?"

"John Rood. R-O-O-D."

"Call me later, but not after five," Harvey said and hung up.

I replaced the phone and sat there thinking about Higgins & Company listening in. I was doing pretty much what they expected me to do, and I damn sure didn't expect to find out anything about Rood they didn't already know. Waste of time for them.

Unless that guy wasn't really Higgins. Hell, maybe it was Rood himself, come to add another turn to the screw. And, finding that concept no more far-fetched than the last couple of weeks of my life, I entertained it long enough to drink another cup of coffee. By the time I finished it I'd made myself paranoid enough to resolve not to talk to Corrie on that phone any more.

I rinsed my cup in the sink and stood gazing out the little kitchen window. The sun looked settled in to stay awhile. I pushed up the window and the storm screen. It was warm outside, maybe fifties already. I looked at the little calendar on the windowsill — the one the car insurance company had sent me. "Live safe — live long!" its little banner advised. Friday. Easter was still two days away, but already there were resurrections everywhere.

I was hungry. I consulted the fridge and found soured milk and some old ham salad that now had the look of a cloning experiment gone wrong. But there was some Swiss cheese in the meat keeper, and in the cupboard I spied a box of Ritz crackers. It got better: on the top shelf sat a can of Skyline chili.

Skyline is a brand of chili made in Cincinnati by Italians who use chocolate in their recipe. That's not a promising premise, but the result isn't bad. In fact, it's habit-forming. The stuff is best when served over the counter some midnight after a Reds game, but it's edible out of the can they distribute to grocery stores. Just what I needed to start the day: food that fights back.

Eating did make me feel better. I stood under the shower for a long time, washing my sins away. I had just pulled on my shirt when the phone rang. I picked it up and heard the click again.

"Hiya, Sam," came a laconically familiar voice. It was Lonnie, my old boss at the university.

"Don't tell me," I said. "You've refigured my severance pay."

"Yeah," he said. "And you owe us."

"Something told me."

"You been getting quite a lot of press."

"And they said I'd never work in this town again."

"Well," Lonnie said, "it looks like you can if you want to. That's what I'm calling to tell you."

I laughed out loud. "You mean I have my old job back?"

"Start Monday?" he said.

"Let me get this straight."

"Don't bother. You have the job if you want it. Yes or no?"

"How'd this come about, Lonnie?"

"Somebody made a call, I guess. I dunno. I'm just the messenger here, as usual."

"Let me think about it," I said.

"Don't think any longer than five today. I gotta worry about coverage, you know."

"I know. I'll call you. Thanks, I guess."

"Yeah," Lonnie said. "Sure." He disconnected.

What was this about? Was Higgins keeping me occupied? The school would never have taken me back on its own. And the interview in the newspaper would have made things worse. The groan I thought I kept hearing must have been nothing less than the sound of strings being pulled.

I buttoned my shirt and stuck it in my jeans. I needed the money, badly. But I also had a priority. I didn't want to be occupied with anything but Corrie. Mac was right: I wanted to save her.

For what? For me? To do what with? To fuck? Isn't that pretty much what everybody else kept wanting out of Corrie, in one form or another? Jack? Her dead mother? Delbert? Rood?

I told myself that whatever was between Corrie and me wasn't physical, but my thoughts wouldn't behave. Some of it was physical. I started computing, as in: When she's thirty I'm fifty-three, and so on. I got some more coffee, sat on the couch and stared at the phone.

Ten minutes of that were enough. I went to the closet and got my Smith Corona down off the top shelf, letting it sit on the counter while I cleaned off the kitchen table. I still had to jiggle the cord to get it going: the damn thing had had a short in it for three years and I'd never gotten it fixed. But it fired up, and I rolled in some paper from the sheaf I'd stuck in the typewriter's case.

I headed the first page "Crystal," and started putting down everything I knew about her — fact and factoid. I filled one page with only mechanical effort: the *C* still stuck and slowed me down. I went on to a second page of more or less chronological stuff, taking Crystal to the time of her death.

Next I did one on Delbert, and then on Rood. I even did one on Corrie, and that was tough. I typed a separate sheet with Selena Blair's name, and put down what I knew about her.

When I was finished I took the sheets over to the couch and laid them out in front of me on the coffee table. I got a pencil and drew lines between corresponding facts on the sheets. I sat back and looked at them some more.

All arrows really did point in one direction: What the hell was it that had happened to these people on the rest of May 4? In the chaos that had followed the shootings, where had they gone? Had they seen each other again? Did Crystal go to Yellow Springs by herself?

I got in my lockbox and dug out the photo I'd brought back from Antioch. There was Crystal, getting off the bus, being helped by the tall man whose face you couldn't see. I looked at Crystal again, at the way her eyes squinted against the sun. I looked at the man, bent toward Crystal, his hand tight around her elbow.

Tight. Was she squinting not against the sun but in pain?

Was I looking at Crystal and John Rood?

The phone rang again. I knew the voice immediately.

"I see you made it home all right," he said.

"Hang up now," I said. "Call the first place." I put the receiver down and got up. I got my coat and headed for the door. It was all I could think of that fast, and I had to hope Delbert would follow me. Call the first place he tried to reach me in Kent. And I needed a pay phone fast.

I ran down the steps and turned right outside, in case. I walked up a block and went into the U.S. Cleaners. My friend Mimi was behind the counter, counting change.

"I need to go out the back, okay?" I said.

She eyed me, but shrugged and pointed with an upturned palm. I went through the rows of clothing in plastic so much like body bags, and out the back door. Across the alley was the south entrance to the Brewery Arcade.

Inside the arcade, I trotted the distance to Mr. Larry's and went in. For once, nobody was waiting to be pierced. I searched the little hall until I found the man himself, making a desultory application of some kind of ugly yellow shit to the head of a middle-aged woman. He wore plastic gloves, which were caked with the yellow stuff.

"Need a telephone," I said.

"There," he gestured, his plastic-gloved hand dripping hair goo. "On the counter."

I grabbed at the thing and dialed for Kent information. I got the number of the first place I'd called in Kent. Damned if that same fucker didn't answer the phone.

"Listen," I said. "My name is Haggard. A guy is going to call there. Maybe he already has. I want him to have this number." I read the number off the phone.

"I remember you," he said. "And so do the cops. Way I'm thinkin', you been to the well once too often already."

"Just give the guy this number. Give it to the cops, too. I don't give a damn."

A pause. Then: "I wrote it down."

"Read it back to me."

"Fuck you."

"Read it," I said, "or I'm going to come up there and blow your balls off."

He read it.

"Thanks," I said, and hung up.

I stayed at the phone, staking out my territory like a wolf. Nothing happened. Mr. Larry emerged from surgery and peered at me with suspicion.

"Has to call me back," I told him.

He shrugged, but disappeared again.

I waited. On the wall in front of me there was a framed portrait of a harlequin, a surprisingly good one to be hanging in a dump like this. I looked around me. Harlequins everywhere: statuettes, mostly, but other portraits, too. Mr. Larry had a motif. I thought about what Corrie had said about seeing a clown after midnight. Corrie. I thought about all the time lately I'd spent waiting for the phone to ring, and most of that hoping to hear her voice. I wondered at what moment back there I'd known I was going to ride this case into the ground, maybe even the grave. Probably from that first time I went to her house; maybe even before.

What made me think the son of a bitch would do it? Why would he call back? I could be setting him up. I owed him nothing.

It rang. I picked up. "This is Haggard," I said.

"Make this good," he said.

"You called me," I told him.

A pause. "Where are you?"

"At a phone that's not wired. This one's safe. Talk to me, and talk fast. I'm out in the open here."

He laughed his dry laugh. "You think I'm not?" he said.

"You're used to it. Get to the fucking point."

"The point is that by this time you've heard the whole story. Or a version of it."

I said nothing.

"Is that correct?" he said.

"I heard some things."

Another chuckle. "And what did you think?"

"I think you're all full of shit. Two women that I know of are dead because of you and another one — who just might be your daughter — is in danger. A lot of danger. What am I supposed to think?"

I'd been talking very low, but now even the empty waiting room seemed to be listening. The line was silent a few beats, and then he said:

"You're speaking of Miss Blake."

"You know damn well who I mean."

"Maybe I'll go see her," he said.

I froze. I could hear the silence in the room now. "Stay away from Corrie," I said.

"I thought perhaps a little reunion. We didn't really get to talk at the pagoda the other day. I missed my chance to see the little tyke all grown up."

"Stay away from her," I said again.

"And then maybe I'll come in from the cold."

"You do what you want about that, but stay the fuck away from Corrie."

"I'll be in contact, Sam. You may be able to help me with my plans. In fact, you have already."

"Listen, I—" But he had clicked off. I put down the phone and stood there. Mr. Larry appeared, still wearing plastic gloves and brandishing what looked like a paint brush.

"Finished?" he demanded.

"Yeah," I said. "I'm finished."

"Good. Just leave your nickel by the phone." He looked me up and down. "Pardon a professional opinion," he said. "But you need a haircut. A shave wouldn't be bad either, unless you're planning to grow that beard."

I felt my stubble. "Maybe I will," I said.

"I could shape it for you," he offered. "Give you a good outline. Four bucks."

"No thanks."

He shrugged. "Suit yourself," he said, and vanished again. I wondered what kept somebody from coming in and carrying off the cash register, but I didn't wonder for long. I got out of there and went back to the apartment. I grabbed the phone and, reading off the torn piece of magazine cover I'd left beside it, I dialed Jack Blake's number. No answer; just the machine. Next I punched in Corrie's number, but, as I'd figured, all I got was the machine there, too.

"Corrie," I said. "Pick up if you're there."

Nothing. Pretty clearly, I was going to Columbus. I slammed down the phone and turned to the bedroom to get my wallet and my jacket. And then I stopped.

The bedroom door was almost closed. I hadn't left it that way. Had I?

The best thing to do is turn and run. Get the fuck out. I knew that. Every nerve in me screamed it. But just as in some horrible dream, I didn't. I walked the rest of the way to the door and pushed it open.

The bedroom looked the same. Just as I had left it. What I saw looked the same. It was what I heard that was different.

In the bathroom off the other side of the room, the shower was running.

I should have run then, too. Maybe I could have gotten out. But I went to the bathroom door.

The shower curtain had been torn down. It lay half in and half out of the tub. There was blood everywhere, running in rivulets under the spray of water from the shower nozzle.

Sprawled in the tub, fully dressed, was the agent named Velie, the one who had driven us down from Kent. His eyes were open and his throat had been slit, with such force as to nearly decapitate him. I tried to look away, but couldn't. For some reason I stared at his shoes. They were tassled Florsheim loafers, black. I had a pair just like them.

"Such a mess," a voice behind me said. "I hope it's the maid's day. Stay very still, Mr. Haggard, and don't turn around."

I didn't move. Somebody patted me down. "He's clean," another voice said.

"You may turn around now," the first voice said. "Very slowly."

I did. The taller of the two goons who had chased Corrie and me was standing there, the shooter. He held a Colt Gold Cup on me. His face was a disaster: two black eyes and a lot of tape over his nose. The right ear looked like it had been through a Mixmaster. But he didn't interest me. It was the other one, the tall man. Though I had never seen him, I knew him immediately. It was John Rood.

"We're going to talk, Mr. Haggard. Or at least you are. Do you know who I am?"

"Yes," I said.

"And you understand what I am capable of?"

"I know the score," I said.

"You don't even know the game," he told me.

TWENTY

We marched back into the living room, leaving the horrid work in the tub behind us. I'd held my guts in to this point, but now my stomach was turning over badly. The guy with the torn up face kept prodding me in the back with his pistol and at one point I thought I was going to heave, but I held it.

"Sit down," Rood said. He pointed at the couch.

I sat and looked him over. He was big, all right, and solid. He wore a dark leather trenchcoat over dark slacks and a black turtleneck, but you could see the muscle outline. He worked out, probably every day. His hair was white and blunt cut, bristling back from a widow's peak. His eyes were dead and cold and brutal. The thought occurred to me immediately: He looks like a much healthier, much scarier Delbert. He sat in the armchair opposite me and watched me awhile. Then he extracted a tiny cigar from his coat and stuck it in the corner of his mouth. He didn't light it.

"This doesn't need to be unpleasant," he told me.

I said nothing. We watched each other a little more. The other guy leaned against the wall, gun trained on me.

"I have reason to believe you may be in contact with an old friend of mine," Rood said.

"What makes you think that?" I said.

Now he drew forth a pack of matches and lit the little cigar. Blueish smoke spiraled toward the ceiling. He put the matches back in his pocket. And then, before I saw it coming, he was on his feet and in front of me. He backhanded me with such force that I felt teeth give. My mouth was suddenly filled with blood. I looked down and saw specks of it on my shirtfront.

Rood got a handful of hair and snapped my head back. I felt the gun muzzle on my left ear lobe. "Move," said the other guy, "and your brains go on that wall over there."

"Mr. Collier is my associate," Rood said. "He is here to assist me in any way possible. If I tell him to shoot you, he will."

I looked into Rood's dead eyes. "I said I don't know," I told him.

The cigar between his lips had not moved. "Let's try again," he said, and kneed me in the groin with such force that now, at last, I did vomit. Rood saw it coming and moved behind me, never letting go of my hair. He slammed my head downward until it connected with the coffee table surface and he held it there. My right cheek was smashed into a pool of my own vomit. The gun was against my neck now.

"Where is Mr. Jones?" Rood said quietly.

"I don't know," I told him.

Rood raised my head slightly and then slammed it again. I was in danger of losing consciousness. "One more time, Mr. Haggard," he said. "And then I am going to kill you and leave you in that bathtub as well. Do you really want to die that way?" He tightened his grip even more. "Do you?"

"No," I said. It was very hard to speak.

"Then tell me where he is."

"I'll show you," I said.

"Fuck that. You tell me. Tell me right now, or I am going to kill you."

"Let me up," I said.

His hold stayed tight a moment, then loosened. I sat up. The gun was in my face now. My mouth and face burned terribly, and my nuts felt like basketballs. Rood watched me with his dead eyes, kneading his knuckles. He still had not taken the cigar out of his mouth.

"Well?" Rood said.

"Need some water. My mouth is full of blood."

At last he took the cigar away and hissed out smoke. He jerked his head at Collier, who handed him the gun. Collier went off to the kitchen. I heard the tap. He returned with a glass of water. He'd used a Reds glass Linc had gotten as a promo the last time we'd gone to a game together.

Linc. I hoped to God he didn't decide to walk in. I drank a little, tasting the liquid mix with my blood and bile. "Gotta spit," I said.

Collier pulled me to my feet and led me into the kitchen. I leaned over the sink and spat out. Rood was on his feet when I turned around, the gun trained on my chest. Then the phone rang.

The machine was on but there was nothing I could do about that now. The three of us stood there motionless while the necessary four rings sounded, and then I heard my own voice, telling the caller to leave a message. There was a silence, and then I heard Mac.

"You okay, Buddy?" he said, and then waited. A long pause, and then: "I'm coming over." *Ah, shit, Mac. No.*

"Who is this?" Rood demanded.

"A friend. He lives close by."

Rood considered, then said: "Let's move. We'll take him with us. Come on. Now."

Collier pushed me forward. I couldn't believe we were all three going to walk out of here and vanish, leaving that mess in the tub and puke all over the living room. I couldn't believe any of this.

"How much time do we have?" Rood demanded.

"Not much. He's in a wheelchair, but he moves fast."

Collier had the door open. Rood still held the gun. "Go ahead," Rood told him.

The other man turned to start down the stairs. I was behind him, but I saw Mac first. He'd used the key I had given him and was wheeling through the door downstairs. I don't know what the hell he thought he was going to do — crawl on his hands up the fucking stairs, maybe. Then Collier saw him and reached into his coat, evidently for another gun. But Mac had seen us and he was reaching, too, down into the wheelchair seat by his useless right leg, and now Mac had a gun: the Magnum, that blunderbuss he'd been waving around in the bookstore.

"Get back, dammit!" he shouted at me, but I was way ahead of him, pushing back into Rood, getting my hands on his gun arm. I heard the Magnum go off, and I saw plaster explode above my head. I pushed at Rood again and this time he pushed back, sending me headfirst down the stairs toward Mac. I caught the side rail as a burst from the weapon in Rood's hand whistled by me. Mac shot again and I heard Collier scream somewhere above me. Rood darted back into the apartment. I knew he'd checked for the fire escape as soon as he'd come in, and I knew he'd found it outside the bedroom window. He was probably gone, but I couldn't be sure.

"Get back outside," I shouted at Mac, even as I saw him wheeling backward. I looked behind me and saw Collier, blood oozing down his shirtfront. Mac's bullet had exploded his chest. I took the rest of the steps and then both Mac and I were in the bright sunlight. I felt like Dracula, emerging from some lair of death and blood and perpetual night.

I must not have looked much better. A couple of boys who looked about twelve were coming out of the comics shop down the street and they took one look in my direction and backed inside again. Then I realized it wasn't me that had scared them so badly: it was Mac, sitting there in his wheelchair holding his elephant gun.

"Put that fucking thing away," I told him.

"Nice way to talk to the gimp who just saved your ass," he told me.

"Thanks. Put it away. We've got five minutes before this place is crawling with cops."

"Since you insist," Mac said.

He rammed the thing down in his seat again. Then we took a crack at walking and wheeling on down the street as nonchalantly as two guys who had just shot up a hallway could be expected to. I mopped my face on my sleeve and picked up mostly flecks of dried blood. We passed the comic shop, where at least four faces peered through the glass at us. We kept moving until we got to the Royal Bar.

"In here," I told Mac, and held the door for him. He wheeled past me into the dark interior of the bar, nearly deserted in the late afternoon. One solitary drinker occupied a stool — a wino fixture whose name I knew but couldn't recall. I did know the name of the woman behind the bar: it was Teeny, and she owned the place. Her real name was Eula, and it had since time immemorial eluded everyone why she should want to go by Teeny, which wasn't exactly a rung up on the name ladder. She gave us a wave but I walked on by, heading straight for the restroom.

The Royal's john was like the rest of the bar: a decrepit mess. I peered at myself in the cracked mirror and felt lucky to be alive. My lip was split and I had a good mouse under my left eye, but I didn't see anything that needed stitches. I ran cold water in the dirty basin and threw it in my face, then used a paper towel on the caked blood around my lip. I didn't look much better when I finished, but I didn't care: I wasn't dead.

I went back out into the bar. Mac, unflappable, had ordered a beer for the both of us and was nursing his at one of the wood tables by the window. The wino whose name I couldn't remember was hanging on the jukebox, trying to make a crumpled dollar slide into the slot — thankless work even when you're sober. I waved at Teeny and sat down beside Mac.

"Another fine mess," I told him and pulled on my beer.

"That's no shit. Who's calling the cops — you or me?"

"I will," I said. I drank some more beer and got up and walked over to the bar. The wino had finally connected his dollar with the slot: *Help Me Make It through the Night* fired up on the jukebox.

Teeny looked me up and down. She was forty or so, blonde, and what was left of her after half a lifetime in a bar was still pretty. "What the fuck happened to you, Haggard?" she demanded.

"Bad trouble. I need to use your phone."

Without further comment she handed over the portable from behind the bar. I took it and dialed one of the numbers I knew best. I got Harvey.

"You better get over here," I told him. "I got two dead, one in the apartment and another on the stairs."

"You're shittin' me," he said.

"I wish I were. It's pretty bad."

"We're on our way," Harvey said, and hung up.

I handed the phone back to Teeny. "We're going to sit over by the window a minute and finish those beers," I said.

"I don't need your trouble in here, Haggard," she told me.

"You won't get it." I walked back and sat down. I felt very calm, and I knew why.

"I have to go, Mac," I told him. "He'll be after her now. You know that."

Mac downed the rest of his beer and wiped his mouth with the back of his hand. "Come this winter," he said, "I'm headin' for the beach. Gonna sit on my ass down there in this chair and peel shrimp. Only thing I'm ever gonna ask anybody is if they want five pounds, or two."

"I gotta go, Mac."

"I don't do the police routine too well these days," he said.

"I can't do it at all. I can't sit and answer those questions when the bastard has a head start. They'll have to come after me. Send them after me in Columbus. She lives out on Whittier close to 70, but she might be with her husband Jack. He's a lawyer."

He looked at me. "You know you're fucking crazy," he told me.

"Yeah, I know." In the far distance I could hear a siren now.

We sat there. *Help Me Make It through the Night* ground to its torturous end. It was the Sammi Smith version, not Kristofferson's. The siren grew louder. Finally I said: "I love her, Mac."

"You dumb shit," he said.

"I wish it wasn't so."

He sat looking at me from a distance of three feet, but it might as well have been twenty-five years. Finally he shook his head.

"Here." He threw some car keys on the table. I looked at them.

"Rita's Honda," he said. "It's behind the arcade."

"Thanks, man," I told him, and rose. "Thanks," I said again.

"Beat it," he said. "But lay a five down here first. You owe me a beer."

"I owe you a case."

"The journey of a thousand miles," Mac said, "begins with a single step. I'll have another Corona."

I looked at him sitting there, his ruined face sunstruck and handsome in the afternoon light. "Mac," I said.

"It's obsession, Pard," he said without turning toward me. "Pure and simple. It's not even obsession with her. You're after somethin' you'll never get back."

"I know that," I said, although I didn't. He didn't really understand. He didn't know Corrie, and he didn't understand.

"People are dying," he said. "If Nam didn't teach us anything else, it taught us that even one death ain't worth it."

"I know you're right," I told him. "I know. But I have to go."

The sirens were a block away. Suddenly, they stopped.

"Don't fuck up the upholstery," Mac said. "It's the only good thing about that piece of shit we call a car."

TWENTY-ONE

R ita's ten-year-old Honda was a mottled vomit green of the *Exorcist* variety, and by far the closet thing I'd ever seen to a slum on wheels. Mac had some lifelong paranoia that every time they went to Kroger they'd wind up stuck someplace, bereft and desperate; so Rita stocked the damn thing full of provisions — meaning whatever came into Mac's head right before they left — and the provisions had a way of just staying in there. I sat in the driver's seat and surveyed the ruin around me: a picnic basket from God knows when full of canned goods; a Coleman lantern — something that looked very like confetti floating out of the open glove compartment. Knotted to the gearshift was a blue cowboy bandanna, the kind Mac frequently wore for a headband. Nothing half-eaten and rotting, at least — but jamming my right thigh I found a jar of bubble soap. Bubble soap: I wondered when Mac thought that would have come in handy.

I got the car going and eased out of town the back way, over the Scioto River bridge. I exited 52 at Alexandria, the original townsite of Two Rivers. But around 1830 those early pioneers had decided that it just flooded too damn much over here, and moved the entire community across the river. Not that it did much good: a levee was finally going to be required to solve the problems of this little town.

I took 104 North, putting an entire river between me and the mayhem back home. It was getting dark. I tried the radio for a report on what had happened, but the thing was dead as Elvis. Careful not to speed and hoping to hell that Rita had updated tags, I drove toward Columbus.

Night fell someplace around the A-plant: I could see its ugly billow to the east, spread against the inky sky. It was going to rain. I continued on past Chillicothe with its paper mill odor and there I turned, taking the highway around Circleville and on into South Columbus. Twice along the way I took a chance and stopped at pay phones, calling both the numbers I had. Answering machines all around. Funny what you notice: on Corrie's, there was a distinctive little tink just before she began to talk. The sound of her voice clutched at my heart.

I hit the city at nine o'clock. I thought about grabbing the 270 outer-belt and driving east to the Alum Creek exit, which would put me blocks from Corrie's house. But then I decided that was exactly what anybody who was interested would figure I would do, so I turned back west at Groveport and took 23 North straight into town. At Whittier, right in the middle of German Village, I turned back east. Alone again with the wrong car and the clothes on my back. Something was very wrong with my timing, if nothing else. I looked out at the spiffy little houses and yards of the Village as I waited for a red light and saw a prissy sort of order in my surroundings which excluded me.

At Fairwood I turned right, trying to remember the layout in Corrie's alley. Hoping, I turned into one alley and drove until it inter-sected with the one that went past Corrie's little driveway. I didn't have a ghost of a hope that she'd be there, but I had to know.

But somebody was there. The whole gang, in fact. Her Blazer was parked in the drive and beside it was Jack's pickup. Shit. Well, hell. The jealous rage would have to wait. I pulled around to the front of the house and parked. I sat there breathing deep for a minute, and then I got out. The porchlight was on. When I was halfway across the yard, I heard the dogs. Then Corrie opened the door.

Framed against the interior light, she looked like some lovely photograph. I could see that she was wearing the same clothes she'd worn the night I'd first come here: the man's shirt — Jack's, no doubt — and jeans. Even the socks; no shoes. Her hair was caught back.

"Haggard," she said. I thought she was going to open the storm door for me, but she didn't. She came outside and met me on the stoop. "You said you'd call first," she said.

"Corrie," I said. "Rood surfaced today. He killed a man, one of those feds, at my place."

"Jesus," she said and clutched her arms around her. I wanted to touch her.

"You have to come with me," I said.

Jack appeared in the doorway. "What the hell?" he said.

"Nobody's safe here," I said. "This guy's a killer and he wants Delbert. Corrie, he'll take you if he thinks it'll get him what he wants."

"Ah, for shit's sake," Jack said. He opened the storm door. I could see his biceps tight against the short sleeves of his polo shirt and, if he wanted to fight, I knew he could take me.

"Go back inside, Jack," Corrie said without turning around.

He kept coming. "Let's lose this guy," he said.

Now she did turn to him. "Go back inside," she said again. He hesitated. I could see lightning now, crackling in the distant sky. Jack shrugged, and turned back into the house.

Corrie stood looking up at me a moment, then pulled the clip out of her hair, a sort of reflex motion. A wind had come up. There was more lightning. I could see the dogs now, their faces pressed against the door. "What happened?" she demanded.

"Rood showed up with one of the goons that chased us. He had already killed one of the feds right there in my place, in my fucking bathtub, and he meant to kill me. Look at my face, goddamn it. You think I got this shaving?"

She peered at me in the darkness. "You're a mess," she said.

Don't you think I know, I thought. "My friend Mac came in and shot the goon. Rood got away," I told her.

"So you have two dead guys in your apartment?" she said.

"One's on the stairs, or maybe not by now. The police came just before I left."

She screwed up her eyes. "Well, why didn't you . . . "

"I had to get to you, Corrie."

She stuck her hands in the hip pockets of her jeans. "This is the second time you've pulled this bullshit, Haggard, and every time you do it gets me in deeper."

"Corrie—"

"Fuck you."

"I . . ."

"No, fuck you. I can't get wound up in this again. I'm due back at school in the morning and work tomorrow night and I'm fuckin' going. I'm going, Haggard!"

There was thunder now and the wind was whipping Corrie's hair. One of the dogs moaned. I put my hands on Corrie's elbows, but she drew away.

"You have to go to the police. You have to."

And, of course, I said exactly the wrong thing. "What's he doing here?" I asked her.

"Jack moved me back over here this evening. He's staying tonight." She brushed back her hair and looked off down the street. "Maybe tomorrow night, too. Hush, Ollie!"

"Rood will come for you, Corrie."

"That's what cops are for. I can't play this goddamn game any more, Haggard. It's your life, but it's not mine. I don't want it."

"Corrie," I said.

And then she touched me, her right hand on my wrist. "No," she said. "I mean it."

"I'm afraid for you," I said. "I don't want you to be hurt."

She took her hand away. "Haggard," she said. "You're so fucked up I can't tell if you're talking about Rood or Jack. Come in here and call the police. If you don't, I will."

Jack appeared in the doorway again, oozing muscles and razored hair. "Corrie?" he said.

"I'm coming," she told him. And then to me she said: "I just can't do it any more, Haggard. If you want to, you can believe I'm not strong enough. But I'm trying to do a life here, man. I deserve a life!"

It was spitting rain. I felt it on my face and saw it on Corrie's. She dabbed at her eyes.

"I can't run any more," she said.

I didn't say anything else. I thought about her mother and her grandfather and the hell of her life, and I knew she was right. I turned around and went to the car without looking back.

"Haggard," she said behind me.

The door handle pulled like it was made of lead. Suddenly she was beside me.

"You got me crying, you bastard," she said.

I reached into the car and brought up Mac's blue bandanna. "Here," I told her.

She took it. "Go to the police," she said.

"Sure." I slid into the driver's seat. It was raining hard now.

"Promise me," she said.

"You're the one who has to watch out. I feel like he's out there right now, watching every move I make."

The rain pressed her hair to her face and ran down her cheeks in rivulets. She smiled something like her smile. "Let him learn a move or two," she said. "You got some good ones."

I drove away. Hands down, the hardest thing I've ever done. I was glad for the darkness because I was sure Jack was trying to get my license number. Or maybe he wasn't: maybe he thought I was driving my own car. Or maybe, like me, he was thinking of Corrie and couldn't have given less of a shit about a license plate. I didn't care what he was thinking. I didn't care at all.

THE WIPERS OF THE HONDA snicked at the rain as I prowled the streets of East Columbus, looking for an ATM. A mile or so back west, on the edge of German Village, I found a Big Bear. I had to dig a hole in my wallet to find the slip of paper I'd crammed in there with the PIN number for my lonely Visa card, but it was there. I shoved the card in, praying I wasn't at my limit, and asked the machine for three hundred dollars. I watched as the little clock on the screen ticked off a minute, feeling the sweat under my arms. But the cash door opened and, like manna, the twenties appeared.

The Big Bear was in fact a big one, complete with clothing. I picked up some Levi's and a couple of workshirts, some underwear and socks. Then I hit the sample sizes, putting together enough stuff to stock a dopp kit, which I also bought. I picked up a couple of soggy packaged sandwiches from the deli and a quart of milk. Then, as further proof that I had lost it completely, I grabbed one of those four-packs of Sutter Home off the wine rack: no corkscrew needed.

"Startin' over?" the wiseass checker asked me as he rang up my purchases. He had a shaved head and a ponytail, a look I've sure as hell never understood.

"Something like that," I said. "Where's a motel?"

"Find all ya want out there on 70," he said.

I didn't want to go that way, though. I drove downtown instead, and found a Holiday Inn just north of German Village.

"How much for a single?" I asked the woman behind the desk. She had neither a shaved head nor a ponytail.

"It's eighty for the night."

I was ready for that. I plopped down a card I'd been carrying for maybe three months.

"Look here," I told her. "This is one of those damn vacation cards. I got it in the mail and I'm paying something like sixty bucks a year for it. I'm supposed to be able to stay someplace sometime for half price, but it never seems to work. Nobody honors it."

She was young, early twenties, but she seemed to know a dangerous lunatic when she saw one. "You're in luck," she said. "Half price."

I paid cash and signed the register Fred C. Dobbs. The room I got was on the eighth floor and it was pretty nice: king-size bed and a wonderful view. After I'd thrown my stuff down I stood at the window and watched the rain fall on the city. I could see the Columbus Dispatch signboard and the Riffe Tower. Below me the rain pounded the pavement, falling through the neon and the reflected light in a forlorn chiaroscuro.

I slumped on the couch and ate my sandwiches and watched the rain, drinking the milk from the carton. I thought about Rood and I thought about dark passages and dead men's faces. I thought about Corrie and what she had said: "I can't run anymore." And of course I thought about another rainy night in Kent, and dancing with Corrie and about what she had said: "You can stay in my room if you want to."

After awhile I opened one of the little bottles, and that one went so well I had a second. Sometime around then I must have moved to the bed, because that's where I woke up, still to darkness although the rain had stopped. I looked at the digital clock beside the bed: 2:35.

I lay there. I had to piss, and I knew I was going to get up to do that. My sleep had been dreamless, but my waking thought was of Velie's death stare. I got off the bed and found my shoes.

I was in the parking lot almost before I knew it. I dug the keys to the Honda out and got the thing going and also before I knew it I was driving through the empty streets. I went east on Town up to Parsons, where there's a bridge across 70. The deep blue Children's Hospital sign beckoned me across the bridge, the brightest thing in the still storm-filled sky.

Down to Whittier. Turn back east. Down to Fairwood. Turn again, and through the alleys.

Both cars were still there. Jack's pickup had been taken out, because now it was pulled in backward beside Corrie's Blazer, nestled for the night. For some reason, the sight of that pickup sitting there nose out wounded me to the soul. Something about the casual assuredness of it, as if it belonged there, now and forever. I turned out on Whittier and drove a block east; then turned and drove back past her house. It was dark, with the exception of one light at the back: the kitchen. Did she always leave it on? Had the two of them been so anxious to jump in the sack they'd forgotten it? *Ah, shit.*

So now I was a stalker. Or maybe I always had been: maybe that element had always been in the nature of the work I do. I drove back to the motel and made my way back through the lobby, past the bleary desk clerk. Back in the room, I sprawled on the bed in my clothes.

Sleep would not come. I drank another of the little bottles, but it didn't help. Around five, I finally did fall asleep, but that was to dreams of such violent terror that I woke again and again. Even with first light I could not shut down my mind. Visions of Corrie haunted my waking sleep, of Corrie and me running through a dark and gnarled wood, and of John Rood — a shadow man in pursuit, ever closer, never far behind.

AT TEN THE NEXT MORNING I CALLED Mac. It had been so long since room service had forgotten the Scioto River Special I ordered that I had pretty much forgotten I ordered it. Rita answered.

"He's not home yet," she told me, and I could feel the anger in her. "The police still have him."

"I'm sorry," I said. I meant it, but it still came out badly.

"How long does he have to ride the coattail of your life?" she said.

"I need to tell you where I am."

"No, you don't."

"I shouldn't have . . . "

"You shouldn't have run," she said. "Who the fuck do you think you are? He's your friend. Maybe the only one you have, Sam. You're one step away from the nut house or debtor's prison or something, and you're dragging him with you."

"Rita . . . ."

"Fuck you. Just fuck you. I hate your sorry ass. The sheriff was here looking for you, by the way. On top of a warrant he's got a restraining order on you about Linc. I guess Val heard your name on the news one too many times."

I took the receiver away from my ear and held it against my forehead. "Ah, shit," I said.

"You can't play around in people's lives, Sam. You can't do it."

That was what Corrie had meant to say, too. I knew it.

"Listen," I told her. "I have to use this car a couple more days."

"You asshole."

"I have no choice."

"We all have choices, Sam. Even Mac. Can you believe that? Even Mac. Hell, even me." She banged down the phone.

I DROPPED MY OWN RECEIVER in the cradle. She was right. What had I been thinking of, screwing around in all these lives? Even Crystal had warned me. But I couldn't stop. Not now. Not till it was over.

TWENTY-TWO

The Corrie watch didn't really begin until that night. Around noon I checked out and drove east through the sleepiness of a spring Saturday. I passed sidewalk sales and, near Grant Hospital, tennis games abound in session, but the overwhelming impression was one of quiet. Saturday morning coming down.

I caught 70 and drove farther east, passing very close to Corrie's house at the Livingston exit. I continued to Bexley, where I found a Red Roof and checked in, this time using the name Harry Lime. Harder to hit a moving target, I figured, especially one that keeps changing names. I sprawled on the bed of the first floor room and this time I did sleep, for nearly five hours. I woke up hungry enough to eat the crotch out of a skunk, so I drove over to Main and found a Lone Star Steakhouse. I skipped the skunk and ordered a sirloin. While I waited I drank Dos Equis and ate peanuts from the big barrel in the middle of the table, throwing the shells on the floor. My waitress's name was Dorothy and she went to business school at Arista. She told me she'd worked for other chain restaurants and not one was as clean as Lone Star, even if they did let you throw the peanut shells right on the floor.

I had bought a *Columbus Dispatch* and I read the front page while I waited for my steak. The inside back page had a fair-sized story, complete with a picture of Mac, of the carnage at my place. There was a little background on me and my recent notoriety when I'd shot my mouth off after Crystal's death. The story said that I was "being sought." No mention of Rood, or any fourth person, for that matter. Rood, the shadow man.

The sirloin wasn't the quality of the peanuts and certainly not of the Dos Equis, but I ate it anyway. Dorothy took my money and offered me a have-a-nice-life smile when I told her she could keep the change. I escaped from "Little Texas" and drove down Main until I hit Hamilton Road, then caught 70 again.

It was dark by the time I got to Corrie's block. I slowed in front of it enough to see the lights were on. Then I made the block and came up the alley. Same two cars parked the same way. It looked like the back porch-light was on, too. What the hell were they doing, sitting out? Helluva night for it: the rain had turned a neighborhood that was already a slum into a swamp, and the April air was still plenty chilly.

I drove back to the motel, brooding on my circumstances. What I needed to be doing was out finding Rood. But how could I leave Corrie? I couldn't, even though she had asked me not to stay. Maybe especially because she had asked me not to stay.

The TV in my room had only bad news, so I flipped around until I found AMC, which was showing *The Incredible Shrinking Man*. I came in on the part where the guy has shrunk so much that his wedding ring falls off his finger. I watched the part where he joins the freak show, then turned it off and lay in the dark, watching the headlights on the highway outside.

EASTER SUNDAY I PASSED IN THE SAME desperate way. But Monday I tried a routine, even though my life was already a history of ruined routines. I got up at six and showered and shaved, then put on my change of clothes. I drove down Livingston until I found a Dunkin' Donuts, where I bought a big coffee. Then I cased Corrie's house. Nothing doing. Cars still in the driveway.

I drove around awhile, finally stopping at a park — probably one where Corrie took Stan and Ollie. I sat and watched the day stir to life. It was nice in the park: the tall trees had greened already and I could look up and see a scuttle of fast-moving clouds moving across the sky. More rain? Probably not.

I wondered where Delbert was. Did he have any sense of what was happening here, of what he had set in motion by coming back from the dead? I thought about Crystal's aged father, withering away in his fortress on the hill, a mottled spider in a jar. I thought about Linc. I even thought about Crystal, about her white-blonde hair and her skeleton fingers and scared, desperate eyes. I thought about Mac and Rita.

At 7:45 I drove back past Corrie's place and got lucky: the Blazer was in front of the house now, and it was running. I drove down a block and turned on a side street, turned around in the first drive I saw and went back to the corner.

Corrie was on her porch, locking the front door. She wore her bomber jacket, jeans and hiking boots. Her hair was loose and looked wet, as if she had just gotten out of the shower. *She's going to catch cold,* I thought. She had a cigarette between her lips and a backpack was draped over her shoulder. She held a cup of coffee: I could see the steam rising from its rim. Thoughts of our predawn drive hit me hard: it seemed so long ago now.

Corrie ran across the front yard and jumped into the Blazer. I thought I was going to have to back up or be seen, but she swung the car in a U-turn and headed west down Whittier toward town. I fell in a block back, sneaking a glance at the alley. The driveway was hidden by shrubbery, and I couldn't tell if Jack was still there or not.

The both of us moved along in eight o'clock traffic, swimming upstream. At Parsons she turned right and I followed two cars back. When she turned left again on Town, I knew where she was going: to Franklin University, a mile or so down. Classes: Corrie was going to school.

She pulled into the school's underground garage, just as I had expected. I found a space a block and a half down, locked the Honda and sprinted back toward the campus. The hell of it was that the thing was essentially one giant building, and I wasn't quite gone enough yet to go prowling the halls. Instead I made for the parking lot and hunted the rows until I found the Blazer. Then I retreated. What goes in must come out.

I was watching from the Honda and a much better parking place when the Blazer exited the parking lot just before noon, back the way we had come and across the 70 bridge. But then Corrie pulled into the Kroger across from Children's Hospital. I parked at the far end of the lot and waited. I watched her get out of the car and go into the store. Ten or so minutes later, I saw her come out, carrying two plastic shopping bags. Maybe they held some steaks Old Jack was going to throw on the grill tonight, along with wine. Maybe champagne, if they had something to celebrate.

On down Parsons to Whittier again, and then home. This time I went around the alley and found that Jack's car was gone. He'd gone to work, too. Tough old world. I thought about banging on Corrie's door right then, but decided against it. I couldn't do her any good if she wound up calling the cops on me. I parked around the corner and waited.

I began to doubt whether I could have gotten away with any of this if the area hadn't belonged to crackheads and dealers. Not the kind of folks to call the police every time a suspicious set of wheels shows up. I sat and watched the afternoon activity for a while, which was nil. A couple of black kids who looked to be about twelve and who certainly should have been in school cavorted on skateboards briefly on the street behind me. An elderly black woman pushing a shopping cart made her way up Whittier, looking like Sisyphus. I slouched in the seat, and at some point I guess I nodded off.

To be awakened — who knows how long later — by a banging on the passenger side window. I jumped so hard I think my head hit the roof of the car.

Corrie.

I rolled down the window on that side. "Hiya," I said. "I seem to be out of gas."

"That's no shit," she said. "Open the fucking door."

I did, and she slid in. She wore her working clothes: tan slacks with low heels and a tan silk blouse and a black jacket. She threw her purse in the back seat and glared at me. "What the fuck are you doing, Haggard?"

"Yoga?" I said.

"Bullshit. And don't say you were watching out for me, because you were sound a-fuckin' sleep."

"*A* for effort?"

"*D* for dumbass. The cops are looking for you. You must know that."

I sat up and ran my hand over my eyes. Then I looked at my watch. Three o'clock. "Yeah," I said. "I know it."

"You gotta get a life, man."

"This is my life, Corrie. If you're not going to watch out for yourself, somebody has to do it."

"Jesus," she said, and faced forward.

"I know this guy, Corrie. I know what he can do."

She was silent for a moment, staring straight ahead. Then she turned to me. "I'm gonna say this just this once more. I can't live my life hiding. That's what I've done since I can't remember, and I can't do it any more. I have to go to school. I have to go to work. Goddamn you, I told ya: I have a life going here. No jerkoff is going to ruin it, not you and not this John Rood and not that fuckass father of mine. You guys had your time. You played your shitty games. Keep playing them if you want, but leave me the hell out of them!"

The slanting sun caught her hair in that way that made it seem almost red. Her eyes looked a little puffy, as if she'd been crying.

"You sleeping?" I asked her.

"Yeah, but I'm sleepin' at night, not at noon in the middle of the goddamn street. You've got to back off, Haggard."

"I will. When this is over."

She slapped me, pretty hard. "You will now," she said, and then: "Oh, shit. I'm sorry."

I said nothing. It was my turn to look away.

"Haggard," she said after a moment. "Look at me." I did.

"The Sixties are over. You know that, don't you? Don't you?"

"Yeah," I said. "I know it."

"And there's nothing to miss about them. Shit, if you had wanted to save some kids why didn't you do it back then? Why did you have us in the first place if this . . . if this shit is all you had for us?"

"I don't have the answer to that, Corrie."

She touched my cheek where she had slapped me. "I care about you. I really do. And I know you care about me. But you have to let go. If you'd get this thing out of your system and then come back, we could . . . "

"We could what?"

She turned away. "I don't know. But it's not going to work this way. Now, get the fuck out of here or I'll call the law myself."

"Where's Jack?" I asked her.

"He's at work. That's what people do. They have jobs." She glanced at me. "Some do, anyway. And then at night they come home."

"He's coming back here?"

She looked down. "Yeah," she said.

"Great," I said.

"Isn't that what you want? Don't you want someone to be with me?"

"Not him," I said.

She exhaled. "So it isn't about Rood at all, is it? It's about me and Jack."

I touched her arm. "No, Corrie."

She pulled away, grabbed her purse out of the back seat, and opened her door. "The fuck it's not," she said. "You never meant anything you said. You're just as goddamn phony as the rest of them." She got out and shut the door, hard. "Don't be here tonight, Haggard. I'll run you off." She walked away.

I'll run you off. I sat and watched her, feeling my life ooze out at the cracks. She crossed the street and went up the alley. I watched the way she arched her step a little, like a dancer. A moment later I heard her car start. I watched as she pulled out of the alley and turned west on Whittier. She didn't look back. I didn't follow. I knew where she was going.

I drove back to the motel and got my stuff, leaving the key in the room. This time I took the outerbelt around to South High Street, and found a dump called the Sleep-Eze. Twenty-five in cash bought me a no-questions-asked room, which proved to be so old and decrepit that

Dillinger might have stayed there. I expected the roaches to collect a surcharge. I tried to work the shower, but all I got was cold water. The room did have a TV, but nothing so enlightened as cable to go along with it. I lay on the sagging bed and watched a *Roseanne* rerun. Roseanne and her husband had caught their daughter with some pot, but it was the parents who wound up smoking it. I wondered what Lucy and Desi would have been like on some good shit. Or the Brady Bunch? No, Lucy and Desi were better. I'd always taken Desi for a speed freak, but that didn't mean that the Mertzes didn't keep a hell of a stash.

Around ten I drove up High to the Brewery District and cased the parking lot at The Purple Haze. The Blazer was there. I parked across the street at The Clermont Cafe and went in and ordered breakfast. The eggs were runny, but the hashbrowns were good. I sat there awhile, and then got up and paid my tab. Eleven twenty.

Instead of driving, I walked across the street this time. The Blazer was still there in the parking lot, right where it had been. I went back to the Honda and climbed in. Stuck down in the driver's side seat was a tattered copy of *The Electric Kool-Aid Acid Test*. There was just enough streetlight to read—sort of. The print on those pages was so small it was like reading hieroglyphics, but I worked at it. The time passed.

At one-twenty Corrie's Blazer emerged from the parking lot and turned onto High, driving south. I picked her up at a safe distance and followed her home, making the block and waiting long enough to be sure she was inside. Then I drove through the alley. Jack's car was there: the Grand Prix this time. No doubt they'd be walking the dogs soon. I went back to the motel.

I watched some shit TV that week; I want to tell you. *Electric Kool-Aid Acid Test* went much too fast, and I found myself far too much in sympathy with its doomed and desperate characters. I could have gone to a 7-Eleven for something else to read, but I knew damn good and well that if I did, I'd just end up driving past that house again. And so I sat propped on the bed in the gloom and watched whatever I was presented with. Sometimes I got lucky: *The Searchers* played Tuesday night — four hours, with commercials. Other nights the best I could do was whatever nature documentary PBS had to offer. I saw a swell one about red spiders eating their mates. I never even knew there were red spiders: they don't call it educational television for nothing.

And every day I followed Corrie. At least part of the time she must have known I was back there, but she didn't confront me again. We just did our dance, the dance of the automobiles. Thursday morning I thought the Honda's engine was going out, and that was a near panic. Didn't happen, though.

Friday after her classes Corrie drove to a medical complex on State Street. That worried me. Was she sick? After I was sure she was inside I checked the register: it appeared that I was in a lair of gynecologists. So what did that mean? Pap smear? Were she and Jack officially screwing now? Was she in there getting fitted for a new diaphragm?

She emerged an hour later, only to cross the street and enter a Rexall Drug. Filling a prescription, my trained detective's eye told me. Birth control pills, no doubt. My heart jounced around in my lap. *She's right,* I thought. *I want her just like everybody else does, and for no better reason.* Something about this depressing experience seemed to kick out my next to last slat, but I stuck with the rest of the afternoon anyway, parking about two blocks south of her house. She went to work right on time: I picked her up about three twenty, crossing the intersection at Whittier and Fairwood. Another Friday night in the big town — The Purple Haze would be rocking. Maybe I'd go in and have a beer, sing a little karaoke. Why the hell not?

I parked on a side street in the Brewery District and pulled out the new reading matter I'd bought myself: *Breakfast of Champions,* by Kurt Vonnegut. I'd found a ragged copy in a used book store on Thurman Street and remembered that when I'd read the thing a quarter century ago, it had made me laugh about as much as the same author's *Slaughterhouse V* had made me cry. I wanted the laughter.

I sat and read until I got hungry, and then I walked across High and bought myself a braut from the hot dog vendor. I was standing there with the braut in one hand and a Pepsi in the other, getting ready to cross the street again when the feeling hit me. It nearly knocked me over. I threw the sandwich into a trashcan and pretty much let the Pepsi drop, already running. I hadn't checked Corrie's car.

It was there, all right, in its familiar spot — not far from the back entrance we'd charged out of that night, weeks before. . .

But this time the driver's side door was ajar.

I walked very slowly over to the car and had a look.

Corrie's purse lay in the floor on the passenger side. Her keys, the big gold *C* glinting, dangled from the ignition.

Sweat was running down my face, so heavily I could barely see. I ran to the rear door and began banging. Nobody answered. The front doors were locked, too. I banged on them. A compact guy with the build of a powerlifter appeared, but didn't turn any keys.

"Don't open 'til five," he said through the glass.

"Corrie Blake," I said. "Is she in there?"

He pushed back his long hair and looked me over. "Not here yet," he said.

"Open the door. I have to know."

"You a cop?" he demanded.

"No," I said.

"Then you don't get in." He turned and walked into the recesses of the club.

Back at the Blazer I tried to hold off panic enough to think straight, but that was a losing battle. She was gone and he had her. Rood had her. What the hell was I going to do now?

I riffled the seats and dug in the glove box. I looked in the side pockets. Lots of Corrie: Pall Mall butts and one earring and a couple of ATM slips — but nothing that looked like a lead. A hair holder — what did they call those things? Squidgies? Shit, I didn't know. Some matches — my gut wrenched: Huckins House. She must have picked them up when we left that night in the snow. A torn ticket, lying there on the floor. Show ticket? Movie ticket? LOID DREA. LOID DREA. Where had I seen that before? *Think, you fucking idiot. Think.*

Yeah, I knew where. And I knew it wasn't Corrie's ticket. This one had been dropped by the intruder. I grabbed up Corrie's purse and ran for the Honda, dodging the traffic on High Street. I took the corner and headed for 71 West, but just before the ramp I pulled off at a telephone on the outer edge of a 7-Eleven parking lot. I dialed information and asked for an office number for Jack Blake, then dialed the number itself. A secretary who sounded like she was all of fourteen answered.

"Is he still there?" I said,

"Who should I say is calling?"

"Tell him it's Sam Haggard, and tell him he'd better talk."

Silence. On hold. Seconds I couldn't afford to lose. Then the man himself picked up the phone.

"Make it good," he said.

"Corrie's gone. I think Rood got her, at the club. I want you to call the cops and tell them to get in touch with a fed named Higgins. Tell him I think Rood might have taken Corrie to Yellow Springs, but I can't be sure. He could just as easily have her here, or anywhere. Her car is in the lot, and that's where she was taken."

"Jesus," Jack Blake said.

"And one other thing. Take care of those dogs, will you?"

Amazingly, he said: "I will."

TWENTY-THREE

The Honda started bucking pretty badly just beyond the little town of Washington Court House. It was 7:05, and dark. I limped on to the outlet mall and found a gas station with a garage that was still open. Fan belt, all right. It cost me thirty-five minutes.

While I waited I reassembled the pieces of the miserable puzzle I was caught up in. May, 1970: John Rood, who may or may not be a government agent himself, either blackmails or seduces Delbert Jones into torching the ROTC building two nights before the Kent State campus explodes. Delbert maybe does it and maybe doesn't, but either way he runs. Maybe he goes to the feds and seeks asylum, and maybe they give it to him. Rood, meanwhile, takes Crystal, who he may have been screwing all along, to Yellow Springs on an amnesty bus. Sometime the weekend before he's hopped his track even further than he already had, now feeling betrayed by Delbert on levels mortals couldn't hope to understand. He hates him. He wants to kill him and would, if he could find him.

Maybe he takes it out on the pregnant Crystal for a while. Who knows what the hell that relationship was about. Were they all three doing each other? But soon enough, Crystal's rich daddy comes for her, and Rood stays, and . . .

The ticket I'd found was just like the ones I'd seen crammed in the jar in the Yellow Springs store. Had Rood recently been a patron there? Or . . . Did he take another identity and get himself a movie house? If so it's a nice cover. And now maybe he's leading a double or even a triple life, working as a mercenary; hiring out to survivalist groups; plying his evil trade, probably getting rich in contract money and squirreling it away, and . . .

And what?

In succeeding years, when Crystal comes there, as she does, to visit Rood, does she park Corrie in her lover's theater where she watches Jacques Tati flicks? What kind of relationship persisted all that time, anyway? And whose kid was Corrie, anyway?

The last was the least important. Corrie was Corrie, whatever her genes. And I had to believe she was still alive: The only reason Rood would take her would be to smoke Delbert out. Twenty-five years later, he still wanted to kill the son of a bitch. As for me, I wanted to kill them both.

I got back on 35 before eight and tried hard not to hit over five miles over the speed limit. One of the last things I wanted was to get stopped by a cop. The highway up there is two-lane, and every fucking farmer in the county had evidently decided to go line dancing on this Friday night. I cursed and shouted and tailgated and, at one point, the unfortunate thought occurred to me that, yet again, I didn't have a gun. For a week I'd been weaponless and worried about it: what the hell would I have done if I had come upon John Rood? But how was I, a fugitive, going to get one? Every time I'd wrestled with the problem I'd wound up avoiding it. Maybe I'd get the drop on the bastard somehow. Maybe I'd get the chance to just shank him and have done with it.

Right. And Lennon's not dead, either. And the Beatles are getting back together at Riverfront Stadium this Sunday night.

And that, for no good reason, got me thinking about Corrie's purse. There it sat on the moth-eaten seat beside me, the same damn bulsa bag she'd lugged into Obsessive Bob's bar that night in the snow. It had seemed heavy even for its size when I ran with it, but I wasn't thinking about that then. Now I was. I jerked on the dome light and spilled the contents onto the seat, sifting through it with my right hand and steering with my left. Corrie stuff: her billfold, an address book and a lipstick, two packs of Pall Malls and one heartbreak of a Zippo lighter. Some wadded Kleenex. A flat pack with a prescription label that looked like birth control pills. Ah, shit: she was fucking that bastard Jack. More wadded Kleenex. A corkscrew. A Milky Way, half eaten. One of those long lighters that you use to start a grill — what the hell was that about?

No gun.

I jerked the bag up. It was still heavy. I set it down and felt the inside for a pocket. Yes. I found the zipper and tugged. I stuck my hand in and felt something wonderful: cold steel. I dug the fucker out, never once expecting some diminutive nickel-plated .25. It was Corrie Blake we were dealing with: no sissy cigarettes and no popguns. What I brought out was yet another .38 just like we'd found in the pickup — also Jack's? Sure, it was — with — yeah, a full load. *Bingo. Thank you, Corrie.*

I felt better. A little, anyway. I shoved the gun in my belt and dumped Corrie's stuff back in her purse. Everything except the Zippo, which I stuffed in my pocket. For luck.

Most of the shops on the Yellow Springs main drag were still open. The restaurants were doing lively business, as was the Trails Tavern. The glassblower's place was lighted and shiny in the night — and my Jerry Garcia lookalike — What was his name? Jake? — was still hawking hookahs at the head shop. I pulled in there.

He was alone, and he didn't look happy when his door chimes jangled. "Closing," he said without looking up.

"Hiya, Jake," I said.

Then he looked. "It's you," he said. "You're hot, man. I been following your checkered career and you're a regular fuckin' Al Capone."

"That a fact." I stood just inside the door.

"Yeah, well, you'll never pass for Pretty Boy Floyd." He laughed weakly, knowing he was in trouble here.

"I gotta know who owns that theater over there, Jake. The Celluloid Dreams Theater. I have to know it now."

He looked relieved, probably glad I hadn't arrived to rip off his stash. "Ain't no secret about that, man," he said. "Leo Pepper. Everybody knows Leo."

"Tell me about Leo."

"You're scarin' me, man," he said. "You look sorta like Bogart at the end of *Caine Mutiny,* if you catch my drift. It's against my nature but I think I oughta call a cop or sumpthin'."

I showed him the gun.

"Well, maybe not," he said. "Look, if it's Leo ya want he lives down there at the end of Birch in that big old house by the sanctuary. Now, I see the guy maybe twice a year and I only know him to speak to, so if you got business with him you ain't got business with me."

"Okay," I said.

"So how about gettin' outa here?"

"What's Leo look like?" I said.

"He looks like a fucking fairy, which is what he is. But he don't bother nobody. He just runs his movie house."

My head felt like concrete hardening. I hadn't advanced a step into the shop, but Jake looked terrified. What was happening to me?

"I want to know what he looks like," I said.

"He looks like fuckin' Roddy McDowell, one of those fuckers," he said. "Now get out of here, man. I got trouble enough. Anybody runs a head shop in this day and age, they got trouble. I don't want no cops. I don't want nothin'. I just want you to eighty-six it." His voice had a tremble in it. I felt sorry for him.

"Okay," I said. "Thanks, Jake. Forget you saw me, right?"

"Right, man. Absolutely."

I backed out of the store, like some desperado in a spaghetti western, hand on Corrie's gun. I felt like a fool. By the time I got to the Honda Jake had doused his lights. No trouble. No trouble at all.

The house wasn't hard to find. Just as Jake had said it sat at the end of the lane, erstatz Frank Lloyd Wright by way of minimum bid. It looked like nothing so much as no place I'd ever want to live, a two-story fortress with a lot of slanting beams and a bow to solar energy. But it looked cheap, just grabass cheap and weather-beaten, as if whoever owned it was never there. Except tonight. Tonight the lights were on. No porchlight, but lights on all over the upstairs.

Cops. I'd called them, after all — so where were they? In my mind I suppose we intersected right here: Corrie locked in the tower room, screaming her lungs out, Rood downstairs loading up ill-gotten gains in a rucksack. The last minute rescue. But there weren't any cops. Just a flamboyant eyesore hugging the night sky — and a much better looking BMW sitting in the drive. Rood's? Well, there was no way Rood fit the description I'd gotten of Leo Pepper. So who was Pepper? A front? A shill? And why the hell hadn't I asked these questions the first time I was here? On that count alone, I was responsible for whatever was happening to Corrie right now.

I tried not to think about that. Rood was a bad man. I couldn't begin to visualize how he might treat her. If he really thought she was his daughter it could be worse: he'd murdered her mother, after all. Tortured her first, probably, and then set fire to her. What I couldn't prove I already knew because I'd met the son of a bitch. It wasn't Delbert who was the devil. It was Rood. Old Scratch. Jumpin' Jack Flash.

I cut the ignition halfway back down the lane and coasted to the side of the road. The nearest other house was a hundred yards away, and it looked empty. So much the better. I got out and walked the distance to the front porch. Then I rang the bell.

I waited. Nothing. Then, just above the bell, one of those two-way speaker systems activated. "Yes?" a male voice, said.

"Leo Pepper?" I demanded.

"Yes?" Very tentative. Very far away.

"I'm from the city," I said. "We've got a reported gas leak over here and I need to check your lines."

"Oh, shit," the voice said. Silence.

Would he buy this? Would he open the door? He came downstairs, at least. A little window opened and he said: "I need to see some identification."

"You'll have to open the door," I told him.

"Can't you just do this from the outside?"

"Not if the problem is in your home. I don't want to alarm you, but you've got boiler heat and I need to check your basement. Look, I'm on OT myself. I've got dinner waiting for me."

Hesitation. "Let me see the identification," he said. He opened the door to the length of the safety chain.

I kicked it in. The chain popped with a satisfying sproing and the man I took to be Leo Pepper tumbled backward into his own foyer. I was inside and on top of him before he could gain his footing. I shoved Corrie's .38 to his temple.

"Get up," I told him. "Get the fuck up."

He looked about as much like Roddy McDowell as I did. Wally Cox was more like it. He was slight, maybe 140, fifty or so and graying. His thinning hair was combed and sprayed in place and his aviator glasses were askew on his nose. He wore a cardigan and slacks and looked about as dangerous as your average adjunct English teacher. He tried to put his hands to his face but I slapped them down.

"Get up."

He did, shaking so badly I had to help him. I pushed him into a sunken living room filled with enough bric-a-brac to stock an antique mall. Something was playing on a hidden stereo: Philip Glass or whale music or some of that shit. He stumbled on the steps and sprawled by the coffee table. I stood over him, holding the gun with two hands and pointing it directly at his heart.

"I want to know where John Rood is," I demanded. "If you don't tell me, I'll kill you. Now."

He glanced around wildly, as if he expected Rood to appear. I put the gun up against his head again.

"Is he here? Goddamn it, tell me or I swear to Christ I'll kill you."

His words came out in an emphasymic hiss. "Not . . . here," he said.

"Where is he?"

"Don't . . . know."

I let go the gun with my left hand and backhanded him across the face. Blood spurted from his lip. "Tell me," I said.

He was crying. Blood and tears mixed in something like a gurgle. "Not here," he said again.

I grabbed his sweater and pulled him up, then hit him in the face with the butt of the gun. Cartilage broke and more blood spewed. "Wrong answer," I said. "Where is he?"

"Why are you doing this to me?" he said. He was still weeping and when he tried to mop at his bloody face I pushed him down onto a low-slung couch.

"I know who Rood is," I said. "I know you're connected. You run his movie house, he fronts you. Maybe comes around and butt fucks you once a month, is that it?"

Leo Pepper wept. I was putting a lot of chips on one torn ticket here. But sometimes a hunch is all you've got.

"I don't care about that," I said. "He has a friend of mine, and he's going to kill her. The police will be here soon and if you're alive you're going to have to tell them everything. But if you don't tell me now, you're dead."

"If you don't kill me," Pepper said finally, "Mr. Rood will."

"That's your problem. Where is he?" I drew back a little. I still had Mac's bandanna in my pocket, the one Corrie had used, and I tossed it to Pepper.

He mopped his face. "Mr. Rood doesn't come around very much," he said. "I don't know where he is."

I was right. *Shit, I was right.* I drop kicked the coffee table across the room and went after him again. The little bastard fell off the couch and started scooting backward on the carpet, a rat in a maze. I brought back my foot to kick him senseless, but he held up a trembling and bloody hand.

"I think he has a place in the Hocking Hills," Pepper said.

Hocking Hills? Shit! That was back the way I'd come, to the east of Columbus.

I put the gun in his face again. "What the fuck are you talking about?" I said.

"He built it. Three, four years ago. A retreat. Someplace in Hocking Hills."

I raised the gun and fired it into the ceiling. The report was deafening. Pepper began to cry anew. "Don't kill me," he said.

I straddled him and shoved the gun in his face again. "Then you tell me the truth," I said.

"It is the truth. I see the man very little. He stays here sometimes. It's a safe house for him."

"Does he own the theater?"

"It's in my name, but he owns it. He pays me to—"

"I know what he pays you to do. Where is this goddamn place?"

"I said, the Hocking Hills. I don't know where. I wouldn't know about the house except they sent some papers here by mistake when he was buying it."

"And you think he's there now?"

"I don't know where he is. Please, I— "

"Give me the keys to that car out there," I said.

He fumbled in his pocket and produced them.

"The police are coming. I want you to tell them the same thing you told me. Exactly."

"Yes. I will."

"Damn right you will. Get up."

"Don't kill me."

"Get the fuck up."

I half pushed and half dragged Pepper to a hall closet and shoved him in. "I'm going to look around to see if you're lying," I said. "Come out of there and I'll blow your ass off." I slammed the door on him, but not before I saw his face one more time. He looked grateful.

I ran to the driveway and unlocked the BMW. The ignition key fit, too. I gunned the thing into life and backed down the lane to the Honda. I jumped out and grabbed Corrie's purse, throwing it on the seat of Pepper's car. Then I U-turned and got the hell out of there. Where were the cops? Had Higgins been that hard to find? Why didn't they move on this without him? Could it have taken an hour and a half to check out Corrie's Blazer? In Columbus, maybe so. I couldn't worry about it now. I had one lead and I had to follow it. I found Highway 81 and drove south, hoping to make better time. I was at least three hours away from Hocking Hills, and I had no idea where I was going once I got there. It wasn't Pepper who was the rat in the maze. It was I. Me. Haggard.

TWENTY-FOUR

If you're going to steal a car steal a good one, I say. I'd always wanted to cruise around in a Beemer, and this was a nice one: '91 model; clean as a whistle. I liked the way Leo treated his car. And I was glad for that poor Honda to have a rest: God knows it was too old and tired to be called into the kind of duty I'd been putting it through.

I didn't think the police would apply the methods to Leo that I had, but I figured he'd talk pretty quickly all the same. I had an hour lead time, if that, and that was fine too, because I wanted a whole convoy of the fuckers around if I actually found this place and if Corrie was there. Hell, I wanted the National Guard, ironic as that was.

For the first fifty miles back toward Columbus, I think I talked most to Corrie's purse. I'd say "I'm coming," and things like that, although I knew good and well that whatever luck I'd gotten had held too many miles already on this night. I'd say "Hang on, Corrie," and try to make myself believe that John Rood really was ensconced in some hideaway in the Hocking Hills and that, even more implausible, I was going to find them.

Hocking Hills is the name given an area southeast of Columbus on the way to Athens, home of Ohio University and one of the great college towns in the world. The Hills themselves were at the bottom of the sea some 350 million years ago, just like everything else that is now called Ohio. All the loose sand that was drifting through those waters had nothing better to do, so over several thousands of years it cemented itself into sandstone — and then some volcanic force erupted beneath the earth's surface which bowed the land upward. That's how Ohio came to be in the first place, and that's why the Hocking Hills are now full of sandstone formations some 250-feet thick.

It's a strange and primitive place, filled with deep woods and water-falls and formidable caves. The Indians loved this area because of the massive deposits of flint that could be found there: as long as they were in that area, they were never without arrowheads. These days the Hills are a tourist attraction, fair game for the RV crowd. But there are also dozens of small cabins dotting the woods up there: weekend retreats and houses used as corporate tax write-offs where the semi-affluent go for fun and games of the secluded variety.

I'd been there before. Val and I had taken off for a weekend in better days, armed with six bottles of Andre and some massage oil. We'd never gotten off the deck and rarely out of the hot tub: we'd brought shrimp and brie and liver pate and a shitload of stuff that we'd never have dreamed of eating otherwise and just chilled out for three days. And then we'd come back to town full of love and promises, all of which got sum-marily broken. But there had been something pure and fine about that brief time that I had never forgotten.

Presently I saw the lights of Columbus off to the north and then I was going south on 23, heading for Circleville. There's a box factory at Circleville which makes the whole town smell like rotting pumpkins all the time, quite an irony when you realize that Circleville is home to a yearly Pumpkin Festival. *Better a rotting Pumpkin Festival,* I always thought. I wasn't at all sleepy but fatigue was gnawing at my eyes anyway, and by the time I found 59 East I was talking to Delbert to keep alert. I might have known it would come to that. I told Delbert about Corrie and I appealed to his invisible better nature to help me out in some way. He got to be a sort of patron saint of the journey for me, not that I was praying to him. Or maybe I was: It has started with Delbert, and perhaps I already knew it would have to end with Delbert as well.

The road into the Hills was winding and long. I punched around at the radio, looking for a report about Corrie and getting nothing. I powerlowered all the windows and talked to Delbert some more. Finally I lit one of Corrie's Pall Malls, but the first drag nearly put me in cardiac arrest. How in the hell did she smoke those things?

At two in the morning, I pulled into South Bloomington, a community, the sign said, of 481. All of them asleep, too, so far as I could see. The town had a restaurant and a filling station-grocery and a bar, but they were all closed. I pulled into the parking lot of the grocery and turned off the engine, then sat there thinking.

By all rights, my luck had run out. I'd taken a sheer hunch to Yellow Springs and it had paid off, but I couldn't expect something like that twice. If Rood did have Corrie up here, he'd have her well hidden. People went to this place not to be found. What kind of luck was I going to have at two in the morning?

South Bloomington was bound to have a cop, probably asleep like everybody else. Maybe I could tell my story fast enough and well enough to enlist the aid of the police. They'd call to check me out, though, and I didn't trust what they might hear.

Up the road came a couple, advancing slowly. She was drunk and he was drunker. I still had the windows down and I could tell that they were arguing. They had come from the general direction of South Bloomington's one bar, and it appeared that they had closed it down.

I made out the woman's words first. "I didn't lock the keys in the goddamn car," she said. "You did."

"But you left your purse in the shitter," he told her. "An' the shitter's in the bar. An' the bar is locked."

"Just like the car, you horse's dick," the woman said.

He looked maybe fifty, a tall guy with a droopy moustache who reminded me a little of Frank Zappa. She was half his height but close to his age: pretty good figure; short black hair. They wore vaguely western clothes, as if they'd set out at some point in the evening to two-step the night away. Too many Buds had spoiled the broth, though. I felt sorry for them: I'd been there.

When they came abreast of the BMW I swung the door open. Neither of them had known I was there before that, and it gave them a drunken start.

"Hiya," I said.

"What the fuck?" the guy demanded. He grabbed for the woman, who retreated into his grasp.

"I wonder if you can help me," I said.

"He'p you what?" the woman said. Her accent was something close to Agitated Appalachian.

"Friend of mine lives up here and he invited me up, but I got a late start. Has a cabin. Name's John Rood?"

They stared blankly at me.

"Big guy. White hair, cut short. Big muscles."

Still nothing. They stood hanging on each other and swaying a little, as if they were still dancing.

"I really need to find him," I said.

"Whazz his name?" the guy said.

"John Rood."

"Never heard of him," he told me and tugged at the woman. "C'mon, Neva."

"Maybe I could give you folks a ride," I said. "I sure as hell got nothing else to do if I can't find this guy."

They looked at each other, considering. Maybe I was the Hillside Strangler, come to prey on unsuspecting Appalachians. Maybe I was the Fool Killer.

"Who're you?" the woman named Neva said. She made it sound like "Whore you."

"My name is Fred Merkle," I told her. "And I think I've got a situation on my hands. I need some help finding my friend."

"Well, we said we dunno him," the guy said. "But we'll take a ride, you wanna give us one."

"Earl," the woman said.

"Well, shit!" Earl said. "It beats walkin'. I didn't leave the daggone keys in the daggone shitter!"

"No," Neva said. "You left 'em in the daggone car!"

"Get in," I said. "I'll drive you."

Neva wasn't happy about it, but she did get in, sort of half-carrying Earl along with her. I helped them get situated in the back seat, then got back in and started the BMW.

"Nice fuckin' car!" Earl exclaimed, suddenly aware of his surroundings. "It paid for?"

"Earl," Neva said again.

"Car like this gotta run twenty-five grand," Earl said.

"It's paid for," I said. "Where we headed?"

"Up the holler," Neva told me. "Straight on there."

I pulled out and drove in the direction she had pointed. I didn't know what I hoped to get out of these two clowns, but what I was doing beat sitting in that parking lot. Half a mile up the road Earl began to snore. I checked the rearview and saw that his moustache was now drooping on Neva's left shoulder, causing the top of her peasant blouse to ride dangerously low. She didn't seem to care. She sat staring straight ahead, in danger herself of glazing over at any moment.

We drove maybe three miles into the woods, and Neva said not a word. Then suddenly she blurted, "Turn right here," and I guided the car onto a dirt road. We humped and bumped another half mile. I still had my window down and the BMW's engine was so quiet that I could hear the sounds of the forest night all around me.

"We getting close?" I asked her.

"Up there," Neva said.

In the headlights I could see a ramshackle house that seemed to be built on sticks, like Baba Yaga's. Our approach had stirred up a couple of hounds, who were now baying and straining on their leashes. A light came on in the house, and I saw the front screen door bang open. A shadowy figure emerged.

"Aw, shit," Neva said. "That's Mama."

"Your mother?" I asked.

"Earl's. It's her place. Me'n Earl, we're just stayin' there while he's in layoff."

She made layoff sound like rehab. I brought the car to a stop. "She doesn't look happy," I said.

"She ain't been happy since Truman was in office," Neva said. "How the shit am I gonna get this lug in?"

"I'll help you, " I said, and got out. I opened the back door and was just getting a grip on Earl when Mama arrived. The dogs were yelping like hell and, on top of everything else, I'd caused a chicken stampede.

"Whut the hell is goin' on?" demanded Mama. She was compact but clearly deadly when she wanted to be: a fireplug of a woman with a bun of iron gray hair and a face which, with the corncob pipe, could have passed for Popeye's. She had to be seventy-five or so, but her arms were muscled and mean looking. She held a 4-10 shotgun, locked and loaded without a doubt.

"Earl's sick, Mama," Neva said.

"Earl's drunk. Who's this bozo?"

Neva had taken Earl's left side and I his right. He weaved between us, still snoring a little. Neva looked at me from under Earl's armpit and said: "I forget your name."

"So do I," I told her. "Look," I said to Mama. "I just gave these folks a ride home."

"He's lookin' for his friend, Mama," Neva said.

"Out here? In the middle of the goddamn night?" She turned to the yapping dogs. "Shaddup, ya turds!"

Mother's Day must be swell around here, I thought. "His name's John Rood," I said. "Maybe you know him."

"Dunno nobody," Mama said. But at least she had lowered the shotgun.

"You wouldn't forget him. Big guy, solid. Snow white hair that bristles. No eyebrows. Very pale."

"Sounds like a friggin' albino," Mama said. "You'uns sure you in the right place, boy?"

Before I could answer Earl pitched forward, collapsing before his mother's laceless Brogans, nearly squashing a chicken. I made to haul him up again, but Mama said: "Lettim lay. Serves the lil' shitass right. Hope a skunk pukes on him."

"Aw, Mama," Neva said.

"Come on," I told Neva. We got Earl by the shoulders and hoisted him up again, Mama bitching all the while. As we neared the house the dogs fired up another chorus, but chained as they were all they could do was bark. We got Earl onto the sagging porch and dropped him on the rainbeaten settee, which sat next to the ancient washing machine.

"Leave 'im there," Mama said. "I ain't draggin' him up no stairs."

That was good enough for me. I gave Neva a hang-in-there nod and started off the porch. Thirty minutes or so down the drain. But then, just as I got to the car, I heard Mama say:

"Don't you come aroun' here no more."

"Sure," I said. "Next time I'll let them walk." I had my hand on the car door.

"I doan want nobody around here got friends like you got."

I stopped.

"What did you say?" I asked her.

"Ya heard me. That pal o' yours run over the best coon hunter I ever had. Did it on purpose, I know it as well as I know sin when I see it."

I slammed the door and walked back. "You know this man?"

Mama stood on the porch. She had brought the gun up again. "I know his big black car. He come down the mountain drivin' like the devil was after him and my hound Clover chased him. Well, that's what dogs do, ain't it? They chase cars! An' on the way back that sumbitch ran his car right over that ridge back up there and kilt my dog. Kilt Clover. Hit 'im head on."

"You sure about this?"

"I'd know that devil anyplace."

"Do you know where he lives up here?"

"I told the sheriff if he dint go git him I would. I'd take his gun and I'd kill the mangy fucker. But the sheriff sez you cain't prove it and you cain't get in up there ennyway. Some big ass ol' house he built himself. Gotta 'lectric fence and all. Stay home, Grace, the sheriff said, and git yerself another dog," she spat. "Shit," she said.

"When was this?"

"March. Just after thet big snow. So what?"

"Where is this house?"

"It's up there. Up at the top of the mountain, above the cave. You see him; you tell him he owes me a dog. Now, git!"

Lucky once more. One more time. Maybe.

"You have a phone?" I asked her.

"What I got is a full load here. Git yer ass in thet pimpmobile and git the hell outa here."

I left the three of them on the porch, peering out in the darkness, looking like some unholy union between Bob Wills and Charles Addams. I nearly went off the road getting the car turned around, gunning it too hard and taking off too fast. I had to calm down. I couldn't blow it now.

I found a No Trespass sign about ten miles up the road that looked promising: there was damn sure nothing else around. I drove on past and found a turnoff half a mile further on. I parked the car there, checked the chambers in the .38, and began backtracking on foot. When I got to the sign I ducked under the barbed wire and, avoiding the road, went straight through the woods.

Dogs were a worry, but I didn't figure Rood for one. He'd be more likely to depend on technology: the electrified fence, some kind of scanner or monitor — maybe even some Claymores planted out here. Scary thought. The woods were strangely quiet out here and the trees very tall: I could look straight up and see a starless sky. Everything around me teemed of humid night blue. There were creatures in these woods, but so far they were keeping their distance from me.

A quarter mile further, I came upon a deserted ruin that must once have been a rent cabin. I got close enough to see a faded sign that spoke of better days: "Dreamland Cabins." There must be others out there at discrete distances — also ruins by now. A small creek ran through the property and I followed it. I wanted a flashlight, some tools — something. I had a gun and felt lucky for that, but I was damned ill equipped to be storming a fortress.

The creek seemed to meander nowhere, so I took to the woods again. At one point I nearly ran into a deer: the first sign of life I'd seen. From across a small clearing the animal peered at me and I at it. Then it bucked away into the trees. I stopped a moment to wipe away sweat: there wasn't a spot in which my body didn't ache. I was still sore from Rood's beating, now nearly a week old, but the creaks and groans in my muscles told me that I was the one who had run this body down the most: I'd put it through more than it could stand. I was an out-of-shape, middle-aged man trying to do the work of a trained athlete. My strength was not up to my task, and whatever resources I had to draw on would be found, if at all, in sheer willpower.

I listened. An owl. Something gliding in the trees, far away.

Music.

It wasn't close, but it was definitely there. I followed my ear. Trees and more trees. Underbrush. I was running now, and at one point my foot caught a rock which sent me sprawling. I grabbed at the gun as I went down, feeling skin on my knees tear. I hit the ground with the palms of my hands, the gun in my right one. Lying still a moment, I looked up. Another five feet and I'd have fallen into a wire fence. Rood's fence, if I was right.

I got up and approached the fence. It was high, eight feet easily. And I had no doubt that it was charged. I wondered how many deer Rood had fried out here, not to mention other more adventurous creatures. The music was a little louder now and there were stretches of it I could almost make out: something classical. Classical wasn't my thing, but this sounded Russian, strident like Shostakovich. I crouched and looked through the fence. I was on top of the mountain, and through the foliage I could see a faint glow. There were lights down there somewhere.

How to get past that fence? I couldn't go over it and I couldn't go through it. But if Corrie was in that house I had to get there. *How? How? Think, Goddamn it!*

I sat on my haunches there in the woods and willed something, anything to come. And it did. Not much, but a chance, anyway. I backtracked to the creek, watching my step this time. Then I followed the creek forward to the fence line. There it was, all right; strung across the creek, which flowed into the property I believed was John Rood's. As silently as I could, I slid into the water, keeping the gun high.

The creek was deeper than I thought. It went above the waist on me, maybe three and a half feet deep. It was hard as hell to see, but when I got close to the fence it appeared that the thing had been run about a foot above the water line. That damn sure made sense: the thing would be going off all the time if it hit the water. I wondered what Rood did when it flooded. The trouble was, I couldn't see for sure. Where was the moon? A starless, moonless night. Just what I needed.

But how much luck could I reasonably expect? I could try to go under the fence, which meant under the water. But if something was rigged down there or if I came up wrong, I was a dead man.

Shit. If I didn't get Corrie, I was a dead man anyway. What difference did it make?

I got a little closer to the fence, as close as I dared. I'd always heard that if you pissed on an electric fence, it went off. What if I managed to splash the damn thing on the way under? What then? Well, hell. What I was contemplating was nothing more than any would-be wetback would be contemplating who wanted to get El Norte. They made it, didn't they?

The first problem was the gun. I would have to toss it over the fence, missing the wire, and manage to keep it out of the water. I couldn't toss it through because the wire was strung too close. It wouldn't have been that difficult in daylight. At night, it could be bitter hell.

I didn't think about it; I just threw the thing. I cleared the fence and then there was a suspended, horrible moment when it seemed to be stuck in the air. But it hit somewhere over there in the grass, and not in the water. Now all I had to do was find it. If I made it to the other side.

I thought about taking off my shoes but decided against it. I'd need them. I took a deep breath, dove as close as I could get to the rocky bottom, and kicked off.

It was easily the longest journey of my life. The water was murky and dark. I went on feel rather than sight. If any part of my body came up at the wrong time I was fried. My back tingled as if on fire, as if I had already touched the fence. I kept pushing against the water for what I judged to be ten yards or so, and then, just as my breath was about to explode in my lungs, I came up.

I was on the other side of the fence.

"Welcome, Mr. Haggard," said John Rood. "I've been expecting you. Won't you come in and dry off?"

TWENTY-FIVE

Rood had all the advantage. For starters, he was dry and I was wet. All wet. I hadn't begun to think about the surveillance devices he might have in place. But I knew now that he'd made me coming under the fence, or before. He stood on the bank less than five feet from me, cool and unfazed in a white turtleneck with the sleeves shoved nattily up on his wrists, arms bulging muscles. And those arms held what looked like an auto-loading sport rifle, infrared lens in place, pointed right at me. He had one of those shiteating little cigars poked in the side of his mouth.

"NSS system," he said. "Best investment I ever made. Camera's in that tree right back there. I picked you up ten minutes ago. Rise up slowly, now."

I did, trying to drip with at least a little dignity. I cast an eye longingly around for Corrie's gun, but gave up that notion quickly. He had me. I'd kept enough luck to find him, but now my luck had run out.

"Sorry I didn't bring a towel," he said. "But you'll dry. Come on up here on dry land, Mr. Haggard. And move very slowly. Hands where I can see them."

I did as I was told. He tossed a pair of handcuffs on the ground in front on me and said: "Put those on. Behind you."

I did that, too. The cuffs clicked into place smoothly.

"I might have known it would be you," he said.

"And why would that be?" I asked him.

"Because you're the only one who cares," he said shortly. "Let's walk. Straight ahead. Toward the house."

I could see it now, straight down a long stretch of mowed lawn that looked like a fairway. It was a two-story structure that reminded me a little of the house in *North by Northwest,* the one up on Mount Rushmore. Four bedrooms at least, and a walkaround deck. It stood dark and stoic against the night sky, the front windows glowing with a hellish candlelight. But hellish or not, the candles had but one reference for me. They weren't Corrie's candles, though. They were Rood's.

"Where is she?" I said.

"Resting comfortably. Keep walking."

It must have been close to five in the morning. I looked for some trace of dawn among the lowhanging clouds, but couldn't see one. The only real light came from the glow of those damn candles. The music was gone, too. I could hear crickets, and that was all.

A wood staircase ran from the base of the house up to the deck. He prodded me with the rifle and I went up first. He kept his distance, watching out for the well-placed kick, I guessed. The deck was empty: no hot tub; no chairs. When I thought about it I couldn't imagine Rood in a hot tub anyway.

"Stop here," he said.

I did, and he pushed open a set of glass doors which led into the house. He gestured me in with a flip of the rifle barrel. The word *insouciant,* unbidden, sprang to mind. I found myself in a vast room with beamed ceilings, shimmering in candlelight. Just the room, nothing else: there wasn't a stick of furniture in all its expanse.

"What did you do?" I asked him. "Piss off the movers?"

He gave a short laugh and prodded me toward a bar that jutted out between the living room and the kitchen area. Once there, he threw a key down in front of me, keeping the rifle trained on my gut.

"Pick it up and use it," he said.

I retrieved the key from the thatch of expensive-looking shag carpet under me, taking some satisfaction in the fact that I was dripping all over it. I uncuffed my right hand.

"Do you see the pole there?" he asked me.

I turned and saw a steel support rod that ran the vertical length between the bar and the kitchen cabinets above it. I nodded.

"Cuff yourself to the pole. Hands behind you."

I did it. Rood checked me, then relaxed the rifle and extracted the cigar from his mouth. He blew a delicate smoke ring. We stood watching each other, hunter and prey. The candles threw ghostly shadows on the walls which danced in the suffused light like the elephant grass I remembered in Vietnam. Corrie was here somewhere, in this house. I could feel her presence.

"This house is my needlepoint," Rood said. "It's coming together bit by bit. When it's done, it will be my fortress of solitude. All mine. Every block. Every stone. This weekend, I'm painting. And that's because I choose to do it all myself. I can afford to live very well, you know, Sam. Better than you ever could have."

He was already talking about me in the past tense. "Where's Corrie?" I said again. "I want to know that she's safe."

"Are you aware," Rood said, "that she bears a lovely strawberry birthmark, just inside her right thigh?"

"If you raped her," I said, "I'll kill you."

He gave his short, soulless laugh again. Where had I heard that laugh before? From Delbert, of course. I saw clearly now what I'd know all along: that the two of them certainly did resemble each other, that they were twins, twins grown old, grotesquely old, like rotted fruit.

"Let us say," he told me, "that I examined the patient."

"You piece of shit," I said.

Rood placed the rifle in the corner by the sliding door and came toward me, picking up one of the candles along the way. It was a squat, square candle, the kind that is easily made inside a milk carton. He stopped in front of me, holding the candle.

"I'm fond of fire, Sam," he said.

Fire is the devil's only friend. "That girl could be your daughter," I said.

"Possibly," he said noncommittally. "But not likely. She is almost certainly the issue of Mr. Delbert Jones."

"Jones won't come for her. He doesn't care about her. He thinks she's yours. You can't smoke him this way, Rood."

He smiled mirthlessly. "You're obsessed with that girl, Sam. And obsession is something I know all about."

The candle burned beneath his face, giving his features that distorted, hollow quality achieved by holding a flashlight under the chin — only worse, because of the constant flicker of the light.

"He'll come," Rood continued. "He wants to see me. But he'll come more quickly if you call him. You must know his whereabouts, Sam."

"I don't. And neither does Corrie. You might as well let both of us go and save yourself a hell of a lot of trouble, because we can't tell you a damn thing."

His stare continued. "I don't believe you, Sam," he said. He reached down, tore open my wet shirt and then pressed the candle to my chest, and I could smell burned flesh even before I felt the pain. Ah, Jesus. In reflex I kicked out at him, but he effortlessly moved back. The area above my right nipple screamed with pain. I felt my knees buckling.

Rood set the candle down and extracted another of his cigars. He bent and lit it in the flame. "Let me tell you about the Sixties, Sam," he said. He exhaled smoke and leaned against the glass doors. "They were filled with bad men. Lots of bad men who saw many opportunities for entrepreneurship. Those opportunities began to come to real fruition with the debacle of the 1968 Democratic Convention in Chicago. I was there, you know."

At least the bastard wasn't at me with a candle. I let him talk.

"I was where they sent me in those days, and they sent me many places. And when the Nixon White House became a reality, my kind of work knew its greatest freedom stateside since — Well, since the days of JFK."

The son of a bitch was apolitical, I'd give him that. "What are you telling me?" I said.

"I am telling you that I worked for people who honored a contract and treated me well. And I did my work well, when left alone to do it. The problem at Kent State was that conditions were imposed upon me."

"What kinds of conditions?" I said.

"The worst kind. The use of nonprofessional personnel."

"You mean Delbert. To set the ROTC fire."

"That is part of what I mean. But I also refer to the deployment of unseasoned troops, and the dependence upon civilians who simply could not be trusted."

"It doesn't sound like your kind of show."

"It was not. I was a fool to participate. But I myself had made a crucial mistake. I had become involved, you see."

"Involved with who? Crystal?"

Through the flicker of the candlelight I could see Rood's shadow on the far wall in grotesque relief, twice the size of the man. He puffed his cigar and said nothing a moment, and then gave his short laugh again.

"Not the woman."

"Then Delbert." What kind of switch hitter was this maniac? Was he fucking them both? What the hell kind of party had been going on up at that haunted house?"

"He betrayed me, you see. He betrayed the idea of what he knew we were. His first betrayal was running; his next was taking the money . . . ."

"Money?"

"Oh, yes. A hundred thousand dollars. We'd already been paid, you see."

I remembered my reading about Kent State. A fifteen thousand dollar settlement on each of the four dead. Fifteen thousand per life.

Rood was studying my reaction. "I see," he said. "You must have gotten the idea somewhere that my friend Del went into some witness protection program, that the agency . . . " He smirked. "Or agencies . . . spirited him away and hid him for safekeeping. No, that run was made on his own, and financed with my money." He advanced on me again. "My money," he said flatly.

His cold, dead eyes bored into me. I knew he was ready to attack me again. "This is about money?" I asked him.

"No," he said just as flatly. "It is about betrayal. Del and I were very close, you see. Very close."

It was a Pandora's Box of terror: you lifted the lid; you saw the maggots. People think about the Sixties and they think Woodstock. They don't think Altamont. Rood and his sick triangle turned my guts. How could Corrie have come from such an unholy alliance?

"Don't you think that twenty-five years—" I began.

"Are enough? Enough for what? Everything ended on that hill that Monday noon, Sam. Don't you see that? Everything ended. Until that moment I was a patriot. Since then I have been a . . . contractor."

"It ended for more people than you, goddamn it," I said.

"I didn't care about them. You need that, Sam, to do the work I do. They were all strangers, you see."

"Strangers?" I said. "Crystal?"

"She was a stranger too."

My chest throbbed terribly and the handcuffs were tight about my wrists. He was going to kill me, I knew that, and then he was going to kill Corrie too. I had no idea how to begin to save her.

Now Rood turned away, as if he had made some decision. He picked up the candle and in the flickering light I watched him retreat into the kitchen, and for the first time my eye made out at least one piece of furniture: a long work bench which I now saw, thanks to the illumination thrown there, held a collection of objects, several of which appeared to be paint cans. Rood picked something up and turned back toward me. Oh, Jesus. It was an acetylene torch. He had the mask that went with it, too, and he put the torch back down long enough to slip it over his head. Then he began walking toward me.

"Rood," I said.

He stopped, torch in hand, and gazed at me from behind the mask. He looked like an alien, The Man from Planet X. "Relax, Sam," he said. "This isn't for you. I know a much faster way to get you to talk." He went on past me, heading for a doorway which appeared to lead to stairs.

"No, Rood," I said. "Goddammit, do you want me to beg? All right, I'm begging."

He didn't look back. "I want you to die," he said. "But not right now. First the young lady will die. And in the process, you will tell me what I want to know.

I yanked at the pole so hard I thought my arms would jump out of their sockets. I could feel blood in my mouth and I knew that I was chewing the inside raw. "I know where he is," I shouted. "I'll tell you."

Rood barked his short laugh, still not looking back. "You're a fool, Sam," he said. "A fool to think I would believe you." Then at last he did turn toward me, the reflection of candlelight in his mask glowing like the flames of hell. "And you're also a fool," he said, "if you believe that one word I have told you is the truth."

"I swear to God I'll tell you," I said.

Rood turned back to the doorway. "That's correct," he said. "You will tell me." And then, somewhere below us, a beep began to sound, strong and insistent, over and over with a deadly monotony.

This time Rood did stop. "Another visitor," he said. "You'd think this was open house." He turned back into the room, removing his mask. He set the torch down on the wood floor along with the mask and went to the glass door, retrieving his rifle. Then he returned to me and placed a key on the bar, by my right hand.

"Uncuff yourself," he told me. "I need to change your accommodations for a while. We'll pick up where we left off shortly." He leveled the rifle at me.

I fumbled to get the key into my shaking hands and then groped for the lock. Sweat was running into my eyes and my chest was on fire. I felt the cuffs click open, and I knew that I had one chance and one only. If I screwed this up we were dead, dead as Crystal and dead as Selena Blair and dead as those four kids on Blanket Hill.

Rood held the gun steady. "Move, Sam," he said.

I pitched right, as hard as I could, sending my body crashing in the direction of the work table. I hit the floor on my back, skidding into the shadows, and felt my right shoulder strike the legs of the bench hard. The cans on the top shivered, and then began clattering to the floor. I felt liquid spilling over me liquid with a smell I knew: paint thinner. Rood was moving toward me, groping his way in the shadows. I felt for the can of thinner and found it inches away, lying on its side, the ooze spilling out onto the floor beneath me. Somewhere in my memory the thought floated through that paint thinner was not all that flammable, but I knew damn good and well that it was the only chance I had. The bastard was five feet away. I dug into my wet and shriveled pocket, groping for Corrie's Zippo. Would it catch? It had been underwater for over a minute and in my pants ever since. Oh, Jesus. Let it catch. I had the thing in my hand. I flicked once. Nothing.

Rood was on top on me. The barrel of the rifle was inches from my face. He was enjoying this. I flicked again. Nothing. *Please, God. This once and never again. I will never, never . . .*

The third time it caught. I hurled the lighter into the puddle beneath me that I could feel but not see, and the room exploded in a terrible brightness. The thinner had caught.

I pushed up hard, handcuff flapping on my left wrist, and caught Rood right at the knees, sending him sprawling backward. The rifle retorted with a deafening roar, the shot spiraling into the ceiling of the room. I clawed at his belt, and he went over backward through the glass door with an explosion of glass and flame. As I struggled to my feet, I saw that his clothing was alive with flames. I looked wildly around for the rifle, but couldn't spot it. And then Rood had me, pulling me back through the shards of glass in a death grip I couldn't break. His massive arms were about my neck and he pulled me to him like a lover, a fiery Phoenix, pulling me downward in a terrible embrace. I got my arms under his and pushed feeling my own muscles popping in hopeless futility. We were on the deck, and the floor was on fire around us.

The lighter was still in my hand, and I thumbed it again. This time the flame caught the back of Rood's hair, which must have absorbed some of the thinner as well. He screamed, the terrible inchoate cry of some animal, loosed his grip and clutched at his face. I pushed away and watched as Rood writhed across the deck to its railing and then over, falling downward and away, back to the hell he came from and where he had always belonged.

I turned away from the terrible sight and back into the house, my fists crashing through broken glass. The front room was a wall of flame. I fought through it and toward the stairs leading down, the stairs that led, I prayed, to Corrie. Sometime in that moment I shoved Corrie's Zippo back down in my pocket. Man, if I ever got us out of the goddam shit, the first thing I was going to do was write a testimonial to the company. I found the stairs and took them two at a time, thinking *How do I know she's not upstairs?* and going solely on the premise that Rood had been heading down. Smoke was already billowing behind me.

At the bottom of the stairs I found myself in a faintly illuminated laundry room, complete with washer and dryer. Where was the light coming from? I whirled around and saw a short, dim hallway, lit by one bare bulb. At the end of the hallway was a door, and I stumbled toward it. I could see a little window high up in the door, covered with wire mesh. A cell. An interrogation room. The holding tank. Rood must have been planning to bring more than one prisoner here. At the door I fought the smoke that was blinding my eyes and peered in.

She was there, lying on a narrow cot. *Corrie.*

I kicked and lunged at the door, probably dislocating my shoulder. It wouldn't give. I battered it again. Goddamnit!

I jerked around, cursing and praying at the same time, feeling the smoke seep into my lungs. "I'm coming, Corrie," I shouted, though I knew she couldn't hear me. "Just wait. I'm coming." And though it crumpled my heart to leave her, I turned and clamored back up the stairs.

Flames leaped at me before I had gotten through the upstairs door. I tore off my shirt and held it over my face and charged into the room, dodging the fire that lapped at me. I had no time, none at all. I fought my way to the bar and pulled the shirt away from my eyes, looking for . . . looking for . . .

There it was. So obvious and austere that I nearly laughed out loud. Beside the bar, just beyond the fridge, a key holder. A big wooden one, in the shape of a vertical key. And dangling from one of the imbedded hooks was a ring of the things. I snatched at it and, clutching the ring, pushed back toward the basement stairs. The flames were everywhere. I could feel my eyebrows singe. The fire crackled and the floor bucked and threatened to bow beneath me. I fell rather than ran down the stairs and fought my way through the smoke back to the cell, back to Corrie. I fumbled with the keys, my eyes too wet with sweat and fear to really see: I was going on touch. Crying and praying, I rammed a key at the lock. No go. I tried another. No. Again. We were dying. The only comfort I had was that we were dying together, but that wasn't enough. The crazy thought crossed my mind, not for the first time, that if I just could have saved Corrie I could somehow have made up for all of them, for all the lost children, for all the graves and all the lives cut short to which my own life had borne witness. The fourth key fit. I shoved the thing home, and felt the lock spring. And then I was inside.

At first I thought she was dead. She was fully clothed, except for her shoes, and she bore no outward signs of abuse. Her hands were cuffed in front of her by a pair identical to those Rood had used on me. But she lay so still and rigid that I was sure that Rood had done his work long ago. Then I pressed my mouth to hers and felt breath, and when my fingers sought and found her carotid artery and felt the precious triphammer of her life. She was alive. Thank God. "Come on, Corrie," I said. "Come on."

She roused a little, enough to bring her wrists up in a motion meant to ward off attack. I scooped her up in my arms and, carrying her, I stumbled back through the dense smoke down the hall and into the laundry room and toward the stairs. No good. The flames had reached us. I turned back and this time I saw what I had missed before: a door, a blessed door, a back door to the outside. I never set Corrie down. I clawed at the deadbolt and got it open and then we were outside, and clean, blessed air, was spilling into our lungs as first dawn seeped through the trees around us. I stumbled and fell twice, but I got us to the dirt road beyond the short driveway and there we collapsed, gasping and choking for air. My own lungs were screaming in pain and Corrie and I both coughed in wretching spasms. But we were alive, and free of the funeral pyre of a house that lay behind us. And somewhere from beyond the trees I could hear sirens. *The bastards*, I thought. *They waited for light to come.*

Presently I saw a flashlight beam, and then a state trooper appeared, looking like a displaced Texas Ranger, complete with handlebar moustache. I hated him and loved him at the same time. He came up to us and tossed aside his flashlight and bent to pick up Corrie.

"Don't touch her," I wheezed.

"It's all right," he told me. "We'll take care of her."

"She's—" I began.

"We know who she is. It's all right now."

I felt hands on my shoulders, pulling me up. Two other troopers were behind me, and they held me between them. "I'm going with her," I said to the first trooper, who was now walking away, carrying Corrie. All I could see of her were her bare feet, dangling limply as she lay in his grasp. The trooper kept walking, saying nothing.

"Take it easy," a voice said close to my ear. "You'll be fine."

"Get those cuffs off her," I shouted after the trooper who had Corrie. "And get her a blanket. She'll be cold." But he was out of sight now, and all I could see was the revolving blur of the red light atop the cruiser which had just arrived.

THEY PUT US IN TWO DIFFERENT CARS, me in the one behind, sitting in the back between the two troopers, and we took 59 straight east toward Athens. About ten miles down the road an ambulance intercepted us, and both the cruisers pulled off on the shoulder of the road. The back doors of the ambulance swung open and a couple of paramedics in white coats bounded out, toting a stretcher. I sat watching as they brought Corrie out of the cruiser and got her onto the stretcher and pushed an oxygen mask onto her face and then she was inside the ambulance and the trooper with the moustache was slamming the doors shut and we were off again, sirens blaring. They'd never even gotten the cuffs off her, which made sense because they didn't have the key. But I knew they would, and I knew she was safe. We were separated, but she was safe. And that was enough, enough for now, and maybe enough for always.

THE ER DOCTOR WHO EXAMINED ME at the Athens hospital looked to be about twenty-five. His hair was burred on top but he sported a hell of a pony tail in the back, just like that checker in the supermarket. All the rage, those cuts. While he worked he whistled, and it was irritating: not just because he was whistling but because the tune was — honest — *Whistle While You Work*. How seeing *Snow White* one too many times can lead to a career in medicine eluded me, but he seemed to know what he was doing. He told me I was going to need a skin graft and for that matter probably a new face. I said I'd settle for the skin graft.

Nobody offered me a change of clothes, so I sat around in the waiting room still pretty damp and watched the sad parade of Saturday morning walking wounded that filed in and out, all pretty clearly casualties of the night before. I didn't have much choice in the matter: a sheriff's deputy who could have passed for Jabba the Hut never left my side. I expected to be arrested at any moment and arraigned on the spot, but nobody made a move to do either one. I tried to speculate on my fate, but all I could think about was Corrie.

Presently Higgins showed up, looking like he needed sleep worse than I did. He flashed his buzzer and the deputy went away.

"So," Higgins said.

"So," I countered, more than willing to hold up my end of the conversation.

He sank down beside me, letting his soiled London Fog flap around him. "Looks like you had quite a night for yourself," he said.

"Yeah. You get Rood?"

"Sure," Higgins said. "We got him."

I looked at him. "You telling me the truth?"

"We got him. You'll have to come with me, you know, Sam."

"Not until I see Corrie."

It was his turn to look at me.

"I'm not kidding," I told him.

"I know," he said.

A half hour later Jack Blake entered the waiting room, looking like Preppy Death warmed over. He must have been there when we arrived. I thought I'd seen that big-assed Lincoln of Old Man Payton's in the parking lot when we pulled in, too, but I hadn't been sure. Family reunion, maybe. Jack stared at Higgins and me a moment, Pozzo and Lucky Waiting For Godot, and then crooked a finger at me and turned away. I followed, and Higgins, the bastard, did too.

Jack led us to a private room at the end of the ER and opened the door. I went in first. Payton was there, all right, silver haired, natty, and older that God, on one side of the hospital bed. On the other was a starchy old nurse, fooling with an IV. And in between them lay Corrie. She was groggy but awake, and she was looking at me. I stood there between Higgins and Jack Blake, the centerpiece in the three most miserable Magi ever assembled.

"Hi," I said to Corrie.

For a few seconds nothing happened, enough time to make me think that maybe that was that. And then, very slowly and painfully, Corrie lifted her hands from the blanket that covered her and held them out to me while the IV wobbled against its tape like a drunken dancer. I went to her and took her hands in mine, trying to touch her as gently as I could.

"You can't—" the nurse began, but Payton shushed her. I sat down on the bed beside Corrie and held her hands. I looked down at her wrists and saw that they were raw from the handcuffs, which I knew they'd had to saw off as they had done mine. Those burns hurt me worse than my own chest did, even though I could see that they glistened with some sort of medicinal salve. And all the time Corrie was watching me with that look I'd known since the first time I met her in the night and the snow, the one that let me know she'd never turn away first.

I didn't know what to say, so finally I let go of her right hand and dug in my soggy pocket and came up with the lighter.

"Here," I told her. "I saved it for you." I put in into her hand and closed her fingers over it.

And then her arms were around me, and her head was on my shoulder. Trying to be careful of the IV I pulled her close, and through the thin hospital johnny I felt her warmth and her life and I tasted her hair which, though it smelled of fire smoke, was still as wonderful as it always had been. After a few minutes the gang behind us must have left the room. I didn't notice, and I don't think Corrie did either.

We stayed like that for a very long time. Then the nurse came back and told me I would have to leave. I helped Corrie lie back and sat looking at her another moment and then I did leave, because I wanted her to sleep. But if it had been up to me, the two of us would have stayed there just like that, holding each other, until the goddam day I died.

TWENTY-SIX

I went home to an apartment that was refreshingly free of corpses. There wasn't even any police tape, and I had Harvey Smoltz to thank for that. I tried to call him, but he'd taken two weeks off and left instructions that nobody was to call him, especially not me.

Higgins drove me, and we had a good talk on the way down. A talk, anyway. And in between his grilling of me I grilled him about Rood.

"I told you we got him," Higgins said, only half-ass watching the road. I could see why he always used a driver: the son of a bitch probably couldn't have passed the exam himself. "He's locked away in a burn ward where only special clearance people see him. Look, Sam. This is never going to make the papers. You're home free, if you keep your head down. Just live your life and forget about John Rood."

"I don't even half-believe your bullshit," I said.

"Believe it," he told me, veering dangerously left. "You have no choice. The world is safe from John Rood."

"And what about Kent State?"

"What about it?"

"The truth," I said. "What about the truth?"

He smiled a little, and this time he did watch the road. "Nobody cares, Sam," he said. "You know that, don't you?"

"Goddammit, I care."

"Then you," he told me, "are a majority of one."

"That's bullshit."

"Is it? How many folks show up at those yearly rallies? A hundred? Two?"

"That's not the point."

"Then what is the point, Sam? How will the truth help after all these years? Will it bring those kids back?" His eyes stayed on the road ahead. "In my line of work, you know," he said. "You learn pretty quick that the truth is often the last thing anybody really wants."

We rode in silence awhile. "And Delbert?" I asked finally.

"We'll find him," Higgins said. "Matter of time."

Matter of twenty-five years, I thought, and didn't believe for a minute that any world I knew was safe from all the John Roods still out there. Hell, if I'd needed any more proof I got it a week later, when the Federal Building in Oklahoma City exploded, sending even more innocent children to death before they had even begun to live.

Corrie, I was told, would be remanded to the tender custody of her grandfather, the last damn thing she needed. I started scheming on that right away, but I was reluctant to do anything that would compromise her. I figured she'd call when she could. I hoped she would. And I called the hospital in Athens every day until they told me she'd been dismissed.

SOMEWHERE DURING THAT CRUEL APRIL the baseball strike got settled and Val, encouraged by the fact that I'd been out of the papers for a few days and happy to hear that I had my old job back, came off the dime about Linc. He and I took in the Reds home opener at Riverfront, just like nothing had ever happened. Well, not quite. But I was so happy to see him and glad that he seemed to feel the same that nothing could have spoiled that windswept Sunday afternoon. The temp never got above sixty, but the warmth between us made the day seem like the Fourth of July. It helped that Barry Larkin hit a grand slam in the bottom of the ninth, and when the fireworks went off over the river nobody was cheering louder than we were. Together.

I think about Linc a lot these days, about how I'd like to protect him, to guard his plans and visions. But I know that can't be done. He has the same world to live in that the rest of us do, and all I can do is hope that he grows strong and wise and that somehow he manages as long as possible to outrun the deadly ambush of time.

I guess it was the Friday after I got back that Rita and Mac summoned me for enchiladas and beer. It was so damn good to be around them again. We played old Stones and laughed at old jokes and never talked about what had happened until late in the evening when we'd popped the cap on the Cuervo bottle and, just like the old days, were passing it around.

"I didn't do right by you, Sam," Rita said at one point.

"Sure you did," I told her.

"No," she said. "I didn't. We've been friends too long for me to start reading you out now."

"Turn 'im to toast for all I care," Mac said. "The fuckin' Honda is pretty much totaled."

"I thought you couldn't stand the sight of that car," I told him.

"Can't stand the sight of you either," he said, holding his hand out for the bottle. "But I still missya when you're not around." He glugged one down and passed the Cuervo on to me.

"So," I said. "What are we drinking to?" Keith had just kicked in to *You Got the Silver,* and I was feeling something like happy.

"The usual," Mac said. "Sex and drugs and rock 'n roll."

"As long as you throw some blues in there too," I said.

But Rita had filled three little jelly glasses with tequila, and she passed them around. And lifting hers, childless Rita said: "I say we drink to the children. All of them. Then and now."

And when Mac gave her his well-honed fishy stare, she looked right at both of us, a little drunk and a little teary, and said: "You guys can do that. Hell, you're nothing but a coupla big babies yourselves."

We all raised our glasses and drank. Even Mac, who can always float a turd in anybody's punchbowl, seemed caught in the moment, taken away.

SHE CALLED AT NINE THE FOLLOWING Sunday morning. I had been lying in bed, thinking about her.

"Hi," she said. "It's me."

"Where are you?"

"Here. Can I come over?"

I sat straight up. "Now?"

She laughed. "Yeah. Now."

I was out of bed. "Yes. Please."

"I've got the dogs."

"Even better," I said, and half an hour later she was there. She wore jeans and a workshirt and her hair was full and free and glistened so that I knew she had just washed it. Stan and Ollie sniffed my place over and judged it all right, then settled in the living room by the cold fireplace, maybe expecting me to do an unseasonal stoking. Corrie and I sat on the couch.

"You okay?" I asked her.

"I'm okay."

"I'm damn glad to see you."

She put her head on my shoulder and said nothing. We sat like that for a time.

Later, she said: "Listen, Haggard, I'm going away for a while."

"I figured," I said.

"On Grandpa's money. The old fart owes me."

"Yeah," I said. "He does."

"I'm going to school out in Santa Fe this summer. I have some friends I can stay with."

"Do they like dogs?

"They damn well better," Corrie said, and we laughed.

She put her head on my shoulder again. "We can write," she told me.

"I wouldn't have it any other way."

"I just can't be here for a while."

"What about Jack?" I said.

"What about him?" she said, and I let it go.

Then she said: "You're my best friend, you know, Sam. The best I've ever had." It was the only time I could remember she had called me by my first name.

I took her hand. "I'm going to miss you, Corrie," I said.

She turned her brilliant eyes to me and smiled and said: "Hey. I didn't say I was leaving today." And then she slid her free hand around my neck. "You know a good way to kill a Sunday afternoon?"

I looked into her eyes, into the wonder of her. I knew at last that the child she had been was lost forever, and that the woman she had become was someone I'd never really know. I understood then that all any of us really have are moments, precious pieces of time.

A long time later we lay beneath the sheets on my bed, the open window streaming April sunshine, and talked about the first time we had met.

"You were a mess," she said. "Still are."

"I know," I said.

She laughed. "But you're a fine mess, Haggard."

The dogs were kicking up a ruckus by then and Corrie got up to find them something to eat. She didn't bother with her clothes, and I watched her body as she moved across the room and remembered the feel of her skin beneath my fingers. In a little while she was back in bed, bending over me, her smile brighter than the sun outside. I looked into her eyes, studying her face, trying to memorize her features, to hold the moment before it slipped away.

ON MAY 4, MAYBE ABOUT THE TIME Corrie would have been arriving in Santa Fe, Mac and Rita and Linc and I sat watching the live coverage of the Kent State twenty-fifth on television. Peter, Paul and Mary were there and so was Alan Canfora, who had been wounded on that day, and even Mary Vecchio, who now deals blackjack in Las Vegas. The crowd was fair-sized, maybe four thousand. The camera panned Blanket Hill just as the noon memorial bell began to toll. It traveled over the faces in the crowd, most of them as old as my own, although there were many young ones there, too. Near the pagoda we got a few close-ups, and suddenly I sat up straight.

"There he is," I said.

"Who?" Linc asked.

"Delbert. Right there. Behind those women. See him? Black jacket. Don't you see?"

"Maybe," Mac said. "Only you would know for sure."

I sat watching the screen, wanting more than its cold objectivity was willing to reveal. Rita and Linc were still transfixed by the image, but Mac had turned my way and was waiting expectantly.

"So?" Mac said. "Is he there?"

The camera had pulled back to longshot now, and I saw the face I had been watching recede and blend, like one of the faces in the photograph from this day in 1970 which had so haunted Crystal, and which had so completely captured me. I scanned the crowd in vain to find the figure I thought I had seen again, but the image had blended into some larger mosaic, some brief tapestry of a moment lost even to memory, but scarred on the soul forever.

ABOUT THE AUTHOR

Jerry Holt is the author of *Rickey,* a play based on the life of baseball guru Branch Rickey, the man who changed civil rights history when he brought Jackie Robinson into the Major Leagues in 1947. *Rickey* has been performed across the U.S., most memorably in Brooklyn at Long Island University and in Cooperstown at the Baseball Hall of Fame.

By day, Holt is Dean of Arts, Sciences and Integrated Studies at Central Ohio Technical College in Newark, Ohio.

The *Killing of Strangers* is Holt's first novel.

LUCKY PRESS, LLC

Lucky Press, LLC is located in Southern Ohio near the Hocking Hills area featured in *The Killing of Strangers*. Established in 1999, Lucky Press publishes books about characters, real and fictional, who overcome adversity or experience adventure, and books on health, pets, and inspirational subjects. For more information visit Lucky Press online at www.luckypress.com.

If you have enjoyed *The Killing of Strangers* please consider posting a review online at Amazon.com. Thank you for being a *Lucky Reader*.

8282007R0

Made in the USA
Charleston, SC
24 May 2011